Dedication

To all the authors who have inspired me, you taught me to believe in worlds that didn't exist. When I began to believe in those, I learned about the power that I never knew I had.

To my incredible husband, Jonathan, who worked so hard so that I could have the time off and live out my dream. I love you more than I can describe.
You are better than any fictional man ever imagined.

Optional Trigger Warning

This book may contain scenes that may be distressing for some readers. On the final page of this book, I have included a list of these scenes and their content. However, listing them will spoil some key events in the plotline of the novel. If you wish to seek information on these scenes, please skip to the final page.

Natural Born

"When the last tree is cut, the last fish is caught, and the last river is polluted; when to breathe the air is sickening, you will realize, too late, that wealth is not in bank accounts and that you can't eat money."
-- Filmmaker Alanis Obomsawin, of the Abenaki Nation

Prologue

In the depths of winter, when the air stings and everything is quiet, the harsh wind and the deep snow show the world for what it truly is. When the ground turns hard and the water stops its journey southward, when there is a sheet of white across the ground and crystals hang from the trees, suddenly you can track every living thing which has passed through. The world shrinks, the other occupants come into view, and the footsteps of others can no longer be ignored.

Then the snow melts, the ground turns soft, and the plants grow once more. A feeling of forgetfulness comes over the land. The trail of the field mouse or the steps of the sly fox can no longer be seen and so are forgotten.

Each season of growth, humanity finds new places to explore. With each exploration, there are fewer and fewer places in this world that have gone untouched and unaltered. Year after year humanity expands and, as we grow, we forget that progress comes at a price.

Humanity forgets that just because we can no longer see the tracks, doesn't mean someone wasn't there before. When the sun warms our faces, we look at the trail ahead, forgetting until winter comes again that we also leave one behind us.

For centuries, a small group of people known as The Believers taught their children to see the land underneath them as more than a means to build something upon. For generations, they taught their children to do nothing, create nothing, destroy nothing the earth could not return to its original form. They lived alone in the depths of the oldest forests, at peace with the earth around them. Although the trees were filled with threats and danger and although the wildest animals or coldest winters could bring death—so also did nature provide life.

They lived within the forest, in balance with the systems around them. Throughout the years, their numbers grew. In return, the forest sustained them and for a time they knew its secrets. Time went on and progress came faster and faster. Every day brought new technologies and new changes, threatening the delicate balance.

Civilization was forever reaching and grasping at the hidden parts of the world. The Believers knew their time in the ancient forests was coming to an end. They left the safety of the trees, but never forgot the gifts it had given them.

Arriving in the New World, they remembered that as important as it was to build roads to cross, so too was it important to protect the rivers and streams that crossed the hills and valleys.

In the wild woods, they found untouched forests; but they were no longer alone under the branches. Their communities grew and spread in this new country, mingling with every culture and every people who sought the safety of its shores. From the Indigenous nations to wayfarers, tradesmen, and artisans, they built their secret communities will all who roamed the earth. They passed down their traditions, told their stories to every child, and urged their people not to forget the secrets of the trees.

The Believers fought for the balance between the progress of people and the protection of land that could not protect itself. More time passed, and they continued to fight against persecution. As with the Indigenous people of the cursed world, their numbers began to dwindle, until they slowly disappeared into the wild woods.

Generation after generation, the desire for progress continued to win. Bustling cities grew, and the forests disappeared. Still, their children were taught to fight. They fought not for the halting of progress but the balance.

Remnants of this battle remain. Spread across the country, across the world, there still exist towns immune to the increasing pressures of progress. The Believers remain in these towns, hidden at the edges of society. Though they may settle only a short drive from a metropolis that swallows the land, the people feel their connection to the earth underneath them. They live in balance with what they need from it and respect what it needs from them.

Chapter One

On three sides of the dilapidated house were the sparkling new greenhouses. They twinkled in the sunlight, filled inside with a faint mist. Each greenhouse was to feature different varieties of plants and flowers. Vernie had wanted plants from exotic places and plants for all types of people. It was well-known that Vernie believed a house wasn't a home without something green in it. However, over the last few years, these greenhouses became more and more vacant. They sat, pristine, but empty, as the couple struggled to make the plants grow on the contaminated land.

Merle was always determined to find a solution to their problem. Each morning he would walk deeper into the woods nearby, following new trails, hoping to find something to explain the death of their plants and their business. Sometimes Vernie would join him, but today she was back in one of their greenhouses. Once again there were two or three azalea bushes that didn't seem to want to live, no matter what their caretakers tried.

Merle's thoughts were heavy at the thought of the azaleas. Their beautiful pink blossoms had already begun to drop from their branches and he still didn't know why. *What kind of gardener can't keep any plants alive?* His thoughts were heavy as he walked further into the dense woods surrounding their house.

The county was involved now. Frantic residents searched desperately for a solution to save their livelihoods. Small farms nearby were closing, unable to harvest enough for profit. Merle sighed, knowing soon their little nursery would probably add to the list of places put out of business by the sickness in the land.

As he walked through the brush the morning sun had begun to peek through the branches and the earthy smell wafted over him. The damp smell of the underbrush filled his senses and brought him the inner peace he had been seeking. The forest always brought him away from the woes of life and it was one of the reasons he loved to start his day off tramping across the undergrowth.

The early morning chirp of the crickets was music to his ears as he hiked the familiar trails. For weeks he had been watching the distressed forest, looking for signs of growth in the ailing trees. Like all the plants in the greenhouses, for miles around the trees and plants withered.

Pulling the rough denim jacket tighter, he gazed at the wilting woods. Trees that were supposed to be sprouting new life sat as bare as they had when icicles hung from their boughs. The fields of wildflowers lay brown. No greens of spring snuck up from the ground.

Merle trudged slowly through the familiar trail, as the cool morning bit at him. He watched as a cloud of breath escaped, sending a chill up his spine. All around him the once-green field had turned gold and brown and the leaves on the trees sat still crinkled and broken. Merle's brow furrowed in confusion and frustration.

The trees should have begun sprouting their new leaves weeks ago.

As he walked on through the sea of brown decay, a thick fog began. It crept along the ground, growing taller and thicker. Although the morning dew wrapped around him the moment he stepped outside, the air soon began to fill with something else entirely. Within moments, an impenetrable wall of white swept across his vision. A veil had been thrown out before him, covering everything in sight.

Acting out of instinct, he abruptly stopped walking. He had no desire to get lost or turned around trying to wander through the haze. A sense of unease crept inside him, as chills spread across his arms and legs. The impenetrable fog had come so suddenly. The hair on the back of his neck stood up. The fog was strange. Worry caused his heart to race. *Is this a new symptom of the contamination in the land?*

He pulled the collar of his shirt across his nose and mouth, trying to slow his breath, expecting to smell chemicals in the air.

When he could hold it no more, he breathed in something unexpected. There was no thick, pungent chemical smell. The air was clean. Merle took a deeper breath this time and dropped his shirt from his mouth. The scent was overwhelming. It was crisp and clean, like climbing to the top of a mountain or stepping outside after a fresh snowfall. His body relaxed and breathed normally again. At least he didn't seem to be poisoned.

Merle could barely see his hand in front of him, as he absentmindedly reached through the mist. Again, he tried to peer through the thick, white wall.

The forest was silent. The insects, the birds, even the wind stood still. They too were waiting. A clap of thunder filled the sky.

It rattled through his bones. It shook the silent birds from their trees and small animals skittered across the ground to safety. The power shook through his chest. His instincts sent him towards the ground.

Adrenaline and confusion rushed through him. Within seconds, a heavy rain began to pour. Merle crouched, panic racing over him. *Should I head for cover under the trees?*

The warm rain soaked through his clothes and filled the soles of his shoes. Confusion and indecision gripped him. He was sure the weather had said clear skies. After only seconds, the rain left abruptly. Within moments the fog had lifted, washed away by the sudden downpour. Merle couldn't believe his eyes. He had been caught in a sudden downpour before, but nothing as quick as this.

A few heartbeats passed, and it was as if neither the fog nor rain had been there. He looked around, turning in a slow circle, awed by the sun peeking out from behind the clouds. The ground a few feet away was barely damp.

He peered as far as he could see. The trees didn't glisten with water droplets as he expected. If it weren't for the squish of his boots, he would never even believe any of it had happened.

Merle stood up slowly, confusion and questions flooding his mind. He had grown up on a farm, and in his earlier years he had been hiking in some of the biggest forests in the world, but he had no explanations.

Soaking wet, he turned around to go back from where he came. He had been hiking for at least an hour and he knew he was done for the day. Merle turned to walk back up the hill he had come from, marveling at the dry twigs and dirt around him. His eyes went to something blocking the path.

Silhouetted by the morning light, sat the dark figure of what appeared to be an extremely large dog. Merle stumbled. He peered through the dark, trying to make out details from the creature's immense shadow above him. With a twitch of its ears, he realized this wasn't a dog. It was a wolf.

His heart pounded violently in his chest. He had never heard of wolves in this part of the country. He dared not step forward. Indecision washed over him, trying to decide what to do, unsure of what the creature would do if he approached.

The creature stood. In one heartbeat, Merle could tell this was no ordinary wolf. The animal was enormous. Merle wagered if he got closer the head of the animal would measure as high as his hip. At least three or four feet high.

Terror seized his gut, threatening to spill his breakfast. Surely, no old man could outrun such a creature. Running was not an option. The wolf began its descent towards him.

When the creature was within arms-reach Merle could see the thick, billowing brown fur as it bristled along the creature's neck. He was right about its height. The animal was a tower. He inspected the creature as the two of them stood and faced down one another. Sharp claws jutted out from its paws. The coarse fur that covered the animal stood on end. In the sunlight he watched the thick, muscular legs move.

For an eternity filled with both uncertainty and fear, the animal stared at Merle. Its eyes pierced through him. Merle shifted uncomfortably, as his eyes searched the ground for a large stick or branch to defend himself.

The wolf continued to stare, and Merle wondered suddenly if he were being judged. His heart was pounding in his ears and he was certain the wolf heard it too.

It's harsh brown eyes never wavered as the examination continued—like a kid being caught by an angry teacher. Its eyes locked on to him, as if considering something. *It's probably deciding what kind of prey I will be.*

As Merle gazed on, he became entranced by the power of it. Its breathing was heavy and deep.

He met the creature's large eyes a few moments more and suddenly an instinctive calm wash over him. He had no reason to believe it, but something told him it would not hurt him.

For a second, Merle reconsidered whether he had been poisoned by the fog. *What is happening?* He stood in awe of the beast, forcing down panic once again, not daring to move from his place on the trail.

After a moment, the wolf lowered its head. It gave a nearly imperceptible nod. Merle brushed away the absurd idea. Surely, he had imagined it.

The creature turned towards a small game trail hidden in the brush. Merle noticed the leaves had been trampled. *Where does it lead?*

The wolf walked slowly at first, looking back once.

Merle took a hesitant step but followed the animal. A voice in his mind told him he had probably fallen and hit his head or been poisoned by the fog and the whole experience was probably some insane dream. The two of them quickly began to journey through the thick underbrush. For the rest of his life, he would never be able to explain it. He would never understand the overwhelming gut feeling he should follow.

The trail began to drop from sight. More than once he thought to himself that he must be losing his mind. He convinced himself again that he was dreaming.

If he was dreaming would his back hurt so much, though?

He didn't stop. He continued, watching the swish of the long, gray tail, pushing aside each bramble and bush.

After a few minutes, they arrived at a large clearing. Once again, he noticed the quiet of the forest. He saw shadows of birds in the trees, though they didn't call out to one another. The two of them neared the center of the clearing and the smell of the earth and the undergrowth overwhelmed him. A sense of calm and peace washed over him, settling on his shoulders like a warm blanket.

The rest of the clearing was entirely different than the forest.

His mouth fell open. He approached the most massive tree he had ever seen. While the rest of the forest suffered from the con-tamination, this part of the forest flourished. All around the tree beautiful flowers grew in a wave of colors. Blues, yellows, reds, and more stretched towards the giant oak. Each branch was des-perate to soak up the sun streaming down through its branches.

The solitary tree stood taller than all the others around it. The clearing under the tree grew in a nearly perfect circle, as if the tree itself had always known how much room it would need to grow. From the base of the trunk, the thick billowing roots stretched along the ground.

Unlike so many other trees in the area, the enormous trunk grew no ivy. As if the tree itself had determined it would always grow taller, completely unencumbered. Year after year the trunk had grown, twisting itself around again and again. A swirl of brown and green trailed up the tree towards its canopy.

The branches themselves were as thick as some of the trunks of the smaller trees nearby. There were too many to count. It seemed impossible the trunk could support them all. Each grew, reaching out towards the heavens in all directions—long arms stretching from a deep slumber.

Merle stopped to examine the tree, realizing it must be ancient—hundreds or thousands of years old. In the silence of the forest, the tree stood alone. Its age showed with every inch of thick, brown bark. It sat in solitude, waiting to tell passersby of all the secrets and stories it had seen throughout the centuries.

Merle was puzzled as he approached. *How had this piece of the forest survived?* He was transfixed by the beautiful landscape in front of him, desperate to take it all in. Slowly, the wolf continued towards the base of the trunk. The hound disappeared, as a low whine penetrated the silence—jarring Merle from his wonder.

Before he knew why, Merle followed around the side of the enormous brown trunk. What he saw, with the large wolf standing protectively next to it, shocked him more than anything else had that morning.

A small child was sitting at the base of the trunk. Merle stumbled towards her. As he approached, he guessed she was no more than four or five, though he couldn't be sure.
She wore a thin, blue sundress littered with dirt and dust from the ground. From under the dress peeked out two tiny, dirty, feet. Her long, brown hair fell in a waterfall around her shoulders and down her back. Merle had no words as she pushed the locks from her face to stare up at him. Her skin was pale in the yellow glow of the morning sun.

Short stubby fingers rubbed the wolf's long ears as she stood. Her eyes were an intense green, like the underside of a leaf, as she looked at him without fear or nervousness. She smiled at him and he couldn't help but smile back.

The wolf's eyes never left Merle's face as it leaned closer to her. The heat of its gaze burned into him.

"Are you okay?" Merle leaned down to the girl. He expected the wolf to growl.

He watched it warily from his peripheral. Inch by inch he held out his hand to her, keeping one eye on the wolf.

"Are you hurt?"

The little girl stared up at him. Her face was full of questions and searched his for answers, confused as to what to do. She looked between Merle and the wolf again and again. After a few moments, she shook her head.

Merle introduced himself as she put a small, dirt-covered hand in his. He knew he couldn't leave her alone in the woods and explained that he lived nearby. For the first time, he saw a flash of fear in her eyes.

As if it understood, the wolf and the girl exchanged a silent glance. After a minute, she looked at Merle with a smile again and took her first steps away from the large tree.

Merle had a feeling if she didn't approve the wolf wouldn't let him take her anywhere.

The two of them walked away from the ancient tree and the clearing. He decided to take her back to the house and go from there. They didn't get far, barely back to the path, before the young child began to lag. Her feet left a trail, as if every step were a chore, obviously exhausted from whatever it was she had been through to wind up this deep in the forest.

Merle stopped their trek to let her rest against a large rock. She was breathing hard from the hike, and he was growing increasingly concerned. The wolf had never left her side, never faster or slower than her pace, walking in stride with them through the thick brush.

As she caught her breath, Merle waited, still trying to process all that had happened in such a short amount of time. He gave her his water and Merle watched as she drained the thermos.

A thousand thoughts ran through his head. She could have stayed lost in the woods for weeks. She could have fallen and been hurt. The nights were cold, and she could have suffered from exposure. The possibilities were endless, but here she was, seemingly unharmed. *It was a miracle.*

With an audible sigh, she jumped down from the large rock.

"Do—do you want me to pick you up?" Apprehension filled Merle's gut as he watched her try to scrub the chill from her arms. "Are—are you cold?" Merle dropped the jacket from his shoulders and wrapped it around her slim figure.

The denim dripped from her shoulders as he watched her warily. The last thing he wanted was to scare her or make her feel uncomfortable. He didn't know much about kids, but he knew he needed to get her to safety quickly.

Her green eyes sparkled as she rose her short arms to the air, sleeves falling like limp noodles.

Her body relaxed against his as he took her in his arms. He tried to force away the stiffness in his shoulders. Wrapped in the denim, she melted into him, at home in his arms. Within a few steps, she was asleep against his chest. As the three of them continued the hike back to the house in silence, his thoughts began to run with all the possibilities. Why was she in the woods? Was her family camping nearby? Who would let their child run away and how was the wolf involved? He and Vernie had wanted kids for so long but had never been able to conceive. If they had been able to have children, he would never allow something like this to happen.

How strange it was this beautiful little girl showed up on their property.

It wasn't until several minutes later he finally noticed the sudden silence of the forest around them. None of the loud chirps or calls from the birds sounded down from the trees. He listened intently, not even the sound of insects trilling loudly like before could be heard.

Finally, they reached the edge of the property. He trudged past the old barn where they kept all their inventory, and the farmhouse and all the greenhouses finally came into view.

Winded by the hike, but relieved at the familiar sight of their property, Merle continued towards the house. At the center, he had an overwhelming and unsettling sense someone was watching them. Like an itch that couldn't be ignored, it told him to turn around.

His breath caught in his throat as he realized the immediate change. All the sickly-looking trees had begun to grow leaves again. The brush and the thick undergrowth, once brittle and dying, already grew again. Branches in each bush along the ground grew, no longer leaning over with the weight of dead leaves.

Next to him, the wolf made a chuffing noise in the other direction, startling Merle. The first noise he had heard the creature make in all this time.

He looked down at the creature and then towards the clearing next to them. A sharp gasp escaped him as his heart suddenly pounded in surprise. Across the clearing, wildflowers had begun to grow. Their wilted petals and closed faces had opened. Purple and yellow faces searched the sky for every ray of sun. The field had become a sea of purple and yellow and within these tall grasses, dozens of creatures stood, watching.

At least a dozen deer stood with their brown fur glistening in the light. A group of red foxes sat with their curious black eyes staring. Their nervous tails twitched behind them. Ground-hogs, field mice, and more lay in the grass expectantly. In the trees it was as if all the birds from the forest were darkening the branches, weighing the thick wood down with their vast numbers.

A cool hand grabbed his. Vernie had walked out the back of one of the greenhouses and stared at the scene in shock. Her mouth was agape, and her eyes were as large as his probably were. Questions flashed across her face as she regarded the little girl in her husband's arms and at the menagerie in front of them.

Suddenly, the wolf let out a loud, angry, bark. It was enough to finally break the stunned silence. He and Vernie jumped in unison as the command filled their ears, startling them out of their wonder. Merle thought in the back of his mind it seemed like a warning.

Within a few heartbeats, the animals disappeared, turning their backs, and blending silently back into the forest. The couple came back to reality, staring down at the sleeping girl in Merle's arms. As they walked back to the house in silence, thinking about what had happened, they could both feel something in the air telling them nothing would ever be the same.

Chapter Two

On the edge of the city, bumping up against an enormous state park, there was a small garden center. Trapped between hundreds of acres of private forest and the lush, green state park, The Gardens had been around for many years. It was one of those places people see, again and again, thinking maybe they will finally stop by but instead forget it exists the minute it fades from the mirror.

Year after year, the older couple who owned The Gardens poured their hearts into keeping the small business alive. Multiple loans had been taken out and new greenhouses built, but despite their best efforts, it didn't seem as though business would be open much longer.

The husband, Merle Kenrick, would always claim they had bought the cheap land too close to the city. Laverne (most people called her Vernie) claimed there was something wrong with the water. Either way, despite both having the greenest of thumbs, nothing on their land or in their business lived long. As the land around them continued to wither, The Gardens was steadily dying.

A car driving by would see that the main building was an ordinary house. Built decades before, and with no extra money to maintain it, the yellow paint of the old farmhouse had faded in the sun. When looking at it from the front, the house itself leaned to one side—as if asking the question, "How could it still be standing?"

Paint chips blew away with every breeze. The once-bright white paint on the windowsills had faded and was now covered in dirt blown in from the wind. Blue shutters held on desperately, torn and battered by too many storms. They clung at an odd angle from both front windows.

All around the house, the large windows let the light shine through, filling the rooms with light and warmth. They were perfect for their indoor plants in the summer, but terrible after an autumn storm. For as long as the older couple had lived there, at least two of the windows had been boarded up—waiting for the money to fix them.

Once the showcase of the house, the wrap-around porch was meant to be a comfortable place to watch a warm, pink, midwestern sunset. Instead, it matched the sad state of the rest of the house, sagging in too many places to count. If not careful, its residents could walk all along the outside, smacking their heads on the low beams. On the other side, sat a minefield of broken boards and nails, waiting to grab the ankles of someone who wasn't careful enough to watch their step.

Every day, the Kenricks worked tirelessly to bring their business new life and every night Vernie would walk to the front door to flip over the bright orange "Open" sign and look out at it all. She would remember how she had always wanted a porch to sit on as she got older. Instead of sitting on a rocker, she would stand in the doorway, screen door half open, a sorrowful look on her face at the dilapidated state of her home. Then, she would let out a long sigh and walk inside again. Merle promised her at least once a week he would fix it as soon as they could afford it. Whenever that may be.

The first thing the older couple asked when they sat the girl at their worn, brown kitchen table, was her name. They also asked her where she was from, who were her parents, how did she get into the woods—every question that came to mind, but she did not speak. She just sat on the rickety kitchen chair and smiled sweetly at them. The two of them sat in wonder as the little girl reached out with hands covered in dirt, touching all the wilting plants littering the table in front of her.

For the first few days, the older couple would discuss finding the girl from the woods with all manner of law enforcement. Local and state police couldn't seem to find any cases of missing children from anywhere nearby, so they took the search for the girl's parents to a federal level. Her face was posted in the local, state, and even in some national news outlets. Again and again, they would ask her questions, but she said nothing.

It was late on the third night after the sun dropped below the trees and the moon began to rise high in the sky. In the large guest bedroom—where the girl had spent the better part of the last three days sleeping—she began to whimper softly.

The wind picked up. Shutters on the front of the house started to slam, and gusts of wind pushed against the thin glass.

Vernie was asleep in their brown, dust-covered armchair, knees crammed up next to the bed. Merle had brought it up for her this morning. The older woman had barely left the child's side once they brought her into the house. She heard the child's whimper and the sudden gust of wind and startled from her brief slumber.

The cool floor of the farmhouse greeted her feet as she closed the short distance between the chair and the bed. She leaned on the soft, feather mattress and a deep sense of dread as she knelt over to check the girl. The smell of sweat hung thick in the air. The once deep and even breath of the girl was now labored and heavy.

Vernie gingerly touched the girl's soft cheek with the back of her hand, remembering how her mother had done so when she was ill. A sense of longing and protection filled her once again as she leaned over the little girl. It was a yearning she thought she had extinguished years ago—an ache she had buried. She had always wanted to be a mother.

Before she had even made contact, the scorching heat reached from her. It radiated from under the covers. The child was on fire with fever.

Throwing back the thick, heavy quilt, she could feel it was already damp with sweat. Hundreds of possibilities swept through Vernie's head as her heart began to race. *Did she pick something up in the woods? Has she caught the flu? Is it pneumonia?*

"Merle!" she called to the other room. Her throat thickened with worry.

Wild-eyed and frantic, he ran into the room, looking half-awake and completely disheveled. His blue-striped pajamas hung loosely from him as he gripped the door frame. His thick, grey beard and thinning hair were sticking out in all manner of ways as he searched the darkened room. His hands fumbled to place the thick, black, glasses on his long nose. The frame had slipped down as he whipped his head about.

A loud crash came from the floor below. The sound of broken glass hitting the floor rattled the silence of the house. They locked eyes. The wind was howling outside, the rain had begun to pound the roof, and something had just broken in the house. A panicked thought passed between the two of them. *What is happening right now?*

A tremor of fear crept up his spine as he hurried to shut the door, "Stay here."

She nodded, running to shut the door behind him. She pushed the door closed, feeling the latch click.

An icy tremor slid down her spine.

Merle ran to the top of the stairs, skidding across the hardwood floor, figuring he didn't have time to grab any gun or weapon. He had no idea who would want so badly to break into their house, but they were certainly determined. Peering down the bottom of the dark stairwell he waited for whatever was coming.

He heard the creak of the floorboards below and prepared himself. From around the corner came a dark figure, low to the ground, a growl spread across the night. The wolf's presence filled the air in the cramped staircase. The sharp noise broke through the silence as its enormous paw touched the first step. The yellow eyes of the wolf stared up at him, glowing through the darkness. Not sure whether to be relieved or frightened, Merle stared down at the beast. He had grown up with dogs all his life and had never been afraid, but he wasn't sure even in his younger days he could have taken down this monstrosity.

The wolf stopped with its enormous paw on the third step as

the two of them considered each other, unmoving. All around them the wind continued to rattle the house.

For several moments it was like it had been back in the woods. Time stood still as he pushed down panic and waited for what was to come.

Around him, darkness enveloped the house. The only exception came from the crack of light underneath the bedroom door.

"Listen...dog..." The wolf crinkled its snout in distaste. A low snarl vibrated through the air. "Wolf it is." Merle corrected.

"We aren't going to hurt you..." Merle whispered to the wolf as adrenaline pumped through his chest. He watched it come up the stairs, and he spread his arms wide. He prepared to block the beast with his body if necessary.

Its eyes changed. He watched as its gaze shifted. Its enormous head was focused on the sliver of light reaching out under the doorway.

A flush of understanding came over Merle as he realized why the wolf, after two days of behaving totally normal, would suddenly crash through their door.

"We aren't hurting her, but she is really sick." He spoke louder, more confidently, down the stairwell.

The wolf turned its enormous head back to stare at Merle. Its yellow eyes glared at him as if waiting for him to continue. "We need to go help her, so you have got to stop breaking things."

A soft whimper came from the wolf. Merle watched in wonder as its stance changed. The fierce predator was gone. The docile wolf returned. Slowly, it raised its neck and began slowly making its way towards him.

The hackles of its thick, brown fur, came down and its large black nose swept through the air, sniffing wildly.

Merle counted his breaths and several moments passed before he was confident—at least for now— the wolf wasn't going to tear them to pieces. Merle lowered his arms and headed back around the banister and towards the room.

He opened the door, with the wolf on his heels.

From behind the door, Vernie came hurtling towards him in the doorway, screaming an attack at the top of her lungs.

"It's me! It's me!" yelled Merle, throwing his hands up in surrender.

The older woman stopped abruptly. Her gray hair flew

everywhere and her pink, flannel, nightgown swished around her. The two stopped. Even the hound looked up at her with confusion and shock.

Vernie threw herself in his arms. She breathed out a rush of relief.

"You were going to attack me with a hanger?" questioned Merle, gently taking the thin, copper wire from her hand.

"It was all I had." She shrugged her shoulders. "But I would have done some damage." She eyed the large wolf suspiciously as it stepped into the room.

Merle nodded, squeezing his wife's hand reassuringly. He knew if anyone but himself had come in the door she probably would have turned it into a deadly weapon.

The three of them rushed back to the bed, leaning over the young girl again. The wolf went around the other side.

Merle noticed how its large frame filled most of the room. Had it always been so large or was he somehow imagining it had grown?

Sweat plastered the girl's long locks to her face and Vernie gently brushed them back. "Honey, honey… it's going to be okay sweetie." She whispered.

The girl took deep, rattling breaths as if trying to push something from deep in her chest. "Go get something to bring her fever down…" Vernie urged, looking back at Merle. "Let's put a cool washcloth on her head."

Merle did as he was told, running to the bathroom, and grabbing one of the worn gray washcloths from the cupboard under the sink. Cold well-water greeted him as he dampened the thick, soft cloth. For once he was thankful for the freezing temperatures, it might not be great when you were waiting for a shower in the morning, but right now it would do the trick.

He came back in the room and Vernie gently folded the washcloth, placing it across the girl's brow. Both sat waiting and watching. They both knew they had no medicine suitable for children in the house.

Ever the pragmatist, Vernie stood up determinedly. "I'm going to call a doctor."

She left the room in a blur of pink as she made her way back to their bedroom. He listened, knowing exactly who she would call. After all, there was only one pediatrician in Kutz.

As if equally impatient and concerned, the large wolf's tail swished angrily against the floor. Deep chuffs left its enormous body, and it nudged gently again and again at the young girl's outstretched hand.

Merle watched as it stared down at the girl intently.

Its tail swished again, thumping against the wall behind it, rattling the glass in the windowpane. It created a gentle breeze, pushing against the thick curtains they had put up a few days before. The thick, black curtains were meant to block both sun and moonlight, so that the young girl could rest these last few days.

Several things happened at once. Years later Merle would think back on the first few days with the little girl. Finding her in the forest was just the first strange thing to happen, but so much came afterward it was laughable to call anything strange.

First, a sliver of moonlight came in as the curtain peeked open with the gust from the wolf's wagging tail. The room quieted. The thunder and wind from outside ceased their incessant rattling. For the first time since they had found her with the fever, the girl moved. She turned her head towards the window, taking a deep, even breath towards the light casting across her bed.

Something happened then that Merle would never tell anyone. He was sure it was sleep deprivation or confusion, but it was too much for him to believe.

He jumped, startled at the girl's movements, and the wolf did the same. The dark eyes of the wolf met his from across the bed. He waited, hardly daring to breathe. The two of them had the same thought. It was as if two voices were speaking across his mind. A headache formed in response, pulsating at his temples. His voice, and a deeper voice he did not recognize, both said 'outside.

Something told Merle this was the right thing to do. He stood up abruptly and began to gather the girl in his arms. The wolf had both of its front paws on the bed, watching him.

Merle sprang from the room, as a bewildered Vernie was leaving theirs. Tears were in her eyes as she said,

"The doctor can't come tonight. Should we take her to the ER?"

Merle secretly cursed the lazy man who wouldn't leave the comforts of his home to help a child. Then, he cursed the hospital for being nearly an hour away. He considered their options, maybe they should go to the hospital anyway? Could they even get there safely with the wind acting the way it was?

He looked down at the moonlight shining through the window.

There was only one thing to do. "We are going to cool off outside." Merle declared before gently lifting the child's sleeping form from the mattress.

The three of them hurried down the stairs. The wolf led the way across the wooden floor, stepping over the chairs and furniture it had knocked over on its way in. Merle followed; glass crunched under their feet as they stepped gingerly across the doorframe.

Merle found that he was too impressed by the wolf's determination to be appropriately upset that he was stepping over his own door, broken off its hinges. Behind him, Vernie walked carefully as well, marveling at the chaos that had become their life.

The moon was bright, its light reaching out to push away the dark shadows of the night. Against the farmhouse, the light illuminated everything it touched. The beautiful reds and pinks of the roses next to the porch had spread their petals open, unable to discern whether it was night or day. The leaves of the tree in the front yard glinted from the dew already covering the branches. The white light shined on the porch and the wooden bench near the flower beds.

Merle stepped carefully, tucking the girl's feather-light form tight against his chest. They walked forwards, out from under the darkness of the porch-cover.

The cool wetness of the grass soaked between his toes as he walked towards the bench. The spring night was crisp and filled his lungs with its chill. The nip of the air spread across his hands and feet. The cold of the night was a stark contrast against the heat still emanating from the girl in his arms.

The soft glow of the moonlight stretched across the night and there was a gentle pressure against his arms. As in the bedroom upstairs, the girl had turned her head to face towards the white glow.

Vernie and Merle waited in the moonlight with the large wolf at their feet. The little girl stretched across both of their legs.

All three of them watched in wonder as, within seconds, the sickly child began to transform back to her normal self.

Pink returned to her sickly pale cheeks. Her breath became slow and even. Despite his worry that she may catch a chill, the girl began to return to a normal temperature. Her body welcomed the night air.

Merle felt the fever leave her as he held her in his arms. He wrapped her feet in his large, warm, hands as Vernie leaned over to grasp her fragile hands. The child's breath continued as her body relaxed and so did the night around them. Vernie was the first one to breathe a sigh of relief. Tears of worry were streaming down her cheeks. She leaned her head against her husband's warm nightgown as the wetness of the bench seeped through her clothes.

Vernie sighed again, wiping tears onto her shoulder, and brushing the long, brown tendrils from the girl's cheeks. "We still don't even know her name..." she whispered as Merle pulled her in against himself on the bench, kissing his wife's forehead lightly.

This time, the girl turned her face away from the moonlight and pressed her cheek against Vernie's hand. The older woman's callused hands met the girl's soft cheek. Their eyes met. The dark green of the girl's eyes reflected off the soft white glow of the moon, as she stared up at the two of them.

After a few seconds, a deep breath filled the girl's chest and a small smile greeted them. The tiny fingers squeezed Vernie's hand, and she wiggled her toes against Merle's warm palm. A quiet laugh left her as she looked into their worried eyes.

"I'm Quid."

Chapter Three

Merle and Vernie got virtually no sleep the night of the fever. They sat outside in the cool air for an hour, listening to each soft breath the girl took.

Quid finally relaxed, and they got their first glimpse of her transformation. Even the wolf let out a sigh of relief. Standing up, he nudged her gently with his long, wet, nose.

"Fen." Whispered Quid, reaching down and rubbing the soft fur of his long ears. Vernie and Merle smiled at each other.

"At least we can stop calling him 'dog' now." Chuckled Merle. "He doesn't seem to like being called that anyway."

"I don't think she should sleep upstairs anymore." Merle looked over at Quid as he spoke, thinking back to how she seemed to respond to the moonlight.

They decided not to take Quid back up to the stuffy bedroom. At Vernie's suggestion, they took Quid to stay in the coolest place in the house.

The four of them walked around the dilapidated porch towards the back yard, all the while Vernie held Quid in her arms, feeling very protective. Together, and with Fen walking at their side, they sat in the old wicker chair in the sunroom at the back of the house.

"I'll get some blankets and pillows." Said Merle as he watched his wife.

Quid quickly fell back to sleep as Vernie rocked her. A warmth spread through him as he looked at his wife's graying hair settling in the gentle breeze caused by the rocking chair. Her eyes were closed, and the sound of her soft humming filled the night. Vernie had always wanted children. He knew Quid must belong to someone, but he also hoped, somehow, this unique child could belong to them.

Vernie wrapped Quid in the yellow quilt Merle had brought down. Her grandmother had made it long ago and a familiar pain filled her chest as she looked down at the familiar colors and her fingers wrapped around the soft material. She had always longed for it to be wrapped around her own child. She stared at the different colored squares, each stitched with a different animal, as her mind tried to wrap around everything that had happened in the last few days.

Within a few minutes, Merle took Quid and laid her on the cot. The air was cooler in the sunroom. The walls were thin and meant for keeping cool in the hot summer, but he made sure to leave her near the window, remembering how she had responded to the moonlight before.

As Merle went to fixing the old wooden door and setting the house right again, Vernie made a decision. She looked at the dilapidated room. The pale walls were covered in dust and cobwebs. Shadows on the wall begged to be swept away by more lighting. Quid might be with them for a while and she would need more clothes than what she had on.

Although she was exhausted when she left the house, that night Vernie drove to the closest 24-hour store around, over an hour away. When she came back, she had filled the bed of the truck full clothes, toys, and other things she thought the little girl might need. She thought to herself as she unpacked that she was thankful Merle had finally talked her into getting a credit card. It was going to take a while to pay all of it off.

The next morning neither Vernie nor Merle had to wake up early because neither had gone to bed. Merle had fought with the kitchen door for several hours while Vernie turned the room into a proper bedroom for Quid.

By the time the sun was rising, Merle had given up fixing the door and Vernie had set up everything in Quid's room except the bed and the curtains, but only because she hadn't wanted to use the drill and wake her. She and Merle had even managed to get the heavy dresser all the way downstairs without killing each other over it.

The sun was beginning to shine through the large windows as Vernie folded the last piece of clothing and placed it into the dresser. She spread a blue dress with yellow sunflowers across the old wicker rocking chair next to Quid's cot before walking through the house to the kitchen.

Vernie wanted to get started on breakfast before Quid woke up. Her eyes were heavier than they had been had in a long, long time. She knew they all needed a good breakfast and not just cereal.

As she walked around Merle, he squeezed her hand gently and she absentmindedly rubbed her hand over the t-shirt he had changed into. She silently placed the box of Apple Jack's back into the cabinet. The two of them needed a hot meal after the night they pulled, and Quid hadn't eaten much since they found her. None of them would recover without full bellies.

Vernie pulled the mixing bowls from the cabinet, listening intently for the sound of Quid stirring awake. The old springs of the cot creaked first, followed by the shuffling of the wolf. His large claws clicked and clacked against the wooden floors.

A few minutes later, Quid came quietly into the kitchen, the blue dress fanning out around her short legs as she walked. Vernie smiled as Quid sat down next to Merle at the old, wooden table. Both watched as she pulled the chair out and waited silently next to them.

Shaking off the awkwardness of the morning, "Time for breakfast!" Vernie announced, to no one in particular, and turned back towards the large white stove.

The hound strode across the kitchen, suddenly making the room shrink. Vernie watched as it pushed the screen door open and headed towards the porch. Whenever the creature was around, she was unnerved. She remembered stories her mother's people used to tell. Like the original fairy tales, she grew up hearing horror stories of wolves luring girls into the forest. The girls would trust their puppy eyes and soft fur, only to get eaten alive. As she got older Vernie always thought the stories were metaphors for not getting involved with boys, but the more she watched the wolf the more she wondered...

Thinking still of the literal wolf at her door, Vernie cracked the eggs into the pan. As she worked, she listened as the sound of giggles filled the quiet morning air of the kitchen. She peeked slowly over her shoulder to see Merle making faces from atop his newspaper. She smiled as she turned on the old gas stove and waited for the big cast iron pan to heat up.

Vernie opened the fridge and pulled out the package of bacon. The heat of the pan radiated out as she emptied the brown butcher paper and sat down the long strips.

The moment the bacon hit the pan and began to sizzle, she heard a loud clamor. Vernie whipped around and searched frantically around the room. The blue of the kitchen walls stood out to her as she searched for the noise.

Quid was standing, the worn wooden chair knocked over

behind her. Her eyes were locked on the bacon on the stove and tears streamed down her face.

Vernie and Merle exchanged startled glances. Vernie's eyes immediately went to the back door, expecting to see the wolf knocking it down, teeth bared. She peeked warily out the window, but the wolf was still laying on the porch, unmoved by this new turn of events.

In a blur of blue, Quid was out of the room, running towards the back of the house and her new room.

"Maybe she doesn't like bacon?" Merle asked, setting his newspaper down and getting up to follow the girl.

Vernie waited a few seconds, feeling confused until she turned around and took the bacon from the stove. She considered tossing it in the trash but thought it was wasteful. Cautiously, she opened the screen door. The springs on the door creaked and slammed as she tossed the bacon towards the wolf. He eyed her and it suspiciously at first but gobbled the strips in one bite. If she hadn't been so wary of it, she might have been flattered at the sudden display of trust.

Reluctantly, Merle made the call to tell the police that Quid had finally told them her name.

Even with a name, it became more and more apparent no one was looking for her. Police suspected she had been abandoned in the forest.

At first, the state wanted her to go to the foster system, but the older couple insisted she stay with them. The local Sheriff Theodore—Teddy—Masterson was a friend of the family, and ultimately ended up vouching for the couple. The Sheriff convinced the social workers he would do regular checks on the girl's well-being.

It seemed like the state Child Services Agency would make a fuss, but, after a few weeks, it was as if they forgot or moved on to something else. Vernie and Merle were officially instated as foster parents. The older couple accepted, and welcomed, that the girl from the woods would be a part of their lives.

They would discuss the strange events in the woods, and the sight of all the animals, for years to come. However, nothing could prepare the two of them for the events of the next few weeks—indeed, the events of the next few years.

Merle and Vernie learned Quid was probably the world's youngest vegetarian. She was so affected by the eating of meat at first that she would burst into tears. Eventually, she learned not to cry but whenever she saw someone with a burger or other meat, she would shift in her seat uncomfortably. The two foster parents became so moved by her plight they too began abandoning it. Except for Merle's occasional fish fry, the entire household adapted to the new changes. Fen was more than happy to eat all the meat from the fridge and freezer, much to Merle's chagrin.

Days and weeks passed, they began to learn exactly how unique their foster daughter was and even more of the changes she would bring to their lives.

As Quid got better there was also an immediate transformation not just in the greenhouse plants, but in the land around them.

In the morning Quid would eat her breakfast—eggs with toast— and then walk through their greenhouses. As she did, it was like everything shifted. The wilted flowers she went near grew petals back, bright, and vibrant, within a few hours. The shrubberies and trees she touched grew taller, their leaves shined brighter, their trunks stronger.

Vernie and Merle didn't know what to make of it, except they realized once the plants were healthy, she seemed to need them as much as they needed her.

After breakfast Quid visited each greenhouse. She walked around, feeling more invigorated and alive with each step through the misty aisles. Her once-pale skin was full of color and glowing with life. Her long, brown hair had before appeared limp and lifeless now fell along her shoulders, shining in the sun, and flowing and bouncing behind her as she went.

Quid loved to visit the greenhouses and she did every day. It became such a big part of her day that one morning they surprised her with a kit they created for her to carry around. It was a large, wooden basket with two rounded handles. Inside was a new gardening kit of her own. There was a shiny new spade, trimmers with bright blue handles, a pair of blue, rubber gardening gloves with pink roses on them, and a small blue watering can.

Vernie often accompanied her around the gardening center while Merle would take his morning walks. No matter what work she had to do, Vernie always took the time to watch as Quid walked slowly along each aisle. Vernie had always had a green thumb, especially for herbs and flowers, but Quid knew what each plant needed on a completely different level. It was like she communicated with the plants in a way Vernie couldn't explain.

As if she could sense what they needed, she was always helping and adjusting them. She would give extra water to some, pouring directly into their soil from her gardening kit or spraying their leaves. She moved the pots that were getting too much water from their automatic sprinkler systems to a drier spot. She turned or moved plants that were getting too much or not enough sun.

If the plant truly needed it, as some of the herbs or plants that had grown too near the forest often did, Quid would take the plant with her to keep them close. Soon she had flowers, herbs, vegetables, all kinds of things in her room. She would keep them with her for the night, or maybe a couple of days, and they would grow.

It wasn't something easily explained, but whenever Quid was around it was as if she were the thing healing the plants and bringing them back from the brink. Life was returning to the business again as everything around The Gardens began to bloom once more. It was as if Quid was helping wipe away the contamination from each plant and with it she was forever altering their lives.

To be near the girl from the woods was to know, instinctually, something was different about her. Even if it couldn't be described, you could feel it, the waiting sensation that something incredible was about to happen.

Chapter Four

Ever since Quid came into their lives almost two years ago, the business was finally becoming what they had always dreamed of. All around the house and across the greenhouses, things were flourishing.

It was a cool, fall morning and light had begun to fill the greenhouses. Inside the largest greenhouse, Vernie was up to her elbows in potting soil. The air around her was already getting warm as sunlight filled the space. She had been preparing the hundreds of bright yellow and red mums, they had ordered for their annual sale, for nearly a day already, and the end was finally in sight.

Vernie heaved another flower into the next of the large, glossy brown pots in front of her, as Merle walked in. He huffed over to her, his face beginning to turn pink with frustration. She could see his thick eyebrows furrow from across the room.

"Have you seen Quid?" he sighed again, desperately looking around the large room. "She was supposed to help me look at the Stellas. They aren't blooming again, and I was hoping to put them in the sale barn before the Fall Sale tomorrow."

"Is it still raining?" answered Vernie, absentmindedly, as she pushed the long, gray hair from her face with the back of her hand again.

"It's sprinkling." He leaned over the display table and laid his face in his hands, letting out a sigh. They had all been prepping for the sale for days. Vernie examined the dark circles under her husband's eyes. As great as they hoped this sale would be, they also needed it to be over.

"Then she is at the top of the barn."

"Of course." He realized. Whenever it rained, Quid liked to hang out in the loft of the inventory barn reading books and playing with Fen.

Merle stood up, leaning across the expanse of the table, to give his wife a quick kiss on her dirt-covered cheek.

Vernie smiled back at her husband as she wagged a dirt-covered finger at him. She knew why he was looking for their daughter. "She cannot see to every plant that doesn't sprout exactly when you think it should…" Vernie stated matter-of-factly, shooting him a knowing, sideways glance. "Or just because you want them to flower again in time for a sale."

She met Merle's eyes with a stern, disapproving, look as the old man looked back sheepishly.

"I don't need her to *do* anything, just look at them, be near them." Merle smiled back at his wife. She thought again that the years of hard work were showing through. His back didn't stand as straight. His hands didn't grip his tools as tight as they once did.

Still, he maintained his eternal optimism. Quid had brought them light and love, but she also brought life back to their business.

"Mmmhmm…" replied Vernie. She continued placing the red and yellow mums delicately in their pots. The tone of her voice told Merle that this conversation was far from over.

As Merle walked across the damp morning grass, he thought about what Vernie had said. Maybe she was right. Whatever it was causing Quid and the plant-life around her to be connected, he didn't want to abuse it. She might be single-handedly saving their business, but he didn't want her to feel responsible for it.

At the edge of their property, before the tree line began, sat the barn. It was graying with age and sat back against the woods. The harsh light of day was just beginning to reach its outer walls. Inviting him in, the towering structure creaked in the gentle wind as Merle walked along its center.

The double-door loft windows had been thrown open. A sprinkle of rain outside promised to cool the air in the barn, which was normally stifling this time of year. The sun peeked from behind the thin rain clouds, promising the warmth of a beautiful day.

He briefly examined the inventory around him. All the nooks and crannies of the barn were filled to the brim. The previous owner had once used the stalls for horses, but The Gardens used each space to organize their inventory. In the first stall were some stacks of boxes yet to be opened, and some boxes that waited to be emptied. Each was filled with small pots of all shapes, sizes, and colors. In another stall, large ceramic pots of all colors filled the small space. Red and green pots that would be part of their Christmas sale were stacked in the back corner, bright blues and pinks were in another, eagerly awaiting Eastertime. There was a space sitting empty near the door, fall colors had already been removed for the sale tomorrow. Each of the larger pots was divided from another, carefully placed on short, black, slats of wood to keep each pot from chipping or breaking.

Merle passed more and more stalls full of Vernie's specialty items. Boxes of trinkets filled the last three stalls. Some were labeled "garden decorations" and were filled with things like lawn gnomes, birdbaths, and signs that said things like "Goddess of the Garden" or "Gnome Sweet Gnome." Along the floor of the last stall were dozens of concrete statues of dogs, cats, fish, chickens, and every shape pinwheel you could imagine. Each statue looked at him as he passed with their cold, grey eyes. All of them waited expectantly to be picked up and sold at Vernie's gift shop.

He shook his head and chuckled lightly to himself as he began the ascent up the barn's new staircase. He wasn't sure which was crazier, that they had turned their entire downstairs—except the kitchen—into the gift shop or that the junk sold just as well as the flowers. The women in his life each had their own bit of magic. Quid had the plants and Vernie magically sold all her trinkets.

He reached the top of the staircase, listening as it creaked underneath him. The thick, sweet, scent of hay still filled the air, though it had been years since it had been kept up here. He walked across the new, yellow slats of wood. The old barn hadn't seen many upgrades, but since Quid enjoyed being up here, they had decided it needed spoofing up.

The floor of the loft had been replaced and electricity had been installed all over the barn. A steep, beautiful oak staircase had been installed last week. They had fought about the necessity of it for a long time. Merle thought Quid would be fine, but Vernie was terrified Quid would fall off the old ladder.

Once the stairs were complete, he had to admit it was worth the steep price. Vernie told Quid excitedly that now Fen could even join her up there—since wolves couldn't climb ladders. Merle hadn't told his wife he had found the wolf in the hayloft many times. Mostly because he couldn't explain how the animal got up there.

The large double windows of the loft were open, and he could already feel the warmth on his face.

As he walked across the room, all around the loft were pots of all sizes, filled with beautiful, healthy plants of various sizes and growth.

Beautiful red and pink bushes, which normally did poorly in pots, were flowering in numbers he had never seen. He recognized one of the ailing trees he had recently potted, now growing leaves.

He bent down to the tree and touched the velvety brown bark. He was shocked, only days before it had been weak and peeling but now appeared ten times healthier.

That's weird, he thought to himself as he examined more of the pots. He had never seen these. A half a dozen tomato plants, brown and wilting in their tomato cages, lined one side of the loft. He recognized the plastic, green pots they were in immediately. He never liked using plastic pots if he could help it. They tried only to ship or buy items in burlap wraps. Another garden center must have sent them over.

Merle thought back and remembered Vernie telling him about a shipment from another local center. Jack's Beanstalks was an operation in the next town over and it had also been hit hard by what the people had begun calling the "contamination" in the land. Jack's specialized in vegetables and herbs, but rumors around Kutz were that it was struggling to stay afloat.

The store was owned by a man—Jack—and his family. Jack was a long-time friend of Vernie's. Yesterday, Jack had sent a truck over. Word had spread about their luck with rehabilitating plants.

Merle waded through the walls of flowers, shrubberies, and potted trees, shocked at how many she had managed to get up to the loft without either him or Vernie noticing. The room was just shy of a jungle. He wandered around, moving between the Quid-sized gaps in the pots.

As he approached, he heard Quid's soft voice whisper as he got closer to the end of the barn. He tried not to move any pots from their places. If Quid moved them together or apart it was for a good reason.

"I'm going to try. I'm ready." He heard Quid declare. Her voice was full of irritation and Merle could almost hear her rolling her eyes as she spoke. "I. can. help." She enunciated each word stubbornly.

Merle gently pushed through the wall of plants Quid had put around herself, wondering who she could be talking to. Part of him was always half expecting to find another strange child without a parent—because if it could happen once…

He found Quid sitting on the worn-out quilt Vernie had given her, looking directly at Fen, who sat across from her.

Silhouetted against the sunlight, Quid sat on the quilt. Her legs and arms both crossed. She stared down at the large wolf, and it kept staring directly at her. The two of them didn't seem to notice him come in. He coughed quietly to notify them of his presence, suddenly feeling awkward, like he had interrupted some kind of private moment.

Merle laughed off the feeling though. After all, it was just an animal.

Quid turned to look at him, not seeming at all surprised to see his head poking out from between her wall of plants. Her face changed instantly from the frustrated, stubborn glance to a large smile as she looked over at him. As always when he was around Quid, he couldn't help but smile back.

"Do you need help with the flowers?" asked Quid, knowingly. She stood up to walk towards him, ignoring the chuff from the wolf. As crazy as it was, although so much in his life had become crazy, Merle thought it sounded like a noise of disapproval.

The two of them walked back towards the staircase with the wolf in tow. Merle wondered for the thousandth time about the strange relationship between the creature and the girl. Sometimes it was as if they were connected—as if they communicated. The hound rarely left her side, and it was always, always watching.

Fen never wandered off except to eat or relieve himself and he was constantly on edge. He seemed as if he was always waiting for something.

At night, Merle often came into Quid's room to check on her. A few times in the last week, he had entered the room and found the hound pacing the room or staring down at her while she slept. The second night that he found the large animal looming over her he made the executive decision to have Fen sleep outside. Its sudden nervousness had made him nervous too.

The next morning, he spotted it pacing again outside the sunroom. Although—as if sensing his approach—Fen stopped when Merle approached.

Merle had grown up with animals all his life. He knew the wolf wasn't domesticated. There was no doubt it still had a lot of wild left in it. But he hadn't pressed the issue, because even when it acted strange—which was all the time— he got the distinct feeling it would protect Quid from anything. After all, the wolf had saved her that day in the woods just as much as Merle had.

As the three of them walked towards the greenhouses, Merle chalked the uncomfortable silence up to another strange thing around here. Quid and Fen kept jerking their heads towards one another, and Quid would sigh angrily in its direction. Merle couldn't shake the feeling that the two of them seemed to be having a sort of silent argument.

Quid and Merle spent the rest of the afternoon tending to different flowers around the greenhouses. Merle always asked her to walk around, "just to visit," but the two of them visited every inch of the place.

As they were finishing up her morning "rounds" Quid walked out to the sale barn to view the plants which were soon to be out of season.

It's not a good idea. Fen pushed the thought into Quid's mind for the umpteenth time that day. Merle had been right, the two of them were arguing, except it was only silent to Merle.

Quid didn't know why, and Fen couldn't—or wouldn't— explain it, but the two of them had always been able to communicate like this. Quid didn't remember anything from before the day when Merle found her by the tree, but she had always had Fen and she had always been able to communicate with him. His voice was always in her head and she always felt him pressing on her, like everything else around her. Fen was the only secret she kept from her parents.

Not for the first time, Quid tried desperately to block Fen from her mind. The three of them walked around the side of the house towards the front.

The state highway ran in front of the house and was always bustling with cars.

The house sat a fair distance from the road, leaving ample space for the large, purple sign and their new parking lot.

As business began to grow over the last year, more customers meant there needed to be more places to park their cars. Vernie had wanted to pour blacktop to put in a paved parking lot, but Merle and Quid had talked her out of it. It was decided blacktop was bad for the local plants and trees. So instead, one morning Merle went out, grabbed some old empty paint buckets, filled them with heavy

rocks, shoved long branches—which had fallen naturally from the nearby trees into them, and roped off rectangles to let people know where to park.

Later that day, Merle had spent three hours spray painting the grass and meticulously measuring each car space. All three of them laughed when he asked Quid to look at his handy work. Within a couple of hours of the girl's walk around the "lot," the grass had grown so lush that all the spray paint was impossible to see.

Between the parking lot and the edge of the house sat the large, purple "sale shed." The inside of the shed had been painted pink and the double doors were always left wide open during the day. Vernie had built shelves all around the inside and all year long she used it to sell flowers, bushes, or decorations that were out-of-season. It was often one of the first places customers would look when they arrived, and Vernie was always working to keep it tidy.

Quid and Merle approached the shed excitedly as Fen lagged. Quid couldn't feel him pressing his thoughts on to her, but his angry sighs every three seconds reminded her anyway.

Vernie walked out of the bright purple shed holding a long, red push broom. Small clouds of dust swirled in the air around her as Vernie swept all the dirt towards the double doors.

Quid walked up to the shed and immediately the small pots of leftover summer succulents perked to greet her in their tiny pots. She couldn't explain exactly how she always knew what the flowers needed, no matter how many times her parents pestered her. They simply called it her "influence."

The plants' needs, their feelings, came to her. Most of the time it was like an itch she impulsively had to scratch. She couldn't ignore the feeling. If she did it only got worse and worse. This time—without even walking to the back of the shed to look—Quid knew Vernie had been over-watering them.

"They need different soil, or they need less water." Quid said, pointing to the small group of succulents in their tiny pots. Each was in a light blue pot that had been hand-painted by a local artist with a smiling, yellow sun on the front.

Vernie bent down to examine the pots, bringing one closer to inspect. There were puddles inside the pots, a sure sign she must have accidentally over-watered them.

"You're right of course." Vernie smiled over at Quid as she

dumped the excess water onto the grass at the side of the shed.

She walked over towards Quid again, "Has he had you in every house today?" Vernie looked accusingly at Merle, who was rewriting prices on the garden statues resting near the front. The old man bent over one of the gray Labrador statues, whistling loudly to himself. He pretended to fix a chip in the dog's ear. Quid knew he also pretended not to hear his wife or feel her eyes pressing into the back of his head.

Vernie watched as Quid began walking around. Her tiny fingers gingerly touched the petals of each plant in the small shed. From the corner of her eye, Vernie noticed the wolf had come to sit outside the shed. Since the day Vernie had begun regularly feeding the wolf meat in the mornings the two of them had come to a silent agreement to stay out of each other's way. Still, though, the way the wolf stood and stared into the forest today made her uneasy. What was it watching for?

Turning to look at Merle, who was adjusting the merchandise in the shed, Vernie put one hand on her hip and pointed the broom handle towards him threateningly. "Make sure she takes a break. She needs a good lunch."

Quid smiled weakly up at the two of them as Merle reassured his wife with a sly smile and a quick kiss on the cheek. She didn't mind helping, in fact, it usually invigorated her.

In the beginning, she could only help a few plats of plants at a time. The plants had been full of so much blight she was often exhausted by the time she was done. In the evenings, Merle often had to carry her, slumped over, from the kitchen table to her room at the back of the house. Now that most of the plants were back to health it didn't take as much out of her.

There were even some animals that came to her when they needed it. The contamination was affecting them too, killing their food and destroying their homes.

Nausea grew in her throat at the thought. She woke up every day feeling more and more of the animals in distress pressing in on her. It was hard to concentrate and often left her with a migraine. Trying to control so many things at once was overwhelming her. Fen didn't understand how bad it was. He didn't understand that she had to try to get control. The only way she knew how to do that was by going to where she felt the most need.

Quid began walking aimlessly around the inside of the small

shed, pushing away the feeling of the animals in the nearby woods.

She greeted each leftover flower, bringing some water from her watering can, moving others into the sunlight filling the shed. The thought of all the plants returning to good health and the pressure of the animals nearby reminded Quid of why she had been so eager to help Merle in the first place.

"I want to take a hike." Quid stared down at the two adults in front of her. She had been waiting all day to say something, but she couldn't wait any longer.

Merle and Vernie had been arguing again over where the best place to put all the pots Vernie had painstakingly filled, but their conversation stopped in mid-sentence.

In unison, Vernie and Merle looked over at Quid, taken aback at the commanding tone Quid had tried so desperately to convey. Wide-eyed, they waited to hear more.

It was so out-of-character for Quid to ask for anything. When she was hungry, Quid simply made food.

When she needed something from a shelf or needed something moved—like the plants in the barn—she found a way to do it. She rarely made requests and she never asked for help. Vernie often joked if Quid found herself stranded in the desert; she wouldn't even ask someone for a cup of water.

"Where do you want to go?" asked Vernie with a smile. She leaned down, placing the broom gently on the ground. "We could go walk around the strip mall after dinner." She brushed one of the long, brown strands out of Quid's face.

"I want to go—" she paused, looking back and forth between her two smiling foster parents and again at the ground. She shuffled her feet nervously. "I want to go on a hike. There's a lake nearby."

Neither of them knew what to say. Quid hadn't been back to the woods, except the small stream by the barn, in the more than two years since Merle had found her. The contamination was spreading. Farms across the county had been fighting off the plight.

"How—how do you know about the lake?" Merle cocked his head, wondering when she could have learned about it. He hadn't been back to it in years. Not even on his morning hikes. It was one of the places most hard-hit from the contamination.

Quid shifted her feet nervously. She didn't want to explain to her parents she knew about the lake because she sensed the need

for it from the distressed animals. She didn't know how or why she could suddenly feel their needs. As she looked into the questioning eyes of her parents, a chill came over her. What if they thought she was crazy? How much could the two of them handle before they sent her away?

"Someone at school told me about the lake near here." Quid answered with the first thing that popped into her mind, but she could taste the lie in her mouth. It was the first time she had ever outright lied to them, and she didn't like it.

As always, the wind mirrored her emotions. It began to whip gently around them, pulling leaves and dust from the ground. Quid took a deep breath as butterflies flipped in her stomach.

Oh, is this what we are doing now to get our way? Lying? Fen's sarcastic tone pushed in her mind again. Quid decided to ignore him, and stared at her parents, waiting anxiously for their reply.

Merle and Vernie exchanged perplexed glances. They did that thing that parents sometimes do. They communicated with one another without really saying anything. A few jerks of the head and raised eyebrows and a decision was made. Quid thought to herself maybe she and Fen weren't the only ones who could silently communicate after all. Probably not though, or Merle wouldn't complain to his partner about "not being a mind reader" so often.

From behind Vernie, Quid could see Fen staring at her, waiting for an answer. Quid ignored his disapproving stare, turning her head towards Merle, who scratched the back of his neck uncomfortably. Fen's stare continued to burn into her.

This is a bad idea. Fen pushed the thought into her mind again.

"The contamination—it killed the lake. There's not much there to see. The land is a dust bowl." Merle shrugged his shoulders as he looked down at Quid. "Are you sure you don't want to go somewhere else? Somewhere that's better..."

"No. Let's go." Quid nodded at him reassuringly, walking towards the old truck parked near the front of the house, secretly hoping to convince him with her determination.

"Okay. Okay. We can all go." Vernie walked after Quid, hugging her shoulders as they went. "But after lunch, Jill is supposed to come over today anyway."

Quid's shoulders sank a little at the thought of Jill. She let

Vernie steer her towards the side door and into the kitchen. At least she got them to agree to take her, even if Jill had to come too.

As she sat at the table and ate lunch with her parents, the animals pressed on her influence again. They were growing desperate. Worry filled her as she wondered if she would be able to help them, to heal them, like she had the plants in the greenhouses.

Chapter Five

Jill sat in the center of Quid's bedroom floor and Quid eyed her warily from the bed. The other girl's pristine pink dress was covered in so many frills and bows that it swept up with every little breeze. The shine of her black Mary Jane's poked out from the edge of the dress as she sat imperiously, waiting for Quid to join her.

The two girls had been forced together again and again since Vernie and Merle first introduced them. Jill's dad, Jack, had grown up with Vernie. The girls were expected to become fast friends. As if it were that simple.

The truth was the two of them were just too different. Jill had grown up in the nicest house in all of Kutz. It was a white mansion, modeled after southern plantation houses. Even though they were firmly in Yankee territory. The house stood back from the road by the length of almost an entire football field, with a pristine rolling lawn that most definitely never had a child's bike drive down it— like most of its neighbors.

Sometimes Vernie would force Quid to go over for play-dates—which was almost worse than having Jill over to her house. Quid hated the feel of the marble floor under her feet and the clean, washed white of everything. Every time she went, she felt like she was going to dirty it somehow. It was the kind of house that never appeared as though anyone actually lived in it.

The Hill family had come from money and then that money grew and grew with the family farm. They had held a monopoly on the local vegetable market for as long as anyone could remember. Until the contamination started wrecking their crops too. Not that Jill would know. She had probably never seen a speck of dirt underneath those purple-polished nails.

Quid remembered back to Vernie's lecture during lunch about "making an effort" and went to sit next to the other girl. The cool hardwood wrapped around her legs as she sat cross-legged from Jill. Her blue jean shorts still had dirt on them from this morning's rounds in the greenhouses.

Jill had pranced in just a few minutes before with the clack of her shiny shoes. She had plopped a pink, bedazzled bag on Quid's bed. It appeared stuffed to the brim with the too-shiny dolls. Quid cringed at the dozens of tiny bodies and outfits now strewn across the floor.

Why are so many of them naked?

From outside the door, Quid heard the deep chuff of Fen's laughter. Already bored, Quid sat down the doll Jill had handed her to play with. Its slick plastic legs were slime in her hands.

"Let's play outside or Mom said we might go to the lake." Quid suggested again. The sunroom was cool enough in the evenings, but in the heart of a summer day, it had grown stifling. Excitement spilled from Quid as she jumped to her feet. She was ready to get to the lake and see what she could do.

Jill's tiny pink nose crinkled in the air. She stared at Quid as if she had grown two heads. "No." She stated it simply. Quid wondered again if she had been born saying that word and had simply never bothered to learn any others.

"And she isn't even your real mom." Jill's quiet voice rang through the air. Quid watched, dumbfounded and hurt, as Jill continued brushing the doll's long blonde hair. A fit of burning anger-filled Quid's chest and warm tears filled her eyes.

I asked. That counts as an effort. Quid thought to herself, shrugging her shoulders as she swept out the door from her room and walked into the backyard. She let the door slam behind her.

I will bite her if you want me to, an angry voice filled Quid's head. She rubbed Fen's ears as they walked away, determined to find Vernie, and get going.

Vernie sent Jill out to help Merle load the truck, though Quid wasn't certain if the little girl would be any help at all.

Quid packed what she thought she might need into her new, brown, rucksack. Well, it wasn't new, but it was new to her. Once Vernie had resigned herself to the hike, she had dug it out from the bottom of the closet. She said she had used it when she was younger when she used to travel a lot, but now it could belong to Quid. The padding on the straps had been flattened, and one of the smaller zippers often got caught, but still Quid loved it. To her, it was like receiving a piece of history.

In their family—or just Vernie— they believed each hiker should be responsible for their own gear. As Vernie filled the bag, she explained to Quid how "…each one of them carried the essentials for a successful hike, no matter how long or short the hike might be."

"Like water?" Quid asked Vernie, as she watched her mom's quick hands grab from the small pile of supplies sitting on the bed.

"Exactly. But so much more." Vernie looked down at the bed in front of them, gesturing to the medical tape, gauze, and socks now littering the bed.

Quid checked the small front pockets of the bag again. Her small hand barely fit inside. The rough zipper scraped across her hand. Quid winced as the delicate skin tore. She would have to watch out for that one.

Inside the first pocket, Vernie put minor medical supplies—things like band-aids, gauze, and something called a tamp-on which you were supposed to shove up your nose if it bled. Inside the other small pockets were other just-in-case supplies.

Vernie explained each one to Quid as she placed each one in its pocket, "The butane lighter is more reliable than a pack of matches because matches could ruin in the rain. The thermal blanket will keep you warm in case you get lost and it gets dark…" Vernie looked at Quid, her face stoic and serious.

"And the most important item…" Vernie held up the pair of thick, blue socks she had pulled out from Quid's dresser earlier.

"What? More important than water?" Quid laughed. Surely, Vernie was joking.

"Nope. Remember, if you get wet—and you can't change, or you can't stay warm—you die."

Vernie's harsh words resounded in her ears as she rubbed the soft fabric of the sock between her thumbs. A tremor of fear went up her spine. *Maybe we shouldn't go.*

As if sensing Quid's sudden fear, Vernie wrapped Quid in a tight hug before placing the socks inside and pulling the strings that tied up the bags.

"Don't worry. We aren't doing any crazy hiking today."

She's right, you know. Being wet and cold is the worst. It's the only real benefit of having fur. She heard Fen's voice declare inside her head.

Still, Quid thought about Vernie's words of warning as she grabbed the bag and checked the zippers again.

The new weight of the bag settled against her back as she slung it over her shoulders. A rush of excitement filled her as she walked from her room into the warm light of the kitchen.

They filled their metal water bottles up at the sink and put them in their bags. Vernie and Quid hurried towards the front door, where Merle was already waiting in his old blue truck. Quid watched as he placed his hand on the steering wheel, about to honk at them to hurry it up. From the corner of her eye, she saw Vernie give him a steely-stare and in an instant the older man was out of the truck, opening the passenger door for the two of them.

The wind wrapped around Quid, mirroring her excitement, as Quid climbed into the back seat of the creaky truck. Her belt clicked and she listened as the engine angrily prattled on. The back of the truck sagged as Fen clambered into the bed.

Quid sat on the soft, worn, leather seats and waited for Merle to pull away. She wrapped her arms around the soft, burlap bag as the house disappeared from view.

I still don't think this is a good idea. She heard Fen's voice say behind her.

The lake was about half-an-hour from their house and Quid watched from the small window in the back of the truck as the golden fields whipped by in a blur. Next to her, Jill prattled on, playing with her dolls again. Quid watched as the trees flew by.

Quid was daydreaming of little plastic heads bouncing from the pavement when Merle began to whisper. As she pulled from her stupor, she suddenly understood what her parents were talking about.

As they drove the land around them had changed. Fields that should be green and filled with life had spots and patches of brown. Enormous oak trees were bare of leaves, some tipping at an angle. Some trees had grown so rotten that their trunks looked as though a giant had shoved its hand through them. The contamination in the land was getting worse and its effect got harder to deny as they got closer to the lake.

A sinking feeling rose in Quid's stomach as she wondered how she could possibly help the plants and animals if the poison had gotten this bad.

The closer the truck got to the lake the sicker Quid began to feel. She watched again from the window as a small, brown sign that read "Rose Lake Welcomes You" whizzed by.

Within minutes, Quid began to not only see the difference in the landscape, but she also felt it wash over her.

It was early autumn and the leaves on their property had begun to change colors. The ash trees typically turned first. The green of their leaves slowly faded, painting the forest canopy. Then, the ground beneath turned the most stunning yellow. The rest of the trees would follow, their brilliant oranges and reds mixing in the earth like a painter's pallet.

She truly loved the magic of fall. She loved how some years the process felt slow, other years she would wake up and the change had happened overnight. Quid was always connected to the woods, but as fall visited and winter stayed her influence quieted. The trees prepared their slumber.

As they approached the lake, Quid was met with an overwhelming emptiness. She knew before getting out of the car the trees weren't fading off into sleep. They were dying.

Merle turned the truck on to a rough, gravel road, tossing Quid about in the back seat despite the seatbelt she clung desperately to. She watched as Jill bounced around next to her, spilling dolls all along the floor.

The land had become hard and rough. All around the truck dust stirred. The truck began its descent. Merle pulled again and again at the little black knob, trying desperately to spray the windshield with fluid and wash the brown crust covering it.

The brakes on the ancient truck creaked in protest as it made its way down the steep hill that would eventually dump down into the lake. Quid fidgeted nervously in her seat as she tried to peer from the window.

"My whole family used to come here when we were kids," Merle spoke to no one in particular. His voice filled with awe as he craned his head over the steering wheel to see better.

A nauseous feeling crept over Quid the closer they got to the lake. The dust cleared as the ground underneath the truck changed again. An empty parking lot stretched before them. Hundreds of vacant spaces, many with their painted lines faded, sat empty. The lot ran along the length of what appeared to be a barren beach. No one spoke as Merle drove towards the beach. The truck maneuvered slowly, swerving around potholes and dips in the pavement.

As they approached the beach Merle slid the truck into park. The three of them left the cab, with creaks and slams of the trucks' doors shattering through the quiet air. Quid's head swiveled around the desolation, trying to take it all in.

As Vernie closed the truck's heavy door with a thud, Fen's rough fur brushed against her side. Her mouth went dry and her feet were suddenly heavy, as she slowly walked towards where the lake should be. She struggled to understand how everything could feel so empty.

"Let's unload the picnic, honey," Merle said to Vernie, walking around the back of the truck to pop the tailgate open.

"Don't go too far..." Vernie shouted to Quid, who had already begun the trek to the beach. Next to her, Jill walked on tiptoes, as if less contact with the ground would keep the dust away from her perfect shoes. Quid could feel her mom's worried stare burn into the back of her head as she walked away, pretending not to hear.

To her surprise, Fen said nothing as he walked next to the two girls. The ground crunched underneath them as the silence fell like a curtain. No birds chirped a warning or greeting. The trees on the edge of the beach were lifeless and broken. Their leaves had long since perished and their trunks split open, revealing nothing but broken insides. The only thing stirring in this wasteland was dust, swept up as the wind reacted to Quid's unease.

The three of them walked across a small concrete bridge that connected a deep trench for sewage and rainwater. Quid looked down into the gap to see if any water flowed, but saw only dry, cracked earth.

Up ahead of them sat a slab of concrete. Remnants of a tiny, crumbling brown building sat haphazardly on one side. A large part of the roof was missing. Along two of the sides, there were empty door frames.

It must have been part of a larger building at one point. Fen motioned with his head at the side closest to them.

The building stood awkwardly in the center, missing giant chunks of walls. As they approached, Quid saw several long, metal pipes sticking out from the ground at odd angles. Though it had been graffitied several times with black spray paint, Quid barely made out the word "bathhouse" on a small metal sign near the empty doorframe.

As they walked along the side of the dilapidated building, making their way to the beach ahead. Quid felt Fen pause. His nose was sniffing wildly in the air and Quid watched as he eyed the structure.

More spray paint ran along the walls. She tried to make out the words and symbols, though none appeared familiar to her. In a dark red color that reminded Quid of dried blood, someone had drawn the name of their gang, Profectus, in a strange cursive script.

Bright orange, crudely drawn, body parts covered a large portion of the wall and Quid rolled her eyes. At the center was a weird picture—a symbol Quid didn't recognize. It was also painted in red. A circle was divided in half by a crescent moon, arrows stuck out from the center toward the sides.

The hair on the back of Quid's neck stood on end as she looked at the strange symbol, but she quickly shook it off. She was here to help the creatures that depended on the lake, not worry about stupid gang symbols.

"That's gross. They should take it down." Jill's face filled with contempt as she looked at the strange building and the trash that littered the ground.

Quid and Fen continued their walk towards the beach, leaving Jill to wander. The knots in Quid's stomach tightened.

Placing a shaky hand on Fen's back to steady herself, Quid focused on how her short fingers felt wrapped in the thick brown fur. They stepped together from the concrete slab and on to the sand. Her tennis shoes sunk into the earth, filling with little grains. Next to her, Fen made a noise of disapproval as he shook the sand from his paws.

Finally, they reached the edge of the enormous, dry, lake. Quid looked out at it. Though the ground descended so she could not see the middle, she knew if she wanted to, she could visit the depths of the lake that had once been untouched. She could walk across the entire expanse of this wasteland.

Another wave of nausea came as Quid examined the huge cracks in the earth. Each crevice was a testament to too much time under the scorching sun. What was once soft mud teeming with life was now a spiderweb of decay.

Let's go back. Fen urged.

It was all Quid could do to shake her head. She fought against the bile rising in her throat and the headache pressing into her temples.

"Wait." Quid whispered aloud. Her voice broke at the pain of the growing pressure. She wasn't sure who she was begging now, Fen, herself, or the lives of everything around her.

Quid met Fen's dark, disapproving eyes as she knelt to the

ground. Slowly stretching her fingers, she rested her palms flat against the jagged cracks in the earth. Closing her eyes, Quid listened and reached with her influence. She couldn't send it far, only a few feet around her, but immediately she felt it.

Something dark, something sick, had poisoned this land. The tendrils had slowly seeped through the earth, killing off fish, clogging the waterways, destroying the ecosystem bit by bit. Around her, Quid felt the animals who managed to survive hidden among the nearby trees. She thought maybe she should go to them, but something urged her to stay near the lake. Even if she could help them like she helped the plants, they would never survive if the lake wasn't restored.

It grew harder to maintain her connection to the earth as Quid grew tired. The pollution, the darkness, was draining her strength. Somewhere in the back of her mind, she knew she couldn't get it all. She couldn't heal this enormous lake. At least not right now. Instead, like the plants in the greenhouses, she focused on a single spot.

She pictured the earth under her palms. She pulled images of soft clay, of the lake full of water and teeming with life like the creek near her home. Her breath rattled in her chest as she pictured boats on the lake, fish splashing in the water, minnows darting about her fingers.

Quid opened her eyes with a start. She thought that she must be dreaming. In her hand, she held thick, wet clay. It was exactly what she had imagined. The black goop fell through her fingers. Her knees no longer knelt on the sharp, painful ground but sank into the earth. The legs of her jeans were coated in thick, wet mud.

Quid looked above her. Gray clouds had indeed swept across the sky, though as she looked around, she realized no water droplets marked the ground.

Again, Fen sniffed the air nervously. His eyes were transfixed on the bathhouse behind them.

Let's go. It's going to rain.

This time, Quid agreed. She wrenched herself free from the thick mud as it suctioned to her shoes, threatening to hold her in with every step she took.

With every slosh, they trudged back towards the shore she wondered again where it had suddenly come from. Each step be came a chore.

Quid's head was foggy as her exhaustion grew. She clung to Fen's scruff to pull her along.

Finally, the mud gave way to softer sand and then the hard, packed dirt. Quid tried in vain to shake off the debris from her heavy shoes. Vernie was going to be mad that she had gotten so dirty.

Quid walked closer to where Jill was crouched in the dirt. Her back was to the lake and her frilly dress pooled around her. Quid heard a quiet clicking noise as they approached.

"Look what I found!" Jill's stubby fingers were wrapped around a small, green lighter.

Quid watched in horror as Jill set a small piece of paper on fire and began throwing it on the nearby anthills that spread across the barren earth. Hundreds of tiny black bodies ran from the little flames.

"Quit it! That's mean!" Anger filled Quid's chest as she jumped at the girl, trying to wrench the lighter from Jill's hand.

Jill hit the earth with a thud. Dust stirred around them and the mud that covered Quid now spread across Jill, covering her dress.

Jill's eyes were huge as she looked at her dress in horror. "You're such a freak! They should have left you in the woods!"

Next to her, Fen let out a low growl at the girl.

It all happened so fast.

The little embers in the papers strewn across the ground suddenly grew. Their flames snatched at Jill's legs, latching onto her dress. The thin frills began to suddenly smolder.

Jill's screams filled Quid's ears as she and Fen watched on in horror. Red welts appeared on Jill's legs and arms as she flailed on the ground.

"Make it stop! Make it stop!" Tears poured from Jill's puffy face as she swatted away the flames.

Enough. Fen's voice was a painful demand that filled Quid's head and a sudden, sharp pain filled her mind. The wolf smacked its head roughly against Quid's ribcage, knocking her off Jill.

Quid tipped to the side, struggling to catch herself. The hard smack of the ground snuffed out Quid's rage. Shock washed over Quid as she realized that Fen had hurt her. It wasn't much, but the realization of it washed over her like a cold shower. Quid's anger extinguished—and with it went the embers around them.

Terror seized Quid as she looked into Fen's furious eyes,

desperate for answers.

A moment passed before Quid realized what had happened. A perfect circle had spread across the grass, charring the plant-life around them. The smell lingered in the air as wisps of smoke danced.

New fear at what she had done spilled from her. She looked again at Fen's eyes. Already, they too had switched from anger to concern. He nudged her gently to her feet with his wet nose as she looked around at the damage and chaos she had caused.

Did I really do that? She wondered again. She had never used her influence on fire before. The destruction she caused by losing her temper seemed far worse than what Jillian had caused, though at least what Quid had done was an accident.

Together, she and Fen helped Jill limp back towards the truck. As they stumbled along, Quid looked at the red and pink welts covering the girl's arms and legs. The smell of smoke and burned flesh filled her nose as the girl sobbed loudly between them.

As they passed the building again Quid felt Fen's body shift.

He curled around Quid, walking between her and Jill and the small structure, pushing the girls away and further down the beach.

The truck is straight ahead!

Water droplets began falling, slowly at first, then faster. Quid welcomed them, hoping to ease Jill's pain.

The rain woke her from her stupor, startling her and making her more alert. The air around her immediately responded to her desire. Like turning on a switch, sheets of rain began to pour around them.

Fear pressed on her even more. She had not meant to urge the rain on. In the same moment though, just like she had with the sudden mud in the lake, the pressure from the animals released. They knew water meant life.

The sound of the rain quickly became deafening. The down-pour fell around them, creating a wall of water that made it hard to see. Quid marveled at what she had accidentally caused. She could hear nothing but the pounding of the rain.

Her temporary joy was erased as she felt the thick rumble of Fen's low growl.

Quid peered nervously through the rain, following Fen's gaze. At first, she could see nothing. Somewhere in her mind, she registered that Jill had let go of her hand. She hadn't wanted to wait for them, for whatever was distracting Fen. Quid watched as the young girl took off running towards the truck.

Quid desperately wiped the water from her eyes, trying to create a shield from the onslaught with her hand. The clouds had grown thick, darkening the day and everything around them.

Fear swept across her as she watched a lone, dark figure emerge from the broken building. Fen sent an angry warning out, all the while pushing Quid behind him. The lone figure continued to walk towards them.

Get to the truck! Fen sent the command out to her. His voice in her mind was filled with anger and something else. It took her a few heartbeats to realize what it was. She had never felt it from him before. It was fear.

She turned towards the direction of the truck without hesitation and ran as fast as she could. Jill was nowhere to be seen.

As Quid's fear rose to her throat, the rain poured even harder around her. Her feet slipped several times on the damp ground and her delicate knees were torn apart by the sharp rocks again and again.

She yelled for Vernie and Merle, hoping they would hear her cries and come help. Somewhere in front of her, she heard the truck's loud, familiar honk pierce through the sound of the rain. Within seconds, she saw two identical beams of light in the distance and knew she must be getting close.

As she sprinted towards the yellow lights the ground underneath her gave way. Suddenly, she was on her back, sliding downwards. The sharp edges of something tore through her back. The skin grated from her legs and hands as she tried to stop the descent.

Quid crashed to the bottom as an intense, piercing pain shot across her leg. Blackness overcame her momentarily as time seemed to stop.

When she opened her eyes, she wasn't sure how much time had passed. The rain wrapped around her and she realized she must be in the ditch.

Quid's leg throbbed as she tried to push herself from the ground. Panic overcame her as she looked up, unable to see the truck's comforting lights. The wind wrapped around the walls, mimicking her panic.

Again, Quid tried to climb the steep edge of the ditch, but the pain was unbearable. She was stuck. Her lungs stung and her heart pounded in her chest as Quid tried to catch her breath. The wind and rain continued their onslaught as they responded to her panic. Water began to rise underneath her. She could feel the current sweeping around the bottom of her shoes. *Why did I want to come here?*

She hadn't been this alone since the morning she woke up in the woods. Since Fen brought Merle to her, she had never really been alone. Warm tears threatened to spill from her eyes as she listened for any sign of her parents or Fen. She silently wished not to hear any sign of whoever had come out of that building.

Let them find me. She thought desperately. A loud, desperate scream strangled from her throat again. She hoped it reached her parents.

As if in response, the rain simply stopped. A strong breeze swept out from the ditch and across the top, carrying Quid's words.

The pain in her leg pulsated as Quid tried for the third time to climb out of her muddy trench. She grabbed desperately at the top of the ledge with her aching fingers when a familiar hand grabbed her. Quid looked up into Vernie's blue eyes, filled with worry.

"Merle! I got her!" Vernie yelled. Within seconds, Vernie had lifted Quid out, dragging her up by both arms. The two of them sat on the soft ground, holding each other tightly. Quid listened to the soothing sound of Vernie's heart beating wildly, as violent sobs of relief shook through Vernie's chest.

Merle came running down the length of the ditch, water splashing all around him. Vernie went to stand, attempting to help Quid. But the minute she was on her feet Quid fell back to the ground, blinding pain shooting up her leg, threatening to steal her from consciousness again. A scream of anguish left Quid as she gripped her leg.

Vernie gingerly lifted Quid into Merle's strong arms. The truck's bright beams welcomed them back as they made their way through the downpour.

Quid watched as Vernie cranked the door of the truck open. Jill lay stretched across the front seat. The carnage of the burns across her legs and arms stood out against the seat as the girl wailed. A few bandages from Vernie's first aid box were already wrapped around Jill's wrist.

For the first time, Quid realized that tiny pieces of green plastic stuck out all along the girl's left arm. The lighter had exploded and embedded itself in her skin.

"Where's Fen?" she heard Merle ask.

Quid's heart skipped a beat. She had completely forgotten Fen and the dark figure. Images of them battling it out flashed across her mind as bile rose in her throat from the panic and the pain.

The pain in her leg was almost too much to bear as Vernie and Merle laid her in the back seat. Still, she struggled to pull herself upwards, peering out, hoping to find a pair of dark eyes staring back at her.

"We gotta find Fen!" Quid screamed, trying in vain to sit herself up against the soft cushions in the back of the truck. The stabbing in her leg nearly caused her to lose consciousness.

Where are you?! Where are you?! She sent the thought through their connection again and again, but the familiar pull of Fen's mind was silent.

Merle walked around the front of the truck and towards the beach as Vernie leaned over the seat to adjust Quid's leg. Quid steeled herself against the pain as Vernie gently lifted it atop the soft, brown backpack.

"Go get him, Merle! We gotta get Quid to a hospital. I think her leg is broken!" Vernie yelled, voice full of panic.

I'm here. She heard Fen reply in her mind from somewhere in the distance. Quid peered over the top of the seat and out the windshield to see him hop the trench.

"Fen's hurt too!" It was Merle's turn to sound out his panic. Quid listened as the old man helped the wolf into the back of the truck. Quid breathed a sigh of relief when the truck sagged with the wolf's weight. The loud crash of the tailgate shook the truck as it was hastily closed.

Quid tried to peer through the tiny back window and into the bed of the truck, but Vernie pushed her gently down.

"He's gonna be okay," Merle climbed behind the wheel. "He's covered in blood, but—it's…it's not his?" Merle's question hung in the air between them.

"What the hell happened out there?"

Jill's wails increased as Merle drove the truck away. Quid looked at her again. Guilt wrapped around Quid's stomach as she watched Vernie look on in horror at Jill's burns.

I lost control. I didn't mean to hurt her.

Fen's sad voice whispered back to her. His voice was full of defeat and shame and when he spoke in her mind fresh tears fell from her eyes. *You cannot afford to lose control again. We all could have been killed.*

Merle continued speeding across the enormous parking lot and back towards civilization.

"What happened out there, Quid?" Vernie asked again as she examined the broken nails and scrapes along Quid's hands.

But Quid's mind was listening for Fen, berating him with questions. *Who was that? What happened? Why did they want to hurt us?* Quid tried to pull her thoughts back together, to answer the questions her parents flooded her with, but as she sunk against the fabric of the seat the adrenaline began to wear off and the pain of her broken leg overwhelmed her.

I don't know, but he got away. She heard Fen's apology whisper across her mind as she faded off into unconsciousness. She wasn't sure which of them was more ashamed.

Part Two

Chapter Six

It had been ten years since the incident with the man on the beach. Quid was nearing seventeen and was no longer the little girl from the woods, as the headlines had read so many years before. However, as they had always been, things were strange.

For Vernie and Merle, the fear of what could have been never left and a new fear set in. Now it was not just a fear of Quid's influence being discovered, but of what her possessing such power could mean. As a result, they stopped forcing Jill and Quid to try to be friends and began living a life of solitude, guarding Quid's secrets more than ever. Jill would tell everyone that Quid "set her on fire with her mind" and most people believed that the two girls had simply been doing something they shouldn't.

For Quid, as most children would, she would only remember the day with the fear that came with almost losing a friend and the shame of losing control. She would remember the sensation of falling into the ditch and the weeks in a cast, but almost nothing about the strange figure or Fen's fight with him.

As time passed, the three of them became a family and soon it was hard for the older couple to remember a time when they hadn't all been together. When Quid turned ten Vernie and Merle legally adopted her, but in truth, she had been their daughter since that first day that she brought magic to their lives.

Summer was nearing its end and in her room at the back of the house, Quid rolled out of bed slowly. The days of morning breakfasts had long gone. Every morning Merle and Vernie would still wake up at the crack of dawn. Merle went on his morning walks with Fen, and Vernie prepared the gift shop. These days the three of them usually greeted each other from behind a cup of coffee or a bowl of cereal.

Inside Quid's sunroom, the air was already stifling, even though the sun was barely beginning to rise. Quid slowly kicked back the thin, blue sheet tangling itself around her feet. As her eyes adjusted to the morning glow coming in from behind the blinds, she looked around the small room to see that Fen must have already left with Merle.

Quid walked over to the faded, white dresser she had woken up to all those years before and sighed. The paint was chipped and one of the knobs had long ago rolled away, never to be seen again. Not for the first time she wondered why she couldn't have a modern one with rolling drawers instead of this old contraption. She disliked the idea of the plastic pieces within the new, fancier ones, but anything was better heaving open the heavy drawers.

She cranked open the old drawers. The wood frame of the dresser heaved back and forth as she tried to pry her clothes free from confinement. Finally, she managed to pull out her favorite dark-blue, jean shorts, and a black tank top. As she opened the stubborn top drawer, she heard a knock at the door.

"I have to run some errands. I will be back after lunch." Vernie announced from the other side of the door.

Perfect. Quid thought to herself. She wanted to go to the pool anyway. It was supposed to be hot today and she could sit in the shade or lounge on the edge and people-watch. If Vernie left soon she could slip out without doing her rounds in the greenhouses and be gone before she got back.

"Okay. I'll see you later." Replied Quid coolly.

Ever since the incident at the beach and the weeks of people asking questions, Vernie was always looking over her shoulder. She was always urging Quid to be more careful with her "influence" over the world around her, even though Quid rarely used her influence on purpose.

No matter what animals or plants crossed her path, no matter how desperate the land around The Gardens grew, she refused to take the chance. She had given up listening to the animals and playing with water—or fire—a long time ago. She wouldn't risk losing control again and hurting anyone else.

Vernie's nervousness at Quid's abilities made it all the more clear that she was just as embarrassed as Quid that her daughter was such a freak. As if her over-protective mom senses told her that something was up, she heard Vernie's footsteps hesitate on the creaky, wooden floor before walking away.

Quid slipped on the yellow bikini she had bought the week before, followed by a tank top and shorts. Vernie would never approve of her bathing suit choice, so today was the perfect day to wear it.

In under an hour, Quid had gotten together all the things she needed for the day, including her homemade sunscreen, a lunch for the day, and her favorite tie-dye beach towel.

As she rolled up the towel, she smiled to herself and thought back to the day when the three of them had each made one. Almost a year after the incident, Merle and Vernie had taken Quid and Fen back to the lake. Word had spread. The lake was once again filled with water and returning to life.

Vernie said they needed to return "for closure." She had invited Jill to come too, but the Hill's no longer returned Vernie's calls.

The three of them dyed the towels the night before and then rinsed them out as usual. They had thought the dye was rinsed enough to use the next day. They were all eager to go swimming. After getting out of the lake, she and Vernie had gone to relax in the sun on their new rainbow towels. It wasn't until half an hour later, when Merle came back with snacks, they realized their wet bodies had soaked up the residual dye. Their chests, faces, stomachs, everything that touched the towel was a mess. Their skin was a kaleidoscope of colors for three days.

Quid ignored the pressure of the hundreds of plants in the greenhouses that sought her attention. She no longer took them back to her room and rarely visited. Still, their business was one of the only ones in the area fighting off the contamination.

I'm a freak without even trying. The sour thought sat in Quid's mind. She was glad Fen wasn't around to snap at her again.

With her large beach tote in-hand, Quid emerged from her room to find Merle in the yard fussing over the new tables again.

"I am going out. Where is Fen?" Quid talked to herself as she crossed the new, paved walkway that connected the new picnic area. She scanned the yard for her persistent escort.

I am here. Spoke the droll, irritated male voice in her head.

"Are you coming?" Quid responded aloud. She refused to share in his mind-melding these days. Sometimes he was almost worse than Vernie. Neither ever agreed to anything Quid wanted to do. Vernie pressed her not to use her abilities, while Fen urged her to practice her control.

Quid walked across the walkway, watching as Merle busied himself. He adjusted the heavy wooden picnic tables for the umpteenth time. She smiled to herself as he moved the heavy table back and forth, inch by inch. He had been doing that all week, never satisfied with the way the seating area looked.

Merle stood up, smiling his wrinkly smile. He looked proudly down at the tables he had painstakingly crafted. On his morning hikes, he brought back naturally fallen wood. He had logs and branches of all shapes and sizes, sanded down and glossed. He had also found a large tree that had fallen during a storm and cut it for the tabletops.

In the end, he had created the beautiful picnic area between the house and the greenhouses. All "without supporting the logging companies," he would loudly proclaim to anyone nearby. He had even found a blacksmith in some craft-town in Kentucky to make him nails from recycled metal.

A few months ago, Merle and Vernie had an idea to get customers to come back and to stay longer. They wanted to be more than a gardening center. Soon they were hosting classes about eco-friendly and sustainable living. They started hosting events on the weekend like soap-making, repurposing old clothes, and how to cut down the amount of trash a family produced in a week.

They had also hired a company that used polished, natural, stones, to create a small picnic area in the shape of a large circle. On the weekends the idea was to get customers to stay for the local food trucks or the gift shop. Local artists and musicians would also come in and sell whatever they were making or playing.

Like most small towns, Fridays were for football games, but they were hoping The Gardens would be the place to be on Saturdays.

"What do you think?" Merle asked, surveying the picnic area again.

"I think it looks great, Dad."

Quid came over and wrapped her arm around Merle's broad shoulders. She leaned her cheek against the soft, blue fabric of his shirt. Without thinking, Merle moved to give her a strong, side-arm, hug. Quid breathed in the woodsy smell of him as they looked at the seating area. Things between the two of them had always been easy, simple. They understood each other in a way she and Vernie probably never would.

When she no longer wanted to visit the greenhouses, he didn't push her or even ask—unless he was desperate.

The realization that Vernie may never get over the shame of having her as a daughter brought back a heavy feeling in Quid's stomach. It was one she never could seem to shake.

"Is it 'lit' enough?" Merle looked at Quid with his crooked smile.

Quid couldn't help it. She burst out laughing at his attempt to use slang. *Where did he even hear that word?* She mused as she caught her breath between fits of laughter.

"If you want kids to come here, you're going to have to put something other than the oldies on, Dad."

"Hey. No one turns off the King." Merle looked around again for the small, yellow measuring tape on the table. "Now, for the lights…"

"Don't forget about the porch though…" Quid gently reminded him. Vernie might never forgive him if he didn't stop putting off fixing the porch.

Quid kissed his wrinkly, grizzled, cheek before heading off. He didn't bother to ask where she was going since there weren't many places she could be going to in Kutz in the first place.

"Be safe," Merle yelled as she walked to the rusty, red truck. Her parents had bought her the truck for her birthday—or 'found' day, since they didn't know when her actual birthday was—a few months prior.

It was a creaky old truck with rust on the bumper and a tailgate that had to be jimmied with a screwdriver. But it had four wheels and Quid loved it. She also didn't have a lot of choices. Her influence and electricity didn't always go well together. She often struggled to control what happened when it came to electronics, especially cars. However, it turned out the bigger, diesel engines with less "froo froo" —as Merle called it—upgrades were less affected by her presence.

Quid climbed up proudly into what she called The Beast and instantly felt Fen clamber onto the bed of the truck.

As Quid drove through downtown Kutz she watched as the town's shops crawled past her window.

The town was ancient, built a hundred years ago by German settlers from Virginia. All along Main Street, there were small mom-and-pop shops, with everything from hardware, to clothes, even a grocery store. Quid watched as the shop owner hung a sign in the window, advertising their fall sale. The shop next to his had long closed its door. Faded-yellow close-out signs blocked the dusty windows.

Like many other stores in town, the poison was spreading through the land and it was affecting everything and everyone.

Storefronts sat empty and vacant, a silent testimony to better times. Quid looked longingly at the stores as she drove by. There was no hope anything new was coming. No one was interested in moving to a town that was dying.

Quid drove, glancing occasionally out her window. As she got to the red light at the end of Main Street, she looked over at one of the only businesses in town not to suffer from the loss of customers. Ms. May's beautiful, Victorian Bed and Breakfast sat regally on the corner.

Quid looked at the tall, white window frames set against the dark, red trim of the enormous house as she drove by. Two young boys in blue jeans and paint-splattered t-shirts held rollers on long sticks, trying desperately to reach the edges of each column at the front of the house. Each summer, like clockwork, the porch and trim were always painted with a fresh coat of white paint by Ms. May's grandsons.

On the lawn stood Ms. May. Quid watched as the older woman gestured to the two young boys. Although she was an almost 90-year-old woman, everyone in town knew Ms. May was a force to be reckoned with. She always wore black, and she was always upset with someone about something. Every child who grew up in Kutz knew to watch out for Ms. May and her cane. If a child came home with a red welt the parents wouldn't even ask questions, just send the child back later to apologize and do some chores. Quid watched the two boys with their rollers and wondered if either one of them was secretly sporting a red mark on their behind.

When Ms. May's mother was alive, more than sixty years ago, the building had been renovated into the town's most thriving business. Much of Ms. May's success was due in part to the city's month-long summer folk festival. People came from miles around. Quid thought to herself the next few weeks would be so busy at The Gardens. Their business depended on the festival too and it took almost the whole summer to prepare. The festival was the only one of its kind and always filled the inn and boosted local businesses. By the end of the festival, it left business owners like Ms. May—who would suddenly remember summer pricing was higher—happy for the rest of the year.

Ms. May was also the only person in town Quid suspected may know her secret. In the springtime, Quid and Vernie treated the landscape around the inn, planting and tending the flowers and bushes all around the large yard. Ms. May was very particular about her yard, but she was also willing to pay extra for it to be looked at and cared for. Several times, there were a few problems after planting a flower or bush that didn't grow right. Ms. May would call the house and ask Quid, specifically, to come to look.

Ms. May might not know exactly why Quid was so much more successful than Vernie or Merle in the garden, but she at least knew her presence was all that was required to help the plants grow. Oftentimes she would call with a problem, but the two of them would simply sit in the garden drinking tea and talking local gossip.

Come to think of it, Quid thought to herself, Ms. May might be her one real friend in Kutz.

Quid finally arrived at the pool a few minutes later. As everyone did when they drove down Main Street and saw so many closed or desperate businesses, she shook her head and moved on with her day. Like everyone else, she pushed away the uncomfortable thoughts. She knew she was helpless to stop any of it.

You're not helpless though, you could do something. Fen's voice reminded her again

Quid decided not to reply, ignoring his insistence that she practice using her influence.

Quid relaxed on a towel in the grassy area of the pool. She could hear but tried to ignore Fen's voice in her head from a distant tree. Fen never would tell Quid everything that happened when he fought the man on the beach, but what he had discovered was he could change forms when he pleased now. Ever since then he had been working on new animal shapes to try out whenever they were alone or when no one would notice his absence.

Today he had fashioned himself into an over-sized, black crow and sat perched in one of the many trees people used for shelter from the summer sun.

How appropriate, she thought to herself, *since crows are the thieves of the sky.* He was constantly stealing her privacy.

Why do you come here? She could feel his petulant whining

intrude on her thoughts again. *There are far too many humans. They all smell of chemicals and sweat. The water itself has been turned into an abomination.*

That's why I like it. Replied Quid. *There are people.*

Ignoring any more comments, she continued in her appreciation of the sun's warm glow as she relaxed on her towel. She had been coming here every summer for a few years and today was her favorite kind of summer day.

It was the kind of day where the water was crisp but comfortable. The sun was warm when you left the water, but not too hot you couldn't sit comfortably on a towel and eat snacks or hang out. There was a cool breeze and Quid relaxed as the wind swept the hair off her neck. It was enough to keep her shoulders from getting too hot, but not so harsh to cause a chill. Perfect.

This also meant the pool was very, very crowded. Although she figured water parks in bigger cities were probably larger, Kutz Community still maintained the three things that enticed families to its waters and kept it in business year after year. There was a place for small children to play, a lazy river for older couples. and a huge pool that for half an hour at a time turned into a raucous wave pool—perfect for the thrill-seeking teenagers.

Quid lay on her towel and closed her eyes. Today she had to put her stuff on what was called "The Hill."

The large grassy area in the park had the most trees, making it a great place to lay down in the shade when the summer days were scorching. It was also directly between the walkway to the wave pool and the kiddie area. It was an ideal place for families to spread out their things in preparation for a relaxing day of sun and chlorine.

Around her, families chattered endlessly in all corners of the park. Mothers chased and yelled after toddlers. Elementary-aged children tried to convince their parents they were finally old enough for the large wave pool and its raging waters. Quid always laughed at this because the moms always said no, but the dads often snuck off, taking them anyway. She liked listening to the families squabble and wondered again what that was like. For as long as she could remember, it had just been the three of them. The large farmhouse was often quiet, even when it was filled with customers. Sometimes, it was so quiet that Quid felt like she could disappear, and no one would notice.

The weight of the knowledge sat on her shoulders. Lately, things between her and Vernie had gotten worse. The heaviness was a rock in her gut. The two of them never agreed on anything. Quid thought back to their last big fight the week before. Quid had decided she wanted to go to the football game. It was something she heard kids around town talk about and she wanted to try. Quid had been homeschooled since she was in the fifth grade. Once there were sensitive computers in every class, there had been no choice.

Quid understood why she couldn't go to school like everyone else. That didn't mean she still didn't want to try to have a normal life.

Even after Merle had tried to intervene Vernie refused to allow her to go. It was like Vernie was constantly terrified Quid would lose control.

Quid's chest was heavy as she thought about their tumultuous relationship. Despite the sunshine on her face, a chill came over her.

Quid usually stayed away from The Hill. She didn't dislike families but also didn't feel as though she fit in around them either. She didn't know what that kind of life was like, to have a house full of chaos or the craziness of siblings and cousins. She loved Merle and Vernie, but what would it be like to be normal?

Quid lay on her warm towel and tried again to relax. She welcomed the warmth against her skin and listened to the sound of laughter in the distance. The local country radio station played across the park blasted the new Taylor Swift song for the third time and began to doze in the summer sun.

A light, damp nudge sloshed against her hip. Startled, she opened her eyes and felt for the ball that had rolled onto her towel. As her eyes adjusted to the sudden onslaught of light, she looked over, hoping to find the owner. A pair of bright blue eyes stared down at her expectantly.

Quid handed the smiling boy's ball back to him. The toy was heavy and wet in her hand. She gave it a little squeeze, water dripping out everywhere. "This is so cool. Is this for the water?" She asked as his tiny hand grasped it excitedly.

"Mmmhmm…" he replied, not meeting her eyes, and kicking at the grass. Quid watched him dash back over from where he came, trying desperately to hold on to his bright red Elmo swim trunks as he ran. He couldn't be more than three or four.

Quid laughed as she watched him run across the grass. He used one hand to launch the ball in the air and the other hand never losing his grip on the shorts. Small wisps of crystal water flew out in shimmers as the colors of the pool toy swirled together in the air.

An older woman in a bright red one-piece that rivaled her fire-red hair, yelled "Sorry!" as the boy rejoined his family. Quid nodded to show it was okay. She continued to watch the family with curiosity.

Whistles blew in the distance. The noise was nearly deafening as the shrill noise signaled to the pool's patrons that the mandatory break was over. Quid watched silently as from all over children and families threw down their snacks and drinks and began to rush towards the water.

Quid waited for the parade of wet suits to run past her. Children screamed for their parents to hurry, clutching goggles, pool noodles, and other toys excitedly as they ran towards the water.

After the onslaught, Quid stood up and meandered around the park again. She wore her bathing suit, but she never went in the waters beyond her ankles.

She loved to sit on the edge and feel the power of the water around her. Since she had been coming here so often, she felt more control over her influence. Usually, she could better predict how a body of water would react to her. Quid sometimes went to the creek by their house. She would swim when the water was high enough, or wade down the stream when it wasn't. Unlike the wind, natural water was always steady. It seemed to know its purpose and it wasn't very often she could influence it one way or another. Not that she normally tried in a place like this anyway.

Fen was right about one thing. There was a lot of man-made influence in this water. It wasn't as connected to nature, or her. It had been displaced from its natural flow and pumped with chemicals. It still responded to her presence, and there was a connection to it, but it was so much weaker than a stream or river. It was a wild horse, excited by her presence. Its behavior was unpredictable.

She watched the families and other park patrons, especially kids she recognized from town, but she never ventured further. In the back of her mind, she was too afraid of what would happen, or what someone would notice if she engulfed herself in the waters.

Half an hour later, Quid was relaxing on the edge of the large wave pool when the howl of "wave bell" sounded loud and shrill like a foghorn. This was the two-minute warning for families with young children, people without life jackets, and others who didn't want to fight the onslaught of waves to leave the pool.

Quid sat at the edge and wasn't bothered by the idea of oncoming waves. She quite enjoyed watching people flail about as they tried in vain to conquer these man-made forces. At times what she called "drifters" would get pulled in from the lazy river to the wave pool by the opening in the wall, connecting the two attractions. It never ceased to make her smile when someone who had been snoozing in the lazy river suddenly realized they were surrounded by eight to ten feet of waves. With her ankles in the rising water, Quid waited for the excitement to begin.

The current began to rock as the water heaved. Quid watched as older people made their way out of the churning waters, and young thrill-seekers swam deeper.

Suddenly, from across the expanse of the pool, she noticed the family from earlier struggle to make their hasty exit. The mom with the fiery hair was pulling a small girl alongside her. The young girl kept losing her balance as they hurried from the waters.

The mom was clutching the girl's hand, trying desperately to help her walk out of the water ebbing and flowing around them more forcefully.

The mom turned and yelled something back at the older teenage-boy and motioned to the water. Quid couldn't hear what she said, and apparently, neither could the boy. He made no move in response. He trudged out from the pool as well, stumbling as he went, watching a group of girls nearby who were also making a hasty exit.

The second shrill siren, warning the start of the waves, resounded its deafening tones all around them. What happened next seemed to happen as only such disasters can, both in extreme slow motion and very-very quickly.

Quid watched as the family members made their way out of the water. The water was rough now.

People screamed their excitement, and the frenzy began. From the corner of her eye, a familiar set of Elmo shorts walked back towards the middle of the pool and Quid's heart skipped a beat.

Quid jumped up, but already people on floaties and rafts were crowding the wave pool, creating a terrifying barrier for anyone caught underneath. She lost sight of the little boy in the literal sea of plastic tubes. The waves were gaining strength.

The mom and brother must have realized their mistake as well. A look of panic passed between them. They raced back into the pool. Quid glanced at them, hoping they would find him first, but they didn't seem to be able to locate him either.

For the first time in the three summers, she had been coming to the pool, Quid swam up to her chest. Immediately, she could feel the response. The waves had been given power by man, but the natural strength of the water intensified when her influence touched it.

WHAT ARE YOU DOING? yelled Fen's voice in her mind. *You are going to put these humans in danger. You know it won't behave around you and you are making it worse.*

Find. The. Boy. Quid replied, projecting an image into Fen's mind of the tiny red shorts. She could feel that he had left his perch in the tree and now flew above the pool.

Quid knew there were only seconds. Maybe one of the other swimmers would notice and help Elmo Shorts. None of the life-guards had. They were busy scanning the top of the water. There was no way they would see someone underneath it.

She could feel the excitement of the water wrap around her. It caressed her in a rapid current and kept her from swimming. It wasn't as strong as some other natural waters would be but still, it tried to envelop her and embrace her. Like when lava meets the sea and creates deadly acid, so too could her influence mingling with the force of the water around her create chaos. A natural force meeting another natural force always had consequences, for better or worse.

Quid ducked under the water and opened her eyes. The chemicals stung her eyes, but thanks to her gifts she could see always see perfectly, even in the muddiest waters.

Left! Shouted Fen in her mind.

She jerked her head in that direction to find the boy frantically trying to swim. His tiny legs and arms barely moving him in the water. He tried desperately to reach the surface among all the legs and bodies above him.

Panic set in as Quid watched the child flail. She knew he couldn't last long. She felt a surge within her chest as panic threatened to overcome her. There was a shift in the water. She realized it was listening and waiting.

STOP! She pictured the water calming in her mind. She wished for the waves to calm, urging them to stop.

The water obeyed. The earth shook, the sudden force slamming everything to a stop. All around her people felt it too. The kicking bodies floating above her paused, surprised by whatever the force was that brought the wave pool to a sudden stop.

She swam towards the boy, dodging feet and bodies, underneath the water. *Go* was all she could think about as she pedaled her arms and legs, pushing through the water. The water propelled her towards him in response. People on rafts were pushed out her way by the strength of the water, toppling from their rafts and into the pool. Quid dodged each flailing body, bending and twisting around them.

She watched in horror as the boy sank deeper into the depths of the pool. *Go, go, go,* she urged again. Time seemed to slow as she reached for him. Each time she got closer a wave would pull him away.

To me. She urged the water with her mind. Within seconds, she had the boy in her arms. She swam towards the sunlight above them. The water pushed her up, as her lungs began to burn. Finally, the two of them breached the surface.

Quid willed that she would reach the edge of the pool, picturing the shallows in her mind, and the water instantly complied. She winced in pain, wrapping herself around the boy's slippery torso.

All around her people screamed as the water from the wave pool crashed to the shore. With it, the patrons in the wave pool came crashing to a halt. Not supported by an inner tube, Quid's legs and knees scraped along the rough, concrete bottom of the pool as they landed at the edge.

People lazing in loungers nearby found themselves soaked. Swimmers struggled to land on their feet as they were thrust from the pool. The kiddie pool filled with the run-off as panicked parents grabbed their children, the water suddenly up to their waist.

In seconds, the wave pool was nearly emptied, only a few inches of water remaining. Some patrons sat, dazed, on the harsh concrete floor of the pool. Other patrons who had been float-ing on rafts stood dumbfounded, faces filled with confusion. One minute they were in the wave pool, laughing at the rough waves knocking everyone about. The next minute, they had been washed from the waves to all ends of the park.

Even the lazy river swelled, depositing several patrons along its shores.

Quid stood up, the warm body still in her arms. The little boy's body was bent in two, coughing and heaving water, trying to catch his breath. Quid watched as he coughed so hard it shook his whole, tiny frame. Relief poured from her. At least he was breath-ing. All around her lifeguards abandoned their posts, trying to dis-cern who was injured and who was simply as confused as they were.

"Sam!" screamed a voice across the chaos.

Quid looked up to see the mom with the fire-red hair running towards them, scooping up Sam in her arms. Big, shaking cries came from her as she wrapped the child in a tight hug.

People around Quid began frantically asking each other what happened. Her heart raced even harder than it had before.

Now that she wasn't immersed in the water, her influence dimmed. Quid raced back to The Hill and grabbed her bag. She had to get out before anyone asked her any questions.

Quid left the park as a man on a loudspeaker announced the park would be closing for the day, "due to technical difficulties." She was hurrying across the hot pavement of the parking lot as she spotted the old, blue truck. Vernie's face was full of confusion as she watched people pour from the park gates.

Quid watched as Vernie cross her arms tightly across her chest as she approached the truck.

This one was going to be hard to explain.

Chapter Seven

Dread threatened to overcome her as she followed Vernie home. The entire drive she stared at the red taillights, wondering what was coming.

"I don't understand why you needed to go there anyway. There are so many people and we would be happy to take you swimming at the lake…" as they sat down to dinner Vernie repeated the statement for the third time.

"Because I want to be around other people. I want to have friends." Quid tried to explain again.

Although the lake had made a recovery, many locals still didn't trust it, and Merle and Vernie had a talent for finding the perfect time when no one else was there.

"You are around people though! Think of all the customers who will be here for the festival. And Jack's kids are here sometimes!" Vernie threw her hands in the air again, as if that solved everything.

"That's not the same thing, mom." Quid let out a sigh as her fork clanged loudly on her plate.

Vernie bent towards Quid, gently brushing a hair back from her face, but Quid shrugged off the gesture with a jerk of her head. "Don't you see that's why we are doing all this? We are trying to make The Gardens a safe place for you and your friends to come hang out."

"But I don't *want* to hang out here. Me constantly hanging out here is *why* I don't have any friends."

Quid saw the hurt flash across Vernie's face and instantly regretted her words. She didn't want to hurt her mom, but she also needed her to understand.

"Well, you won't have to worry about hanging around here for a while anyway. That's what I came to tell you this afternoon before all this nonsense happened." Vernie's voice dropped low and she shifted uncomfortably in her seat.

Quid's eyebrows furrowed in confusion as she looked across the table at her mom. Vernie was seldom uncomfortable or unsure. Merle took his wife's hand before gingerly kissing the back of her palm—a silent sign of support.

Despite her annoyance, Quid felt a twinge of appreciation

towards her parents. They might be annoying, but they were true relationship goals.

"An old friend of mine has passed away…" Vernie sighed, running her long fingers through her graying hair. "The funeral is tomorrow, but it's a few hours away. We are going to leave in the morning. Your father will stay and tend to the shop."

At this Merle stood, squeezing his wife's hand one more time before beginning to clear the dinner plates.

"Why do I have to go?" Quid asked. She didn't mind road trips but sensed her mom had ulterior motives.

"We won't make it in time for the funeral, but we are going to camp out with some…friends," Vernie paused. She made a face as the word came out. Like it tasted odd in her mouth. "We can camp with them for a few nights."

Quid began to groan. Although she loved camping, being trapped in the woods with a bunch of her mom's friends did not sound like a good time.

"There will be a lot of kids your age there. He belonged to a unique community. It should be a good time." Vernie bent down, pulling a worn white kitchen towel from a small drawer. Next to her, Merle began washing the dinner dishes as Quid put away the left-over broccoli and rice casserole.

Quid placed the leftovers in the fridge, appreciating the cool breeze as she opened the door. The old farmhouse was stifling lately.

"Besides," she heard her mother say as Quid left the kitchen. "It will give all of this pool business time to blow over…"

"So, my punishment for saving a child's life is that I have to go to a funeral?" asked Quid incredulously for the third time that morning.

Quid followed her mom to the truck again, arms full of boxes of camping supplies.

Vernie let out a long sigh as she shot Quid an irritated glance over her shoulder.

"It's not about punishing you. It's about giving you a chance to get out of the house and about us spending some time together."

"And why can't I take Fen?"

"Honey. We just don't have room." Vernie slid another box into the back of the pickup.

I could always make myself very small and you can put me in your bag... Fen silently suggested.

Are you going to stay in either bird or mouse form for the seven-hour car ride and the three days at the campground?

Except for the incident at the pool, and a few sarcastic comments back and forth, this was the first time Quid and Fen had communicated like this in weeks. The truth was she wouldn't mind being away from him for a while. She was already going to be stuck with her mom. She didn't need them both annoying her. She didn't need another voice constantly telling her to get control.

"Fen can stay here with your dad. They'll both be fine."

Merle came across the yard, carrying their sleeping bags and coolers. Each of them said their goodbyes as the two ladies loaded up the truck.

Quid watched as Fen's tail flicked against the broken hardwood planks of the porch, irritated at being left behind.

I do not like this idea, was the last thing Quid heard him say as the truck turned away from the house.

Chapter Eight

They had missed the funeral, but Vernie made a few phone calls and soon they were headed down some backwoods roads, headed to wherever Vernie was taking them.

After a few miles, Vernie pulled the truck off the state highway onto a dirt road. Within a few minutes, the scenery changed. Quid watched with curiosity as the caravan drove under the shadows of the towering hickory trees above. From the window, Quid watched as a brown sign zoomed by which read "Bald Eagle State Park."

Quid recognized the name, briefly remembering some fourth - grade project. Her body relaxed as they drove deeper into the forest.

Unlike water, she found it was much easier to be around trees and plants, even ones that had never felt her influence. As always, she had to maintain control, but at least she knew what to expect. After all, she was the girl from the forest, and the trees were her home.

As they drove, the forest reached out to her. At first, it was overwhelming, the power of the ancient trees pressed on her. This was a forest where nature was in its truest form. These trees and plants and animals had been around for generations. They had been growing for hundreds of years and they were largely untouched by man. Their presence affected her more than she expected.

At home, there were plenty of old trees on the property. Quid learned the older the tree, the clearer she could feel it. As Vernie drove through the old forest, the sound of it all, trees, animals, streams, plants, sounded in her brain. Like the dull roar which envelops your senses when you drive through a tunnel, it took her mind a minute to adjust to the onslaught of noise. For a few heartbeats, it threatened to overwhelm her. She fought against the increasing pressure as she evened her breath. The ache in her head dulled as she adjusted.

The plants and animals around her greeted her, hoping to share needs no one else could hear, not with words but just with the feelings she got from being around them. She could feel when the forest ached for water because of a drought. She knew before she even got close when a fungus had made its home deep in the trunk of a tree.

She pushed calming thoughts out to them, urging them to wait. She had learned the trick when she was younger, reaching out with her mind when she needed to find an animal in trouble.

Quid closed her eyes and covered her ears with her hands. She didn't hear nature, but the pressure seemed to help her headaches when she was overwhelmed. *Thank you. Please. Easy.* She urged. This continued for several minutes until Vernie finally pulled off at a large clearing.

"Do you have a headache, sweetie?" Vernie asked Quid, reaching out to rub her shoulder. Her voice was filled with worry, and her eyebrows furrowed as she leaned across the seat.

Quid swatted her hand away. Vernie was such a worrywart and Quid wasn't ready to forgive her yet for not letting her explain what happened at the pool.

"I need a second." Replied Quid softly. Quid took several, long, slow breaths. The wind around them was stirring, mimicking Quid's annoyance. The last thing they needed was for Quid to cause a storm around their campsite.

Finally, the dull roar quieted, until it became an itch at the back of her mind. Now that they were stopped for the night, Quid hoped the trees would start to get used to her presence.

Quid kept her eyes closed, listening to the sound of Vernie opening the tailgate of the truck and unloading their supplies. She was still annoyed at being dragged all the way out here, but it was hard to be angry when she was surrounded by the forest. After all, she loved camping.

Quid watched as the rush of unfamiliar faces got out of their cars and began to unpack. Men with long, black ponytails and several women who were dressed head to toe in "fashionable camo" heaved suitcases and tents from their cars. Quid counted not two, but five camo-colored purses.

Not everyone was dressed the same though. Many men and women were dressed in normal clothes, jeans and t-shirts or flannels. As Quid watched she noted how odd it was that so many of them were adorned with beads or shells. Some had bags, clothes, and hair draped in beads and shells of all colors. Quid watched as Vernie's long, straight gray head walked past the truck. Shell earrings bounced against the old woman's neck as she walked.

Is Vernie one of them? Quid wondered to herself. For a

moment, she considered refusing to leave the cab. She reminded herself she loved camping, even if it was with all these weirdo people.

When she had calmed and distracted herself, the wind settled again. The effect of the forest was once more just an itch at the back of her mind.

Quid watched as an older man in a dark, red jacket piled wood inside a large circle of rocks at the center of the camp. Tents of all shapes and sizes had been erected around where the campfire would be, leaving a large space in the middle for people to get out their chairs and gather.

The shadows of the trees continued to stretch as the sun waned and people began preparing dinner. The smells of different foods filled with garlic and spices drifted through the air towards Quid, who sat in her favorite orange folding chair watching the commotion.

Her parents often took her "glamping." Vernie was the one who demanded Quid and Merle participate in glamorous camping. Vernie wasn't as committed to "roughing it" as the rest of the family. She would only go when she could take all the comforts of home. Although the three of them rarely strayed far, her parents had long ago committed to the fact that Quid belonged in the woods. Since her mom wouldn't let Quid have normal social habits, the three of them camped all year long.

At first, when Quid was about six, Merle had bought this orange and black monstrosity of a tent. The thing was huge. It was meant to sleep twelve people in it comfortably. Designed in a giant 't' shape, each section had individual zippers to divide up the space, so each of them could have their own "room," even Fen.

They used the tent for a summer, and everything was fine. After all, it was plenty of space for the three of them and all their stuff. However, there was no tent in all of creation that was going to keep out the winter's chill on a Pennsylvania night in January. The first night Vernie had gotten even a little chilly, she showed up the next afternoon in her very-own pop-out camper. She said she "loved her daughter but could not live without heat and air conditioning."

A small Serro-Scotty, it was a tiny thing even their old truck could pull. Quid stayed out under the stars if she could, but when it came time to go inside, she had to admit it was a lot warmer and more comfortable than the cold, hard ground.

Sadly, three months ago, they realized that the beloved thing had sprung a leak during the last storm and soaked the mattresses. Merle had been fixing it again and again ever since. These days, Vernie was stuck with the enormous tent and blow-up mattresses.

The two of them got the tent up in record time. As Quid stood to unpack the large wooden box labeled "cooking," she listened to the swish of Vernie's feet as she shuffled around inside the tent. She knew that Vernie had wanted to bring the camper, but as she looked around, she realized how out of place it would have looked. Obviously, the people around them were more used to roughing it than her mom.

Quid listened as Vernie huffed and puffed inside the tent. The wall next to Quid bulged as something smacked into it. There were several distinct crashes as things were thrown from the boxes.

Vernie's angry voice filled the campsite and Quid tried to ignore the curious looks from the older couple unpacking next to them.

"Have you seen the pump for the air mattress? I *knew* we should have brought the camper. I don't even care if it leaks!"

An hour later, her mother emerged from the enormous tent, arms full of cooking utensils and pans. Vernie's face was beet red but she smiled triumphantly as she dumped things on the folding table that Quid had erected.

Quid peered into the box before her, "Oh good, because everything in here is cleaning supplies." Remarked Quid, pulling a mason-jar full of thick, green homemade soap from the box.

The smile immediately left Vernie's face. "Your father went on that trip and must have packed them all wrong." She said through gritted teeth, brushing the gray strands of hair back from her face and rubbing her temples. "We are never going to find it all before it gets dark…"

Quid looked around the large campsite. People of all ages unpacked, and as they finished, they walked around greeting one another. Most of them knew each other. It was a parade of polyester. Tents of all colors and shapes filled the edge of the woods, and she could see more in the distance. She realized this gathering was much larger than she thought. *Did Vernie really know all these people?*

At the center of the ring of tents sat a large circle of rocks, piled three-high and filled to the brim with crisscross logs and sticks. As Quid continued unpacking the truck, she watched the wooden pile grow as two young men heaved log after log.

As Quid pulled her heavy animal-quilt, and the soft, furry, gray body-pillow, from the truck she looked up to see the taller boy staring at her.

Even from the short distance, she could tell he wasn't much older than her. Maybe seventeen or eighteen. As she caught his glance, she realized he was also extremely handsome.

He stood next to the large log pile. His skin was tan and brown, glinting with sweat in the sunlight. His arm muscles bulged invitingly as he heaved log after log higher on the pile. His long, brown hair was pulled back in a loose ponytail, but some of the strands had fallen loose, framing his jawline.

Quid wasn't exactly short for her age, but as she stood there looking at him, she didn't feel her height. *I'm finally not taller than a guy.* She thought to herself.

For several seconds she stood, half in and half out of the tent before she realized how awkward it was that he was staring back at her too.

A flush came over her cheeks as she ducked into the tent. She moved around absentmindedly, adjusting pillows and blankets.

Quid made a show of unpacking the campsite as she reemerged. She looked at the boxes before her, though she could care less what was inside, painfully aware he was still standing there.

From her peripheral, she watched as he stood, waiting for the other boy to rearrange the logs. One of the enormous logs was wrapped in his long, sinewy, arms like it was nothing.

Once again, Quid realized she was staring. This time though, he was looking at her intensely. A sly smile spread across his face as he adjusted the log in his arms.

Neither of them looked away until the other boy, who was a full head shorter and far less built, reached for the log. The younger boy was dressed almost identical to the older, taller one. He had the same faded jeans and the same white undershirt. Quid thought he looked to be around twelve or thirteen, but his clothes reminded her of someone trying to convince others he was much older.

"Liam!" the young boy snapped, waving a dirty hand excitedly in the older boy's face. "You gonna throw that last log on there or you want me to take it? I don't think we have room on the pile after all."

Liam seemed to snap back to reality, as did Quid, who again pretended to busy herself with things around the camp. She began shuffling around their section of the campsite, pulling things out of boxes, and setting them on the tables Vernie had erected.

All the while, Quid also tried to pretend she wasn't watching the two boys.

For a second, the boy called Liam didn't move, but the young boy kept his arms out like he was going to take the load. Liam made a motion like he was going to throw the log at the other boy. The younger boy flinched, jumping backward.

"You think you can handle it?" Quid watched as a mischievous grin spread across Liam's lips.

The younger boy didn't seem as amused. "Whatever, I'm going to unpack." He snapped. A dejected look flashed across his face. His pride was obviously wounded. Quid watched as he marched off towards the edge of the circle of tents. He disappeared in a flurry of angry denim.

Liam quickly tossed the log next to the circle. She thought she could be imagining it, but he seemed to smile in her direction before running off into the woods after his smaller counterpart.

Inside the tent came the clang of metal hitting the ground. Quid again peeked through the front flap. Vernie had furiously dumped out three boxes inside the tent and was now surrounded by the contents. Near her feet, Quid began to pick up pots, pans, soaps, and several rolls of toilet paper—which had now rolled across the uneven ground.

"Why do I even bother labeling anything?!" Vernic yelled to no one in particular. Quid tried to help her mom sort the items back into their boxes as she entered the tent, laughing at the adult temper-tantrum before her.

Quid and Vernie got everything sorted into their proper boxes in under an hour. The sun had gone behind the trees and twilight had set in.

Quid was busy preparing the different fruits and veggies for their salad as she watched more and more people come towards the center of the ring of tents.

Within a few minutes, tables of all sizes had been placed along one side of the campsite. Quid watched with fascination as young children began draping hand-woven tablecloths with beautiful geometric designs along the line of tables. Quid smiled, as she recognized the young boy from earlier motioning to the young children on how to fix the cloths properly. He had found somewhere *he* could be the boss.

As the final light of day dimmed, the sounds of crickets increased all around her. More and more people from each tent came and set bowls and foods along the tables. Slowly, they gathered around the tall, unlit pyre. The campsite was suddenly teeming with people.

The sun was setting, and an older gentleman walked from between two tents, bent down, and the carefully constructed fire was lit, illuminating the faces of everyone around her.

"I should have known," Vernie said quietly. She came to stand next to Quid, watching the group as well, but smiling broadly.

The tables kept getting longer and longer. More were being erected as people poured from between the trees.

There must be multiple campsites. People kept appearing from the darkness. As she searched each face she wondered where the tall boy from earlier was. She couldn't help but eagerly scan the crowd for his face.

Vernie came up next to her, thrusting the large salad bowl into her arms. "It's a potlatch."

"A potluck? Like where everyone brings food."

Vernie wrinkled her nose as she watched the crowd. "Kind of the same idea. Indigenous people of this area and many others would host a potlatch to honor a specific family or member. Many of these people are probably descended from Indigenous nations near here. Maybe even different nations…" Vernie's voice trailed off. She nodded her head absentmindedly. Her brows furrowed like she was realizing something. Slowly, her smile disappeared.

Quid looked at Vernie, wondering why her mother was so knowledgeable. Quid had only seen a few pictures from when her parents were younger but knew her mom had once had long, straight, black hair. Quid studied Vernie's long, arrow-like nose and wondered again what her mother had to do with all these people. *Was this her family?*

Vernie didn't talk about her life before Merle a lot, but Quid remembered back to an incident in her fourth-grade history class. She had to write a report for history about the Native Americans

from their area. Vernie had scolded the project itself for its of-
fensive language. She told Quid people needed to use names that
gave the victimized people back their power. Vernie called them
Indigenous people, not Native Americans, and Quid also learned
they were called nations, not tribes. Vernie even scratched the
name off on the projects' requirements sheet and made Quid give it
back to her teacher with the corrections.

Quid thought back to how angry Vernie had gotten at her
teacher for the points that had been taken off. Mr. Knoble had tak-
en two dozen points off because her drawings didn't meet his requirements. Vernie's face was cherry-red when she showed up to
the parent-teacher conference and listened to the history teacher
'explain' that he took off points because in Quid's drawings "the
Indians weren't even in headdresses or riding horses." Vernie had
told the teacher in no uncertain terms where exactly he could shove
his ideas of what was "historically accurate."

"Let's get our salad together quickly." Vernie began pulling
the lettuce from a large glass bowl. Quid leaned down, grabbing
out more jars of the fruits, veggies, and nuts from the large, blue
cooler.

Quid watched Vernie as she worked, occasionally handing her
ingredients from the jars. Soon the two of them were walking over
and placing their bowl along with the others.

Unaccustomed to large crowds, Quid grew nervous as more
people gathered. She sat, watching the sea of faces. The gathering
was filled with people of all ages. Some faces were wrinkled with
age, talking and laughing, while young children whizzed by,
chased by older siblings. They all seemed to know each other.
Many stood around, laughing, and talking in little groups.

Vernie did exactly like the others. Quid watched in awe as
Vernie moved comfortably around everyone.

Her smile never faltered as she greeted some and hugged others. It was obvious she knew most people there, especially the older adults who stood back, watching the crowd.

Quid tried to hang back, but Vernie pulled her from group to
group. Quid nodded as she was introduced again and again. She
shifted awkwardly as she stood smiling next to her mom, overwhelmed by it all.

*How did Vernie know all these people? Why have I never met
or heard of any of them before? How much more did Quid not*

know about her mother's past?

The wind reacted to her unease and breezed through the camp, fluttering the plastic of the tents and the thick cloths on the table. Quid took a few steps back towards their tent, trying to calm herself and the breeze around her.

Vernie pulled Quid towards the middle of the circle. The intense heat from the fire reached out to greet Quid as she approached. The two of them watched as a family emerged from a large, green, tent near the edge of the clearing.

"That's Ayasha. Her husband is the one who passed away." Vernie gestured towards a woman with long, gray hair that walked between two older gentlemen.

Vernie placed her hand around Quid's shoulder. This time Quid forgot to shrug it off. She was too curious to remember she was still angry at her mother.

"Who are they?" Quid whispered in Vernie's ear as a hush fell over the crowd.

Vernie either didn't hear or ignored Quid's question altogether, "These people only gather together at important events, weddings, funerals…big meetings." She whispered to Quid.

Quid stared at Vernie, watching her eyebrows furrow again, deep in thought.

"Everyone participates, bringing food, but they also bring gifts for the host family. Sometimes to lend help or support, sometimes to give respect to the person who has passed. Sometimes to show their support of a transference of power…"

Vernie's thoughts seemed to drift off. Vernie crossed her arms in front of her now. Her eyes never left the strange man as he walked through the center of camp, towards the fire. Quid watched as her mother pursed her lips, surprised by Vernie's obvious distaste.

Quid examined him intently, as did several others in the crowd. He was a giant, hovering over all the members of the crowd. Although he appeared to be in his late seventies, nothing about him was feeble. As he paced around the fire, he nodded to some in the group and avoided the eyes of others. The air filled with his presence.

He walks like he owns the place. Quid watched him circle close to them again. He came close to them again and she amended that he was *far* from dressed like a boss.

The faded green cotton shirt he wore had been bleached by hours in the sun. His pants were worn, blue denim. Across his broad shoulders was the fur of a large, white arctic fox. Its head was still visible.

Its lifeless eyes stared back at her from across the fire. Her heart pained for its death and anger simmered in her chest that its life had been subjected to a fashion statement.

A gust of wind pushed back his greasy, black hair. The fire before them grew. Its tendrils reached towards the night sky but also spit angry sparks towards the ground. Quid felt Vernie squeeze her shoulders in warning. They both knew Quid's history with fire.

Everyone gasped at the display of the fire and wind, but the old man spoke loud and clear as he paced around the blaze. People around her silenced once more.

Quid waited in wonder as he spoke, urging herself to be calm. She watched as he raised his enormous arms above his head towards the sky and then to the crowd around him. "We are not here *today*..." he spoke calmly.

His voice filled with authority.

Quid wondered to herself if the authority came from those around her or his inflated sense of self-importance. He seemed to emphasize each word as he continued, "We are not here *today* to address the problems facing us. No, today is a day of celebration. Tonight, we have come to celebrate a life."

The crowd bowed their heads around her and closed their eyes, almost in unison. Somewhere, a drumbeat began, followed by a soft flute melody. Several female voices began harmonizing. It wasn't a tune, but soft notes. Quid listened and let herself relax in the large crowd. The song was low. Its soft melody was a heart-felt goodbye to Ayasha's lost husband.

There was nothing but the gentle music and the crackling of the fire. Even the crickets stopped their music to listen. Entranced by the music, Quid watched the spectacle around her.

A pair of piercing eyes glinted at her from across the blaze.

Just passed the old man stood the older boy from earlier. He didn't have his head bowed or his eyes closed.

He looked directly at her. She felt his gaze on her face. A hint of curiosity hid behind his eyes. She had this overwhelming feeling he wasn't looking at her but through her. He looked at her like he already knew everything about her.

He doesn't even know your name. Quid reminded herself.

Quid watched as the orange and yellow flames danced across his eyes. A thousand questions pierced the armor she had been so desperately clinging to since their arrival. His dark eyes melted away her desire to run.

Heat spread across her skin and she knew it wasn't from the inferno in front of her, it was from the one building inside her.

She couldn't shake it off. She examined his long nose and thick, furrowed brow as a sense of familiarity came over her. She couldn't understand it, but a sense of familiarity came over her. As if they knew one another. Her heart pounded in her chest, so loud she was sure he could hear it too. A flush came across her cheeks. Her mind reminded her that they were surrounded by people, but his eyes took her away. They pierced through her until she forgot the noise around them. Her heartbeats were fast in her chest as she met his stare. He looked at her as if he had been waiting for her for a very, very long time.

She was locked in by something in his eyes, mesmerized by the questions they contained. She didn't look away until the people around her were yelling.

Chapter Nine

The moment passed suddenly, as everyone cheered. It must have been the signal for everyone to eat as there was a flurry of movement towards the tables of food. All around the campsite large, standing kerosene lights came to life. Light began to fill the spaces the fire didn't reach.

Quid looked back, and the boy across the fire was gone.

Before she could contemplate it further, Vernie was calling her name from across the campsite, having found a place near the beginning of the line.

Quid chuckled to herself. *How did she get to the front of the line so fast?*

She headed towards Vernie's wildly waving arm, feeling kind of proud of her mother's little trick.

Quid joined the throng of people near the front of the line. She took one of the wooden plates and a set of silverware from Vernie, shoving the metal fork and spoon in her back pocket as she waited for the line to move.

Neither her nor Vernie liked to use plastic bowls, and Merle had become a pretty fantastic woodworker in the last few years. All three of them had a unique, hand-made set, especially for camping. Quid rubbed the smooth edges of the bowl absentmindedly as they waited in line. Vernie chatted to someone in front of them and Quid pretended again to not be looking around for the strange boy.

Quid watched as the widow, Ayasha, was escorted to the table of food. She was a few people ahead of them in line. Her head was hung low, her long, gray hair in a tight braid down her back. An older gentleman guided her by the shoulders. "The family that is being honored eats first, but then it's get it while you can," Vernie explained. Quid thought again that Vernie sounded like someone who had been doing this for a long time.

The two of them made their way slowly along the length of the table. The cool night air changed from the musky smell of camp to the smell of fresh vegetables and stews. Quid's stomach rumbled as she looked at each exquisite dish. Quid had never seen so much food. As she peered down the table it was hard to even see where the table ended. It was a rainbow of culinary knowledge.

Usually, because she was a vegetarian, she was skeptical of banquets or potlucks. It was often hard to tell if something had meat ground up in it or what the mystery foods consisted of. The thought of eating an animal when she could connect with it and feel its pain made her physically ill. In fact, in elementary school, she had packed her lunch every day because one time, the school lunch ladies had mislabeled the spaghetti with meat sauce. Quid threw up in the girl's bathroom for the rest of the day.

"What are the green cards for?" Quid asked Vernie, noticing several of the dishes had small green paper cards placed in front of them.

"They're to mark the ones that are vegetarian." Said a loud, bright, voice from behind her.

Quid turned in the cramped line to see a tall girl with long brown hair standing right behind her. She stood a full head taller than Quid, who had begun feeling smaller and smaller the longer she was in this crowd of giants.

What did they all eat that made them grow so tall and where can I get some? She wondered as she faced the beautiful Amazon.

The girl smiled at Quid who was immediately taken aback by the girl's appearance. The girl's shorts were cut-offs, fraying at the end and clinging tight to her long legs. She had on a bright-pink tank top, as she turned Quid came face-to-chest with the purple sparkles that read "PEACE" across her enormous breasts. The bottom of the shirt had been cut off at the bottom, revealing her bare, flat stomach—complete with purple kitten belly button ring.

She looked like she just stepped out of a city catalog, not walked from the woods like most of the camo and denim wearing people around them. Quid wondered if she was intentionally trying to stand out from the crowd.

"A LOT of people here are vegetarian." Said the girl matter-of-factly through her overly glossed lips. She smiled a friendly smile at Quid, who eased. Vernie kept forgetting Quid existed, but maybe Quid wouldn't be alone this entire time if there were friend-ly, young, faces in the crowd.

"So that means there are actually options for once?" laughed Quid, suddenly excited for the first time about the banquet in front of her. She looked down the row of dishes and bowls. More and more green tags stood out.

"Girl! You are veg? Me too!" squealed the girl excitedly.

"Yeah, my whole life." A wave of calm soothed over her. Normally, she was nervous around people. She had been growing increasingly nervous around this crowd, but as the giantess leaned down to scoop up something with beans and rice into her plate, Quid relaxed.

"I'm Quid." She said to the girl sheepishly. "Maybe you could show me what's good and what to avoid?"

"You know it! I'm Nia." exclaimed the girl, stepping in front of Quid.

Quid shuffled the plate, trying to reach out and shake the girl's hand. Nia shook her hand, as someone tried to squeeze between the two of them.

"Nua!" yelled Nia, pushing the young boy back with her elbow and blocking him from the table. "Go back with the little kids and don't cut in line!"

Quid realized immediately this was the younger boy from earlier.

"We are the same age, Nia. And I'm hungry..." Whined the boy, trying again to squeeze between them.

"Uh-uh." Said Nia again, this time booty-bumping him out of line.

"Fine!" replied Nua indignantly, once again storming off. This time he slumped towards the end of the line, which trailed so far back Quid couldn't even see the end.

Nia took two more scoops of dishes marked with green cards. She put a scoop on Quid's plate as well.

"Sorry. That was my brother, Nua. He's such a freaking pain."

Quid laughed as the two of them shuffled down the line. Nia scooped dish after dish, some for Quid some and then some for herself. She casually explained when she skipped certain veggie dishes. Some were "not green enough." Some had "too many colors to not be full of artificial preservatives." Others Nia claimed they were "too brown to be edible." The two of them stopped when their plates were piled high and could absolutely hold no more.

At some point in the long line, Vernie also filled her plate and walked off absently toward the other adults. For a moment, Quid stood awkwardly, shuffling her feet, and inwardly debating on following Nia or going back to her campsite to eat in the tent.

As if sensing her hesitation, Nia turned and gently nudged Quid towards the fire. "Let's go sit and eat!" she yelled to no one

in particular. Quid followed her. She had a feeling she was going to like hanging out with Nia, who seemed to have boundless
energy and unrelenting joy. Nia didn't just walk. She seemed
to bounce from place to place.

The two of them sat by the fire, eating their food. Quid listened as Nia pointed people out, telling Quid bits and pieces about
each person. She knew who had beef with whom, who was related
to one another, and even who everyone had "dated" or "been
with." Nia would wag her eyebrows when she explained each
one—she even knew about the adults. Apparently, life in this
group was filled with complications and drama.

Quid was fascinated by all Nia's knowledge and was excited
to people-watch now that she was learning more and more. The
two of them were whispering and laughing at an older couple who
were dressed in identical red flannels but were having some sort of
silent fight.

The wife was sitting in a folding chair at least a foot away
from the older man. He was leaning away from her in his chair,
looking dejected with his baseball cap pulled low in his face. The
wife would periodically kick or bump him, to make sure he was
awake for her to be angry at. Quid watched the older couple, wondering how long they had been together and thinking about her
parents.

Merle and Vernie were very good at silent fights. Vernie could
communicate exactly what she wanted in very few words. She had
even done exactly that when Quid asked Merle why she had to go
to the funeral. All it took was one look from Vernie for Quid's fate
to be sealed.

Quid was looking around for Vernie, trying hard to remember
that she was supposed to be upset that she had to come when the
two boys walked up.

"How did you get through that long-ass line so fast?" Nia
pursed her lips knowingly, looking Nua up and down.

"Because Liam actually loves me." Replied Nua, sticking his
tongue out at his sister and shoveling his mouth full of food.

"Uh uh, little brother. The ground." Nia said, pointing at the
hard dirt as Nua leaned down to sit on the log.

"Let him sit." Liam let out a sigh. He took a long swig of his
thermos, rolling his eyes at the two of them. Quid wondered if he
was used to the two of them bickering.

With a huff, Nia scooted closer to Quid to make room on the log. Nua sat down next to his sister but leaned around to give Quid a flirtatious grin. "Soo…who's this?" he said the words long and drawn out, flashing her a toothy smile, and lifting his thick, black eyebrows.

Quid couldn't help but smile as she stuck out her hand for the young boy. He was certainly a charmer.

"This is Quid," Nia's voice was filled with annoyance as she cocked her head to the side. She stared down at Nua. "And she doesn't want or need any—" she wagged her finger in a circle, motioning up and down Nua's torso, "of that."

Quid couldn't help it. She burst out laughing at their banter, accidentally choking on the small grains of rice.

The rice raced down the wrong tube in her throat. A fit of coughs almost caused her to spill her plate. She bent over the side of the log, desperate to clear her throat. Panic made her realize she hadn't brought a drink over with her.

"Here…" Liam responded quickly, handing her his silver thermos. The metal was cool in her hand as she took it. Heat flushed across her cheeks in embarrassment.

Get it together…She chastised herself as she nodded her thanks.

Acutely aware of how ridiculous she must appear choking on food like a small child, Quid took a quick swig of the thermos. The warm, soothing sensation of jasmine tea glided down her throat as she stopped coughing.

"Thank you…." She murmured, looking up at him and placing the metallic thermos into his outstretched hand. When their fingers brushed together along the edge of the thermos, a spark passed between them. The thermos slipped from her hand towards the ground.

"So—sorry!" she exclaimed, but Liam had already recovered. He grabbed the handle of the bottle and screwed the lid back on, still smiling at her.

Quid blushed and began inspecting her plate more intently as she ate, trying to ignore the amused smile across his eyes.

Next to her, Nia continued to point out people and prattled about their stories. Meanwhile, Nua inhaled rather than chewed his food and sat next to his sister, nodding, and making agreeable noises, while sneaking food from his sister's plate.

All around them the potlatch continued as people ate and talked. Quid made her second trip back to the table of food once the line had died down. She had already eaten all the rice dish that had made her choke. Despite its perils, it was the most delicious thing she had ever eaten.

"So, you like it?" asked a voice from next to her, as she scooped another spoonful of the brown and white dish onto her plate.

Quid looked up to see Liam standing next to her, scooping a spoonful of baked yams onto his plate. He was close enough their shoulders touched, and her heart raced in response.

She reminded herself forcefully that you were supposed to respond when cute boys ask you questions. "I really do love it all. I've never had so many vegetarian options before."

"Yeah," Liam replied, smiling at her again with his crooked grin. "Most people's idea of a 'vegetarian' meal is 'make them a salad.'"

"Exactly!" Quid said excitedly. She thought back to when the only restaurant in Kutz began advertising its 'Vegetarian Menu' last year. When she asked to see it the only available options were house and Caesar salad, now available with or without chicken strips.

"I'm Liam." He said, extending his hand out to shake hers.

Quid hastily set down her plate and shook his hand. The rough calluses across his palm pressed against her skin. His hand must be used to hard labor, but it shook hers gently. His touch sent a shiver up her spine as he smiled.

The two of them walked away from the table, Quid carried her plate in her hand but immediately forgot her hunger as they meandered around the circle.

"I haven't seen you around before." Liam watched her curiously as they walked along.

"We weren't at the funeral. I don't really know anyone..." Quid trailed off, once again feeling out of place around the crowd of people who were all familiar with one another. "But I guess my mom knows people?" It sounded more like a question than an answer. Vernie still hadn't explained exactly how she knew everyone here.

Instinctively, Quid looked around for her mom in the crowd. The kerosene lamps created as many shadows as they erased.

Finally, she spotted her at the side of a large, green tent with Ayasha. The two women stood facing one another and even in the darkness Quid could tell Vernie was angry. She stood facing the other woman, shaking her hands in the air angrily. The two of them were talking quietly, but she could tell by looking at her that Vernie was upset. She had been on the receiving end of those angry arms many times.

She watched for a few more seconds, wondering if she should go over and check to make sure everything was okay. *What on earth would make Vernie so upset that she would get into an argument with a widow the same day as the funeral?*

Quid might be mad at the way her mom always seemed to want to run her life and she wished Vernie understood her better, but that didn't mean she wouldn't have her back. Thoughts of rescuing her mom from whatever had happened were interrupted as Liam said from next to her, "I didn't know Laverne had a daughter."

Quid looked at Liam in surprise. It never occurred to her that he might know of Vernie at all.

"I'm adopted." She stated. She reminded herself it was the truth. She could never tell him or anyone she hadn't come from some sort of fancy adoption agency but had been found wandering in the woods with a wolf as her guide.

"You don't have to say, 'congratulations' or anything." Quid replied as the silence hung awkwardly between them. It was her standard joke-reply. Telling people, she was adopted always seemed to make them uncomfortable. She often told Fen it was like if someone told you they were herpes-free now. People didn't quite know what to say.

Liam didn't laugh, but he did smile, which helped ease the awkwardness.

They started walking again towards the log by the fire. The blaze was beginning to dim to a dull glow. Nua had walked off, *probably in search of more food,* thought Quid. Nia looked at them questioningly as they approached, raising a well-manicured eyebrow at the two of them.

Both Quid and Liam ignored Nia's questioning glance as they sat in silence. Quid picked at her plate absentmindedly, thinking of her mom next to the green tent and of the tall, warm body sitting shoulder-to-shoulder with her on this hard log.

A few minutes later Nua emerged from the darkness, carrying an armful of sticks and three woven bags swinging from both arms. A hoard of children chased behind him. Little hands stuck out towards him with marshmallows in their hands, ready to roast.

Like his sister, Nua left a trail of bouncing excitement. He popped over to the two girls, thrusting their hands full of the long, thin sticks picked from the underbrush.

Suddenly, a dozen smiling faces were surrounding them, pleading to them for help roasting their sweet treats.

Quid laughed as Liam peeled himself away from the throng of young children, literally lifting one of his legs over the head of a little blonde girl who was stuffing her cheeks with uncooked marshmallows. His long legs lumbered from between two small bodies, almost tripping, to get away. "I'll get a log for the fire." He stammered, running away.

"Liam is not great with kids," Nia stated matter-of-factly as she speared a third marshmallow onto the stick.

Quid shrugged her shoulders in response. She could count on one hand how many times she had been around kids, including the incident with Sam at the pool. She probably wasn't very good either.

Liam brought back two logs and a hand full of sticks to the fire. He tried again and again to stoke it back to life, but the wood was wet with evening dew and the fire struggled to regain its glory.

Several older men came over to try to help. Quid watched as they bickered over where to lay logs, how many sticks were too many, and whether or not placing leaves and paper on the fire was a good idea.

Quid knew she could probably get the flame going in the fire. The embers would make it easy for her and she had secretly been practicing her control in her bedroom with candles for years. Fire was the element she was most afraid of. She thought back to the weeks after the lake. Visiting Jill in the burn unit had been terrible. If Jill hated her before the lake, there was nothing like looking her in the eye afterward.

Her influence over it was as unpredictable as the flame itself. Considering what happened at the pool, she couldn't risk it. Who knows, she might start a forest fire or hurt someone. Either way, she couldn't do it with everyone around, so she sat listening to the men bicker.

The children around her were beginning to pout, eager to roast their marshmallows, as an older woman emerged from the crowd.

She wore an old, gray sweater that matched her long, braided gray hair. She wasn't a large woman. She had a small hunch in her back and hobbled slowly over to the edge of the ring of bricks. The men around her stood to help, but she took no one's hand. The faint light from the embers illuminated her face and Liam rose to greet her. Quid watched as his face lit up.

"Grandmother Dana." He said it with reverence and leaned down to wrap his long arms around her gently. As he stood back up Quid felt a twinge of appreciation at the obvious love he felt, and the fact he obviously wasn't afraid to show it.

The woman touched Liam's cheek gingerly with her palm. She smiled back at her grandson and Quid saw the love reflected in her gray eyes.

"Fire." The old woman turned slowly to look at the faces of the men crouched around the pit, "Takes patience. It takes understanding. You cannot force it to do what you want. The spark is only fed when it has exactly what it needs."

The old woman bent down over the fire, taking Liam's hand from beside her as the crowd watched. Liam's face lit up in a way Quid hadn't seen before.

In a moment, Nua was back. His hands were full of boxes of graham crackers and chocolates. Even Nia sat silently, watching, as Dana adjusted a few sticks around the fire.

Something about this woman demanded respect. Every word she spoke made you feel like you were anxiously waiting to learn something new.

Dana puffed on the glowing embers at the base of the fire. She shuffled again to the opposite side. She let out a puff of air into the fire, which set the embers ablaze, instantly igniting a thousand flames that wrapped orange and yellow tendrils around the pieces of wood. Within seconds, the fire was once again reaching into the night sky.

Quid stared at the woman as she leaned back from the fire. It may have been a trick of the light, but she could have sworn the older woman's eyes glowed.

Seconds later, the men descended on Grandmother Dana, shaking her hand, and hugging her.

"Grandmother Dana has magic." Nua whispered to one of the

small children next to him. The child laughed, grabbing his marshmallow stick and heading towards the fire.

Neither Quid nor Nia said anything to him this time. They sat in silence, helping the children pierce their marshmallows onto their thin sticks and keeping clumsy feet from the heat of the blaze.

Quid didn't even know these people, but she had a strange feeling he wasn't wrong. Something was certainly different about them.

"So... how do you know each other?" Quid asked no one in particular, as she looked at the different faces around the camp. People were laughing and smiling again.

Suddenly, Grandmother Dana was sitting next to her on the log. Liam had helped her over and Quid made room, waiting for the older woman to sit.

No one seemed to notice, except for Liam and Nia, but the old woman spoke softly, leaning down close.

Her intense glare met Quid's as she spoke.

"We are all of one people. Though we have had many names. Our families call themselves The Believers."

Quid listened intently. For a reason that she couldn't explain her heart began to pound. It was as if her body knew whatever she was hearing was extremely vital.

"Believers worship nature and balance. They believe humans should always work to keep the balance. They keep the balance by worshipping the Great Mother. Because they worship the Great Mother, they believe some members are bestowed gifts, such as foresight. In the way that Believers value the natural balance above all else, so do the Profectus value progress above everything. For thousands of years, the Profectus tried to keep the masses enslaved and uneducated. They wanted progress but only their own.

History claims great events were accidents, or worse, it paints us as the villains. But, we know better because our people were there. Our people always paid the price. The history books call the burning of the library of Alexandria a casualty of war, but our people know better. Our stories tell a different tale..."

A hush fell over the group. From the corner of her eye, she saw a young woman with short brown hair, not much older than herself, nudge a friend who was talking. Immediately, the young girl stopped and turned to watch the old woman. Vernie and a group of older adults watched near the edge of the large, green tent, each with the same silent stare.

Quid looked around the small camp, across the bonfire all eyes were on them. She thought to herself she wasn't sure which they were showing so much reverence to, the old woman or the story she was telling.

The old woman's eyes never left Quid's face. Quid found herself drawn in, waiting for Grandmother Dana to continue, "We have come in many forms and have fought many battles. Druids fought with their lives to keep their homes in the forests. Our people..." the old woman paused, eyeing down two older gentlemen who had scoffed at her words and sat in two folding chairs, rolling their eyes and their arms crossed. Quid stared at them, shocked and bewildered at their disrespect.

"Our people who came from England..." Dana continued, staring down the two older gentlemen—daring them to interrupt her again. "...called themselves Keelman. Before their families came to the New World, they fought the coal trade for better conditions, trying to protect themselves and stop the pollution of the rivers. Hundreds of years later, in the newly industrialized cities, another group of our people demanded better conditions in the factories and less pollution in the air. People mocked them, said they were against technology and progress. History called them Luddites."

All around her the crowd of people was sitting or standing, all faces leaning in and listening as Grandmother Dana spoke. Quid looked around, she wasn't sure what kind of games were at play here or how this strange community worked, but whatever point Grandmother Dana was making, everyone was listening.

"History remembers these groups as the anti-progressive villains. Time and time again *our people*..." She emphasized these words again. "...fought for humanity. We never wanted people to be uneducated and we never wanted our people to go without. We must fight so humanity is not so blinded by the glare of technology that they cannot see the withering flowers before them."

Like a connection she had with her audience, Grandmother Dana looked across the group of young people around the fire.

Quid had heard several cell phones vibrate as she spoke. From the corner of her eye, Quid watched as Nia pushed the long rectangle sticking out the back of her shorts in a little deeper.

"All we have ever wanted was for progress and nature to be balanced. Our people have spent thousands of years suffering and dying so humanity will finally pay attention to its Mother. It is a battle we seem to be losing and will continue to lose if we do not work together. If we do not come together as one and use all the gifts the Great Mother has bestowed upon us."

Grandmother Dana stood and walked around the fire again. As she spoke the last words, she looked at Quid. A chill went up Quid's spine as a soft breeze greeted her nervousness, blowing her hair about. Quid tried to brush off Dana's stare, but in that second, she couldn't help but feel this strange, old, woman, knew her secret. Slowly, the woman's gray eyes traveled over her shoulder to meet Liam's gaze.

The old woman walked back up towards the tents and into the darkness. People all around them slowly came back to their senses. Within a few moments, music was playing and conversations had started again.

Quid looked at the space where the old woman had walked away, and then again at Liam. Unease sat in her stomach like a rock. How much did Grandmother Dana know and why had she looked at Liam the same way?

Her heart raced as a mix of nervousness and excitement filled her stomach.

Does Liam share some sort of secret too?

Chapter Ten

One by one people began to wander off, headed back to their tents. Quid grew weary as she watched the fire die down again. When only embers remained and the warmth from the fire no longer kept away the cold of the night, she left the log to head back to her tent.

Liam had disappeared shortly after Grandmother Dana had. Quid ignored the growing feeling of disappointment that he had never come back.

The adults had disappeared long before the kids went to bed, and Nia had led quite the dance party around the fire. Quid had danced a few times with different people, but eventually fatigued. No one could out dance Nia, who never tired.

As Quid walked away, she realized that Nia and a boy with flaming red hair were the last ones around the fire. He hadn't bothered to introduce himself to Quid, who shrugged it off. She had met plenty of people tonight and probably wouldn't remember half their names anyway.

Quid looked away as the two of them began kissing. The two of them were obviously relieved to be alone. They had been on the verge of making out all night and Quid didn't even bother to say goodbye as she walked away.

Quid trudged up the hill as Jordan Davis' "Slow Dance in a Parking Lot" came on the small, rectangular Bluetooth speaker sitting on the log. The large, silver kerosene lamps had long ago been extinguished. Quid looked back as the two of them began to grind slowly on one another. The embers of the fire glowing red against their slow-moving shadows as the song wrapped through the air.

Unnatural jealousy sat in Quid's chest. She wished she had Nia's outgoing nature. The girl appeared to always be both in control and a little out of control. Quid knew it was something she could never experience, the sudden letting go of inhibitions. Who knew how her influence would affect her if she ever did something like that with a boy? She had never even been kissed. For all she knew she could kiss someone—she pushed away the thoughts of Liam's full lips as they flashed across her mind—and send a lightning bolt through them both.

Inside the tent, Quid changed sleepily into her fleece pajamas, using the dim light of their small, kerosene lamp. She was ready, anxious to climb under the soft blankets and heavy quilts.
Like a pro, Vernie had made the wise choice to fill the air mattress as soon as they had unpacked the tent.

After all, Quid thought to herself again, *Vernie really was a pro.* She had done this, been around these people, many times before.

A noise came from outside the tent as Vernie came in. She was already changed for bed. Normally Vernie wore her typical worn, flannel gown to bed, but tonight she had on thick, yellow pajama pants and one of the purple t-shirts they had made for last year's Harvest Festival. She placed the hot, kerosene lamps outside the tent, extinguishing their light and leaving the two of them in near darkness. The only light was the soft white of the moon reaching down through the netting above them.

Quid watched as Vernie shuffled over to the air mattress. The swish of the plastic underneath her heavy feet was slow and thoughtful. The two of them had decided earlier to sleep on the same mattress. The night might not get too cold, but the tent had many doors and windows and they had opted not to put on the rain cover, since so many stars would be visible. Without Fen or Merle, the two of them would sleep together in the middle, to ease their 'women alone in the woods' anxieties.

Quid listened as Vernie climbed into bed. The air mattress sank, and Quid gripped the hard plastic to keep from rolling off as the bed settled.

"Are you having a good time?" Vernie asked through a yawn. Quid felt her pull on the covers as she settled in. Quid couldn't help but smile. She hadn't slept next to her mom since she was little. She always forgot what a blanket hog Vernie was.

Quid relinquished the heavy quilt to Vernie but stole the softer blanket for herself. Vernie's warmth filled the small bed and Quid was comforted by her presence. Even though she wished the two of them could get along better, and even though she felt like Vernie shouldn't have been so upset about the pool, she had to admit she was having a good time. Which was a weird thing, considering these people had all just come from a funeral.

"I am." Quid whispered next to Vernie. "But who are these people? How do you know them? What is their deal?"

Once the words were out, Quid's mind was once again awake with questions.

Vernie seemed to know Quid would have questions. Her words sounded scripted as she spoke, as though she had practiced them before. "You know about the Puritans, who came over from Europe, right?"

"Yeah. They wanted freedom from the Catholic Church." Quid replied, suddenly flashing back to fifth-grade history class and Mr. Wilson's balding head reflecting images of History Channel documentaries.

"Yes." Vernie continued speaking slowly, like a teacher to a student. Like Grandmother Dana earlier, she spoke from memory. Quid wondered to herself how many times Vernie had told the story and how many times it had been told to her.

"People forget for decades before and after, there were other groups that came, seeking asylum from oppression. Others have made the journey as well. They came from all continents, traveling thousands of miles…"

Quid listened, the weight of Vernie's words pressed on her, reminding her of the way Grandmother Dana's had also filled her with their weight. Her heart raced as she listened to each word. Like watching the news to see if something important or something terrible has happened, she waited once more.

"History says the people found danger no matter where they went… just because they were different. Still, for hundreds of years, they came in droves across the ocean, seeking refuge in the unending forests of the New World. Their pursuers called them Druids, Gypsies, Witches. Ultimately, they found a kinship with some of the Indigenous people of the new world. As time passed and the Indigenous people became fewer and fewer those who remained, those who remembered and worshipped The Great Mother became a new people. They called themselves The Believers."

Vernie squeezed Quid's hand underneath the thick blankets as she moved closer. Vernie's warmth radiated from under the thick fabric and Vernie's pulse pumped against Quid's as she waited for more. "I know that you know my mother died when I was ten."

Quid looked across the black of the tent. Though she knew Vernie couldn't see, still she nodded. She had never heard Vernie talk about either of her parents. She remembered asking one time when she was young. All Vernie said was her mom passed a long time ago. "I never knew my father. My mother didn't like to talk about it. I think she was ashamed of the fact she had to raise me on her own when he left. I think my sisters blame me for him leaving.

They were old enough to understand. My mother came from a unique group of people."

"People like this?" Quid wondered aloud, suddenly the pieces coming together in her mind. She remembered Vernie walking around, greeting older members of the group like they were good friends.

"Yes." Vernie had a smile in her voice as she spoke. "I grew up with these people. It was a…unique experience." Vernie chuckled to herself.

"I learned a lot about respecting and caring for the land you live off. I learned to fish, to hunt, to grow things. The community traveled a lot when I was younger, and they travel even more now. Some of them never take a real home. They work as migrant workers, planting in the spring, harvesting in the fall. Others own large farms, hidden away, and passed down from generation to generation."

Quid thought back to the way Liam had easily lifted the logs, and of the thick muscles on his arms. *Was he a migrant worker or had he grown up on a farm?*

Vernie continued. Her voice was now a whisper against the quiet night. "But our community was not always welcome when we got there. We would be chased from town by police, who were often paid off by big businesses. Our people would try to get these companies to stop polluting nearby rivers or to change the way their huge stacks would cover the air in smog.

In one city, the residents blamed us for shutting down a local factory that supplied most of the jobs for the community. They woke us from our beds and ran us out of town. Men with guns followed us all the way to the state border in the dead of night. It was the most terrified I have ever been, until the day on the beach when you broke your leg." Vernie paused and Quid knew that they both were remembering that day and how scared they had all been.

"By the time I was sixteen, I ran away. I wanted something different."

Quid listened intently as Vernie's voice broke through the hum of the night. Her voice was low, melodic, against the chirping of crickets and frogs outside their tent. She hadn't known this part of her adopted-parents' lives and even though she knew they weren't related by blood, it felt like learning about her history too.

"I didn't see anyone again until I was in my twenties. I came back when I received the news my mother was dying." Vernie let out a long, hard sigh. She shifted on the mattress uncomfortably. Vernie released Quid's hand and she must have moved it underneath her head as there was a sudden shift at the top of the air mattress.

"What happened?" Quid asked softly. She didn't want Vernie to be sad, but she also wanted her to continue. *How did this history all fit into what was happening now? Did it have something to do with Vernie and Ayasha fighting?*

"She was really out of it by the time I got there. Waving at people who weren't there, talking about things only she could see. Some of The People aren't a big fan of doctors, but I convinced her to go. They told us it was cancer and that she didn't have long. I stayed with her for weeks. My sisters were poor and lived all the way in Oklahoma. They couldn't afford a plane ticket and we wanted to wait until we were sure it was the end before they drove out here…"

"Before long, she was in and out of consciousness, tired and weak. When she was awake, she was always telling stories. Our people love to tell stories."

Again, Quid heard Vernie's voice lighten. She listened as Vernie chuckled to herself. "Mama loved to tell stories. She told stories all day. She had a story when she washed dishes, when she folded laundry, or when she was in the field. If she got into an argument, she would tell you a story about how you were wrong. The sicker she got, the more stories she had. Stories about things I'm not even sure really happened."

"One night, she woke up, sat up in the bed, and started talking. Clear as day. She told me the story of how she had met my father by the time she was in her early 20s. He was a factory worker and I think she loved him because he was the opposite of everything she had grown up with. She settled down and had two daughters, one right after the next. I was the third, at the end of their third year of marriage. She found out she was pregnant with me early on in her pregnancy."

Vernie paused again, trying to decide if she should continue,

"The midwives had a lot of ways to know when a woman was pregnant, if there would be complications, and if the child would be a boy or girl. Mom had always wanted a lot of children. She was so excited at the prospect of another baby. But, within a few weeks, The Great Depression hit, and my father lost his job at the factory. When the job was gone, so was he."

"My mother began mending and washing clothes to help make ends meet. She was walking home when she suddenly felt a strange pain in her side. She didn't think much of it until she saw a strange woman looking at her from across the crowded street. She said the old woman had such a sad look in her eyes, and she just stared."

Vernie took a deep sigh. "My mother recognized her immediately as someone from her old life. One of my grandmother's people. You see, when my mother met my father, she left her old life. I guess a lot of us do…"

"Even still, when she saw people from her old life it was because they lived mostly in small communities on the edge of town, but it was rare to see them in a wealthy community." Vernie adjusted again, almost toppling Quid from the air mattress. Her body sunk lower as Vernie's weight lifted from the bed. She listened to the crinkle of the plastic beneath them as Vernie paced. Although she couldn't see her, Quid knew that Vernie was probably standing, wringing her hands.

After a few moments, Quid pressed gently, "What happened to her?"

Vernie hesitated but finally climbed back onto the air mattress to lay down. They both stared at the top of the tent, lost in Vernie's story.

"She saw the old woman several times over the next few days. Always with the same sad look on her face. Finally, she saw her at a local park where she had taken my older sisters to play and confronted her. At first, all the old woman would say is that she was sorry. She was so sorry. The old woman told her she was sorry for making her uncomfortable, but she had to say something. She had been sent to tell my mother something, to give her a choice. Quid, always remember, people think they want to know their future, but often realize too late that it was a terrible price to pay."

Quid sat, confused by her mother's words, Vernie went on to explain, "You have to understand, Quid. My mother, we both, belonged to this unique community. Believers worship nature. They worship The Great Mother and believe that humans must fight to keep the balance between progress and preserving the natural order. Some of them believe that this means we shouldn't use any technology that isn't absolutely necessary. Others believe in the middle ground.

But a select group, part of the oldest groups of Believers, believe that the Great Mother watches out for us because we work so tirelessly for her. Because of this, they believe that some members are bestowed gifts such as foresight. They believe that they can tell the future."

Quid could hear the skepticism in Vernie's voice as she spoke. But as she continued, Quid also heard something that she hadn't heard in Vernie's voice in a long time. Fear.

"This woman who had been following my mother claimed to be blessed with it. She told my mother that she had seen her future. She said that her fate was going to be sad and it was coming soon. But she also said that because my mother had come from a long line of Believers, she would be allowed to barter her fate.
The woman told my mother that she and I would both die in childbirth, leaving the other two daughters behind to starve. However, she offered my mother a deal. A gift from the Great Mother, she said. She would allow both mother and daughter to live, but it required balance. None of her daughters would ever conceive a child. They would all live out their lives desperately wanting.

"The woman told her that she had until the last breath before the baby was born to decide."

"When she told me about it, I never really believed her story. I grew up with these crazy stories, but I never believed them. By the time I was a teenager they were just more fairy tales."

Vernie's voice was filled with anger, as she got louder. Quid felt Vernie throw her hands up in the air in frustration as she spoke.

"I thought it was just another story, this time brought on by the cancer. I always thought it was a coincidence or something genetic that neither myself nor my sisters were able to have children. It wasn't until Merle brought you from those woods, and until we realized how unique you are, that I began to wonder how many of those stories were true…" Vernie's thoughts trickled off there. Words were left unsaid.

She turned away from Quid to the empty side of the tent, lost in thoughts and memories that Quid couldn't see.

Quid wanted to press her but sensed that now wasn't the time. A flood of questions raced around her mind as she lay next to Vernie. *Were Vernie and her sisters truly cursed? Was her Grandmother saved by the Great Mother? Was Quid's influence over her surroundings somehow connected to these Believers?*

Could they help her? If so, why had Vernie kept her away from them for so long?

Chapter Eleven

Quid woke up as the sun began to warm the tent. Vernie had been tossing and turning all night until Quid had finally decided to steal the heavy quilt and sleep on the ground.

She stepped gently around the tent; every sound magnified by the swish of the plastic under her feet as it cut through the quiet morning air. Quid put her shorts on over her yellow bathing suit, filled with excitement as she thought about how Nia had invited her to swim with them all later that day.

She was pulling the thin, blue fabric of the tank top over her yellow bikini as she emerged from the tent. Within seconds, she felt eyes on her in the low morning light that was filling the large, round space. She looked around the quiet campground but saw no one else. The sea of plastic tents around her were still zipped tight, sleeping soundly as the sun rose. She knew she must be the only one awake. It couldn't be more than five or six. Still, even though the air was warming, a chill went up her spine as she scanned.

The air wrapped around her as the wind greeted her, caressing her neck and shoulders. In her mind, she sent a greeting, picturing a tranquil breeze. Quid walked deeper into the woods. The trees and brush continued their gentle reaching. The pressure on her head was minimal. Some part of her kept it at bay. She would always be grateful for that part of her influence. It might just be self-preservation or some instinct that protected her. Without it, she knew she would be easily overwhelmed. With it, she could focus on a little at a time—on the parts of the natural world that needed her the most.

As Quid walked, she touched the thick bark of the trunks around her. This part of the forest was slowly getting used to her presence and she was finding the tall, ancient trees to be a comfort.

Within a few minutes she got to the small group of toilets and she silently thanked whoever had the foresight to both provide the group with portable toilets and to keep them away from all the tents.

After she was done relieving herself Quid began to feel the familiar itch in the back of her mind of an animal nearby that sought her out. She couldn't read its mind. However, she closed her eyes and reached out with her influence like a radar. She walked deeper and deeper into the thick, green brush. Following the trail as it got stronger.

She could feel that the animal was in pain, but its connection was strong, which was a good sign. Injured animals were often the hardest to track.

Her steps crunched underneath her, breaking through the quiet of the woods. All around her birds chirped from high on their perches, greeting her with their songs. She could feel that other animals were coming near, seeking her out. She could feel the influence of their energy and their minds weigh on her, but she focused on the one she had been following.

Pushing through a thick patch of honeysuckle, Quid bent low to the ground. Slowly, she pushed the thick vines out of her way, but they reached to greet her.

Like sunflowers turning in the sunlight, so too did the plants turn towards her. Once again, she was reminded that these weren't greenhouse plants. They weren't used to her and she needed to be careful until she learned how they would respond to her presence.

Let me see, she silently urged.

With a groan, the thin trunks parted, and stalks leaned away, giving Quid a view of the small, brown rabbit that lay on its side in front of her.

As the thick trees moved, Quid's heart skipped a beat. She had never seen plants move like that and once again she wondered if her influence was getting stronger. She wasn't just connecting to the natural world, but like with the waters in the pool, she commanded it.

The soft, damp earth sunk underneath her, and the sharp sticks crunched under her knees as she leaned closer. The rabbit's soft, slender ears perked as she got closer. It kicked wildly, just as surprised as her at the sudden movement of the plants.

"Easy Thumper…shh…" Quid leaned back on her heels, her voice a whisper. She waited for the animal to calm before leaning closer again to get a better look. She moved as slowly as she could. Even though she felt the animal's panic, and even though it had sensed her, she knew that she probably looked like an enormous predator.

Within a few seconds, the rabbit stilled. Its black eyes never left her face as Quid pushed plant life out of her way.

The long foot of the rabbit had gotten caught in a vine as it climbed through the underbrush. She slowly pulled at the thick, brown vine that had twisted itself as it grew across the ground. She wrapped both hands along the soft wood and pulled the thick pieces apart. The rabbit was free. Quid watched as it skittered off through the woods in a panic. It's influence on her mind faded as it ran deeper into the sea of green.

Within a few minutes, Quid had walked back and was nearing the circle of tents again, brushing off the dirt and sticks that she had gathered as she walked. She leaned over. Her knees were still dirty from leaning down on the ground, and she attempted to sweep off the forest grime. Again, she felt a tickle at the back of her neck. The tiny hairs along the back of her neck stood on end. Someone was watching her. A sinking feeling filled her with fear as she slowly stood up.

Quid turned on the spot as she heard the cracking of a twig. Her heart skipped a beat when she realized someone was standing behind her. A blast of wind shot across the short distance, shaking the leaves in the trees above her as she turned around.

It took her mind a few seconds to catch up as she realized that she had caused the blast of wind. After another few seconds, she was grateful the blast had missed as Liam emerged from between two enormous hickory trees.

"You scared the hell out of me." Quid spat at him as he walked closer.

Liam's whole face laughed as he smiled, but quickly faded when he realized she wasn't laughing with him. His brows furrowed as he walked next to her.

"I didn't mean to scare you." He held both hands up in surrender as he approached. His face was a mask of confusion.

"Whatever." Quid looked him up and down, feeling suddenly suspicious. *Why was he constantly disappearing and reappearing?*

"Have you been following me all morning? I felt you earlier. How long have you been watching me?" Quid couldn't help it, her mind buzzed with questions as her pulse raced.

She stuck her finger out at him and left it there, poking it into the thick muscle of his chest. Even though he was a head taller than her, she looked him up and down as she considered her new suspicion. His dark green t-shirt was soft against her finger. In the middle, a landscaping company's logo was printed. A tall, yellow Oak sprouted beneath her finger. She eyed him suspiciously as surprise crossed his face.

Quid told herself to ignore the fluttering in her stomach now that she was so close to him. She also told herself to ignore how warm he was.

Liam's eyes never left her face as he took a step closer to her. They were inches apart before he stopped. Warmth spread across her body, as he looked down at her. To her surprise, her heart didn't clamor. Instead, it calmed in his presence. His breath was slow and even under her palm. He cocked his head to the side as he waited for her to continue.

She tried again to remind herself that even if the guy did look like some sort of hot, Indigenous God, that didn't give him an excuse to be creepy.

Liam wrapped his long, thick fingers around her hand and held both of their hands to his chest. The warmth of his callused hands covered hers as he spoke.

His thick, brown eyebrows furrowed at her. The tip of his arrowhead nose nearly touched hers as she looked up at him. "I am sorry that I scared you. I have just come out here though, and I have not been following you." His voice was low and sincere. She found herself believing him.

He shook his head as thick brown locks fell into his eyes. Part of her wondered what it would feel like to run her fingers through those long strands.

Would it be coarse? No. He definitely looked like someone who conditioned. I bet it's soft, like silk.

A slow smile crept across his lips as if he could read exactly what she was thinking. She wondered if he could tell how quickly her heart raced.

"Okay." Quid cleared her throat awkwardly, inspecting the ground intensely to try to quiet the heat rising through her. Maybe what she felt earlier was nothing, just some animals in the tree line.

The two of them stood like that for several heartbeats, until the sounds of voices and zippers opening tents in the distance brought them back to reality.

Quid took a step back as Liam released her hand. They walked back to the circle of tents in silence.

She couldn't help but notice that he continued to smile in her direction.

Liam walked Quid back to the outside of their bright-orange

tent, glaring in the morning sun. As they approached, she

tent, glaring in the morning sun. As they approached, she wondered what she was supposed to say. *Sorry for accusing you of being a creeper* or *thanks for walking me back to my tent, even though I was a jerk?*

Liam seemed to read her thoughts again as they stood awkwardly in front of the tent. Quid shuffled her feet nervously as he smiled at her. This time he seemed to smile with his whole face. He had the most expressive face she had ever seen. Every line told a story and right now his dark, brown eyes illuminated his warm brown skin.

"Would you like to go swimming with us?" he asked. "We are going to hike out to the stream, but we need to leave soon."

"I'd love to." Quid replied much too quickly. Embarrassment flushed across her face. She hadn't meant to sound quite so desperately eager.

"Great. I'll let you get ready and come back in half an hour?"

"Sure." Quid said, shrugging her shoulders this time in an attempt to appear more nonchalant, as her stomach did flips of excitement.

Liam turned to walk away, and Quid reminded herself to move slowly until he was out of sight, but he turned back around as she began to unzip the tent.

"Hey! By the way, I have lunch handled, so don't pack anything." He smiled at her mischievously again before running off. Quid watched for a second as he ran. Maybe she wasn't the only one who couldn't control her excitement.

Within fifteen minutes, Quid was ready to go with her bag, water bottle, sunscreen. She had resisted the urge to put on earrings since they were going swimming but left on her favorite opal necklace. The shining blue reflected in the compact mirror she had borrowed from Vernie's bag.

Vernie was finally awake, getting dressed in one of the sections of the tent. The inside of the tent had grown too hot to sleep in any longer, but Quid couldn't help but notice the bags under her mother's eyes, as she zoomed in and out of the tent. Quid ran around, trying to gather everything she would need for hiking and swimming, as she frantically explained to Vernie what was going on.

She explained, pink toothbrush hanging from her mouth, that she would be gone most of the day. She intentionally failed to mention who she was going with. Quid scurried once more from the tent, spitting water out the side to rinse out her mouth. She mentally prepared herself for the coming argument.

Silence filled the tent as a light wind pushed against the thin, plastic sides. Quid stopped in the middle of all her fervor and eyed her mother suspiciously.

Vernie sat on the hard ground inside the tent. Her gray hair was disheveled, hastily put up in a weak ponytail. Quid watched as Vernie struggled to put on a pair of worn, brown tennis shoes.

Quid knew something was up as she looked at her mother, who stared absentmindedly at the long, brown strings like she didn't know what to do next. It was then that Quid realized Vernie also wasn't wearing socks and that she had just put her shoes on the wrong feet.

"Are you okay?" Quid leaned down next to Vernie, as worry filled her. Quid rested her knees on the hard ground of the tent as she helped her mother take the shoes off. From behind her, she grabbed the pair of white socks that lay forgotten.

Vernie pushed Quid's hand away, but shook her head to the side, seeming to refocus on her daughter. Quid looked at the lines around her mother's eyes, at the exhaustion in her face. "I'm fine…" Vernie slowly brushed a strand of Quid's long, brown locks from her face. She looked at Quid and smiled weakly, but still looked past her, at something else weighing on her mind.

"Do you want me to braid your hair real quick?" Vernie absentmindedly touched Quid's hair, pulling it gently from her shoulders with both hands.

"Are you okay?" Quid asked again. "Do you want me to stay here with you?" She grabbed one of Vernie's cold, slender hands. Her bones were brittle. Her skin was forever thinning with age.

"No! You should go!" Vernie insisted. "Have a great time. I'm gonna hang out here with the old people." Vernie laughed but Quid noticed how it didn't reach her eyes.

"Okay…" Quid replied nervously but remembered that Liam would be here any minute.

"Let me do your hair! Like when you were little." Vernie exclaimed, holding out the plastic, pink Wet Brush that had saved years of crying over knots in her thick hair. Quid's hair grew long, lush, brown locks—if she regularly "recharged." No matter what though, it didn't change that she had a tender head.

It has been so long since we did this. Quid thought to herself with a smile as she sat before her mother, whose deft hands gently pulled her hair from one side to another.

Quid sat and waited outside the tent in a folding chair as Vernie stood behind her. Vernie's skillful hands plaited her hair along the sides and down Quid's back. The braids were tight against either side of her head, to keep them from getting tangled in the water.

Liam walked up as Vernie wrapped the tie-off around her hair. Again, Quid reminded herself not to be too eager, as she nearly leaped from the chair as he approached.

"Good morning Mrs. Kenrick." Liam smiled at Vernie and tipped his head politely.

True to form, Vernie eyed Liam suspiciously as she nodded her head in a curt response.

Hoping to push through what was sure to be a permanent and embarrassing scar from her teenage years if Vernie started grilling Liam, Quid quickly grabbed her worn, brown satchel.

Quid slung the bag over her shoulder and gave Vernie a quick kiss on the cheek. She looked at her mom with a wide-eyed expression, hoping Vernie would get the clue and leave it be.

Vernie's nose flared and her eyebrows raised, as if she were suddenly reconsidering her decision. Quid thought to herself that whatever was bothering her mother must not be too bad if she was back to her over-protective self.

Without missing a beat, Liam smiled as he waited patiently behind the folding table that held all their supplies. A look of patient understanding rested across his face. "The others are meeting us back at Grandmother Dana's. My brother and sister and several others are coming as well."

Quid watched as Vernie appeared to deflate, relieved that she wasn't letting her daughter go off into the woods alone with some boy she didn't know. "Too bad we don't have Fen…" she heard Vernie whisper as she waved the two of them off.

"Thank God we don't have Fen." Quid mumbled as she walked across the campground with Liam at her side.

Chapter Twelve

Quid and Liam walked nearly ten minutes before arriving at an enormous grey and brown RV. Liam knocked on the hard metal side of the door. Nia came out, banging the door wide open—a supermodel making her appearance on stage for the first time.

Nia's smooth, brown skin was luminescent in the morning sun. She had on a bright pink bikini top that barely covered her enormous breasts and jean shorts that were cut so high up her thighs that Quid considered whether they could even be classified as shorts and not some sort of loincloth.

Quid was suddenly feeling insecure next to Nia's gorgeous, flashy look and absentmindedly adjusted her shorts. She should have worn those earrings after all. Nia's smile was infectious behind her glossy lips and immediately put Quid at ease.

"I'm ready. Let's go!" Nia whooped loudly, one arm circling in the air as she jumped down. Her matching pink Converse hit the ground with a thump, stirring dust around them.

Quid laughed to herself as she watched Liam roll his eyes at his sister's performance. He walked away, making a loud noise of disapproval.

Nia quickly hooked her arms with Quid, dragging her around the grumbling Liam. Before she knew what was happening, the two of them were running. Liam's quiet grumbling became yells for them to wait up.

Quid couldn't help it. Liam yelled to the two of them and she looked back, scrunching her nose, and sticking out her tongue. The flash of surprise that filled his face and the way his nose crinkled when he laughed sent butterflies through her stomach.

At an insane pace for this early in the morning, Nia guided Quid towards a small break in the trees. It was the start of the trail.

Together the three of them walked for over an hour. Nia was filled with unending energy. She stayed ahead of the two of them, leading them through the maze of green. Sometimes the trail would narrow, or turn, and Nia would lead, running up ahead and out of sight.

"Is this even classified as a trail?" Quid mused aloud. She knew that she would never, ever get lost in the woods. She could always follow her connection to the trees back to the ones that felt more familiar, but that didn't make the hiking part any easier and she wondered how Nia never got lost as the thick brambles started to blur together.

Quid pushed her way through, careful not to push her desire for them to move too hard. The last thing she wanted Nia or Liam to see was her command these plants to do something.

Quid's breathing got faster as the trail got closer around them. She stopped for a second to catch her breath as she struggled to find where her hair had been captured. She looked ahead at where Nia pushed through the branches but all she saw was a wall of green. Suddenly, a branch pulled painfully at her scalp.

"Don't worry. I got you." Liam's voice whispered behind her. Quid struggled to turn to look at him, but the area was too overgrown. He bumped up against her on the path, his chest was against her back as he squeezed between the brambles.

Liam gently touched the end of her ponytail as he leaned down to inspect the tangle. His breath was hot against her neck as he fumbled with the thick strands. Bumps rose across her skin as she waited for him to untangle it, listening to the sound of his heavy breathing against the quiet of the trees.

Within a few seconds, it released. "Thank you." She breathed heavily, her heart pounding in her chest.

Liam cleared his throat nervously as he pointed up ahead, where the thick sunlight shined through the branches. "We are almost there."

Quid nodded but didn't say anything. She couldn't decide if reaching their destination was good or bad. Right now, she didn't want to move.

Quid's heart was still pounding as she emerged. The sunlight temporarily blinded her as the opening came into view. She heard the familiar rush of water as her eyes adjusted to everything around her.

"Welcome to Kid Camp!" Nia's joyous voice resounded over the soft murmur of the stream and the voices that came up from the bottom of the hill a few feet away.

Scattered around the clearing were four small lean-tos. Each one was hand-made from branches and rope and acted as shelter from the warm sun streaming down through the trees. Quid walked closer to one and looked inside.

Of course, they're prepared... Quid laughed to herself. Each of the huts also had exactly the kind of "supplies" that you would expect from a place called 'Kid Camp.' Large, wooden boxes filled with cookies, sodas, and at least six types of potato chips sat against the back wall of one of the huts.

Nia walked past Quid quickly. She had removed a rolled-up beach towel, and some sunglasses, but tossed her large, yellow, bookbag to the floor with a thud.

"Quid, you can put your stuff in here." Nia motioned with her thumb back to where her neon-yellow bag sprawled across the ground.

Quid sat her stuff on the ground, following Nia's example, and grabbed out her towel. *After all,* she thought to herself, *she did say we would go swimming.*

Quid followed Nia to the edge of the hill where Liam had walked down. As they walked closer, the sound of shouting came from below. She tried to make out what they were shouting to one another, but the words were lost by the roar of the creek below.

Nia began her descent down the steep path, and Quid slowly followed, holding on to tree roots sticking out from the bottom of the trees as she went. Near the bottom, Liam stood and helped Nia hop the final couple of feet, reaching his hand out to ensure that she wouldn't fall on to the flat rocks along the creek bed.

Quid neared the bottom, each step carefully chosen so as not to embarrass herself. As she walked, the earth beneath her turned softer as the soil became loose mud. The farther she trudged down the steep embankment, the more she could feel the creek pull on her influence. The water greeted her, feeding off her excitement. With it, the rapids rose.

From the center of the stream, Nua yelled in fear and surprise as the water suddenly rose to his knees. The two boys stood on either side of the creek, desperately holding on to their thick, wooden poles. Nua and a group of boys were knee-deep, each boy spread out in a line across a wide creek bed, grasping on to what appeared to be a line of sticks tied tightly together. The white water pushed past them as they held on to the wooden fence buried deep in the water.

Flashbacks of the wave pool spun in her mind. Normally natural waters were better behaved, but this creek was eager for her to join. It pressed on her. Her heart pounded in her throat. If this water got out of control the boys could be seriously hurt. The boys weren't on rafts like the swimmers in the pool. They would be dragged along the sharp rocks.

Quid stopped on her trek down the embankment. Out of instinct she closed her eyes and took a deep breath to calm herself—and the rushing water.

The sudden noise from the rising water quieted to a gentle roar. Quid opened her eyes. Nua and the other boys were laughing, readjusting the strange, wooden, fence-thing. Nia was already laying on her beach towel. Her slim, brown, bikini-body glistened in the summer sun.

Quid felt a sense of relief. None of them seemed to notice anything odd about her or the water.

The steep trail continued, and Quid looked down towards the shore. Liam stood much closer now. His thick eyebrows pulled together. His face was full of questions she couldn't answer. He looked at the water and then at her. She knew he was trying to figure out what had happened.

Quid didn't know what to say, so she continued to walk down the steep hill. As she reached the bottom, before the final hop to the smooth rocks below, Liam stretched out his hand for Quid, just as he had done for Nia.

She smiled and thanked Liam, ignoring the questions lingering in the air. His long fingers wrapped around her palm as she hopped the last few feet.

Quid held Liam's hand and immediately felt an overwhelming sense of calm— a cool wave of relief washed over her. Like a cold shower, her anxiety calmed and the pressure of her influence on the creek became a dull itch in the back of her mind.

Next to her, Liam stopped as well. She watched as another look of surprise flashed across his face. He took a deep breath. His wide chest grew and shrank.

Shock hit Quid like a bolt. She waited for her heart to pound, for her blood to rush, and she knew she had to regain control when it did. But whatever passed between the two of them, it made her feel calm. In control. Two things that she rarely felt. After all, it was hard to relax when you influenced every natural thing around you.

After a few seconds, she realized that she was still gripping

Liam's hand. Much too quickly, she ripped her hand away. Trying to recover from the sudden awkwardness that comes from holding on a little too long, she walked up the bank, towards the boys and their strange contraption.

Quid quickly kicked off her worn, black Converse, leaving them to lay in a dismal display next to Nia's shiny pink ones, which appeared to have gathered almost no mud while they hiked earlier. Throwing down the neon-dipped towel, Quid walked to the edge of the water. It had receded to a normal level and splashed coolly around her feet.

The current tickled her feet. The thick moss on the bottom of the creek bed squishing between her toes. She walked around the front of the line of thick sticks. The long sticks jutted from the water and had been tied together, creating a net of wood and rope.

"You have to make it into a W!" Liam shouted from next to her. He had also abandoned his shoes and splashed into the water. His steps were clumsy as he walked across the stream. Quid watched as he picked his feet up much too high in the water, splashing as he moved towards Nua at the center of the stream.

Quid glided across the moss on the bottom of the stream. She was steps away from Liam as she realized what was about to happen. His clumsy steps nearly landed him butt-first in the water.

His arms flailed out like broken helicopter blades to keep himself upright as Quid grabbed his arm, keeping him from tumbling into the water.

Bursts of laughter from the boys exploded all around them as Liam righted himself, barely missing the water. His face was flushed as he stood, adjusting his stance.

Once again, a sense of calm came over her as she held Liam's hand tightly. She couldn't help but smile and forced herself to hold back the laughter threatening to burst from her as he looked at her, wide-eyed.

"You have to glide, not stomp," she explained, pointing down at her feet through the clear water. She exaggerated her step, showing him how to move across the water, all the while pulling him along with her.

Liam did as he was told. Quid peered through the water, watching his large feet glide along the mossy rocks of the creek. He gave her hand a gentle squeeze as they walked across. She looked again at their hands, then again at Liam. The mischievous smile was back, spreading across his face. Neither of them let go. The two of them met Nua at the center of the stream. The thick, wooden net now formed a large "W."

Nua struggled against the current, losing his footing before securing his center pole between two rocks. Liam quickly joined him. Quid tried not to show her disappointment as he released her hand. He shuffled back awkwardly until he reached the middle of the fence, working alongside Nua to lift the thick net of wood from the water. Finally, the two of them managed to secure the wooden poles.

Two other boys stood at either end of the wooden net, following Nua's lead. All three took slow, deliberate steps until the center of the net was lined up with the center point of the 'W' in the rocks. For several more minutes, Quid watched as each boy on the end lined up the net again, completing the shape that formed alongside the rocks.

Liam returned to her, awkwardly splashing his way through the water. She reached out twice to catch him as he stumbled but finally made it. Nua and the other two boys were soaked, but joyous. Nua smiled from ear to ear and looked over his creation. Again, Quid wondered what this was all for.

"Congratulations, you…made a W." Quid teased Nua. She playfully splashed water up at him with her foot, gesturing to the net before them.

"It's a weir." Nua smiled triumphantly, spreading one arm wide as if to display the strange contraption.

"It's for catching fish," Liam whispered next to her.

Quid nodded. She didn't like the idea of other people catching any sort of animal to eat, but she wasn't going to insult them by saying so.

Next to her, Liam shrugged his shoulders like it was no big deal, but Quid could tell by the way he smiled at Nua that he was proud of his little brother.

"Our people…."

"…have been building these for centuries." The two young boys walked closer now, finishing each other's sentences as they went. Quid looked them over and finally realized that they must be twins. One had dyed his hair a dirty blonde, but their sharp, angular noses and their matching green eyes gave them away.

"I'm Flint, the better-looking twin. This is Sap, who wishes he was better-looking." Sap quickly elbowed Flint in the ribs, but each boy shook Quid's hand. The one called Flint smiled broadly at her, the front left tooth missing. Quid recognized him as the boy that Nia had been dancing so closely with the night before.

Quid blushed as he wagged his eyebrows at her. His smile was flirtatious as Quid met his eyes. She thought he smirked a little too confidently in her direction and thought back to the way he had been making out with Nia only hours before.

The five of them stood in an awkward circle as Nua and Sap looked at their masterpiece. All the while Flint's predatory gaze didn't leave her.

Liam cleared his throat and turned his towards Quid, "So, Quid. Do you want to go swimming?"
It took Quid a second to realize that Liam was asking her. He had said her name but glared across at Flint. His eyebrows furrowed together, as his eyes flashed a warning at the younger boy. Quid couldn't help but wonder if Liam really didn't like him, or if maybe he was feeling a bit jealous over Flint's obvious attempt at flirting. She tried to push away the feeling that she kind of hoped he was jealous. *Why should Liam be jealous of Flint's flirting?*

"*You* are... going to go swimming?" Nua, who had been adjusting the wooden net, stopped suddenly, and stood up. He looked at his brother, obviously surprised.

Liam turned and looked at Nua. "Yes. I am going to go swimming." He spoke slowly, shrugging his shoulders like Nua's question was ridiculous. Quid wondered what in the world was going on, did Liam not know how to swim? Why was Nua so surprised? The heat of the day was pressing down on them and the hot summer sun was brutally oppressive.

"I would love to." Quid replied, eager to figure out what was going on. The heat from the day covered her face and the sweat dripped down her head. Relaxing in the water, especially now that she was in control of it, sounded perfect.

"Let's go. The swimming hole takes about fifteen minutes to get to." Liam looked back at her and smiled, finally turning away from Flint.

Nua stared at his brother's back questioningly but didn't press any further.

"*We* are going to go check and see if there is anything else that might block the fish upstream, Nua declared. "I haven't seen so much as a tad-pole all day."

He was already several feet away, gliding confidently through the water. Again, Quid wondered at the odd friendship or relationship between the boys. Nua said it like a command and the twins followed.

Sap shrugged and followed Nua without a word, the two of them heading upstream. Flint flashed another toothless smile at Quid and blew a taunting kiss towards Liam, who had turned downstream to wait for Quid. He hesitated in the water, watching her and Liam, but finally began trudging along after the two boys.

As Flint trudged through the water, splashing up the stream after the two other boys, Quid struggled to shake the uneasy feeling she had about him. The burning in her chest grew, angry at him for whatever this display was. She might not know why the two of them had such obvious distaste for one another, but it was like he was taunting Liam, trying to make him angry.

Maybe someone knocked out that missing tooth... Quid thought as her irritation rose. To Liam's credit, he ignored Flint's taunts. The only sign of his growing irritation was the small circles that he drew with his thumb across the back of her hand.

Liam turned towards Nia, who was still lazing about, sunbathing at the bank of the stream. Quid felt a twinge of guilt. She had completely forgotten the person who invited her in the first place. Nia's sunglasses gleamed against the sun, as her long, tan legs stretched across the ground.

"Nia!" Liam yelled to her across the stream. "You want to come swimming?"

All he got back though was Nia's well-manicured hand, waving him off. Apparently, she was content to sunbathe.

More guilt grew in Quid's gut as she realized how glad she was that Nia had wanted to stay on the shore. Now it was just her and Liam.

The two of them began walking down the stream. At first, it felt uncomfortable to be alone together and Quid tried to focus on other things. Like not embarrassing herself further. The water

trickled down the creek, filling in the gaps in the silence between. Uncertainty threatened to overwhelm her. She wasn't sure if she should try to start a conversation, but after a few minutes, she decided the silence was okay.

The air around them cooled the farther downstream they walked. The trees around them grew closer, casting their shadows all along the water. She slowly felt herself relax.

She was at home in the woods. She felt at peace in the muddy water. The current grabbed at her ankles, pushing her onwards. Minnows danced under her toes as sharp rocks threatened the soft soles of her feet with each new step. Still, she didn't mind.

Next to her, Liam struggled several times to keep his balance on the slippery bottom. His long arms were out to the side, flailing around every time he slipped unexpectedly. After a few times of watching Liam flail, Quid did something that she never thought she would be brave enough to do. She walked closer to him and stuck out her hand again for him.

Liam's smile sent a wave of warmth across her body as he gripped her hand in his. This time the two of them laced their fingers together and again Quid felt the sense of ease come over her. She knew it came from her hand being wrapped around Liam's.

Quid took a deep breath. She listened to the crickets around her, and the birds chirp in the trees. For once their influence didn't scare her or worry her. Walking along the creek, with the sunshine warming her face and Liam holding her hand, felt exactly like where she needed to be.

They reached the swimming hole a few minutes later. Liam released her hand to peer over the waterfall to the water below, but Quid hesitated. She was not a fan of heights. Not quite a phobia, but if she could avoid any chance of falling to her death, she generally took it.

As if sensing her hesitation, Liam looked back at her, sticking out his hand for her to grab. "You didn't let me fall. I won't let you fall…" Quid could hear the confidence in his voice, and it was the only thing that made her grab his hand again.

Quid peered down into the white water a few feet below her. The drop couldn't be more than ten or fifteen feet. Her head swirled as she looked at the pool below. The sun was warm on her neck as she tried to gauge how deep the water was. She couldn't quite see to the bottom. The blood drained from her face as her heart threatened to leap from her chest.

The water pushed at her ankles. Out of instinct, she leaned

away from the edge, grabbing on to the soft green fabric of Liam's shirt with her other hand.

Liam wrapped his warm arm around her waist to steady her. His hand touched the soft skin of her lower back, sending chills up her spine. Her fear of the water completely dissolved. It had been replaced with a new, intense, desire to never remove her hand from Liam's broad chest.

Liam looked down at her and the grip she held on his shirt. His eyes explored her face, asking questions he was too afraid to speak aloud. Quid's breath caught in her throat as his eyes lingered a little too long on her lips.

Their eyes met for a second and Quid couldn't help but examine his face across the short distance. His nose was sharp and angular like Nua's, but his cheekbones were higher and more defined. His lips were large and full and revealed his emotions in a way that surprised her. When he was angry his lips became a thin line. When he was happy, they filled his face with glee like a child's.

Quid followed his sharp jawline. Her stomach flipped nervously. They stood so close that she noticed something that she hadn't before. Across his neck was a pattern of scars, leading down his collar bone and under the collar of his t-shirt.

Liam was the one to break their intense moment, releasing her and stepping towards the shore.

"Ready to swim?" he asked her. Once again, he smiled at her with his whole face. "We can put our stuff over here." Liam walked over to the edge of the water to a large rock that was flat on the top.

Quid nodded as she undressed slowly. The idea of taking off her tank top and shorts and being in only her bikini seemed extremely intimate. She had worn a suit to the pool plenty of times—but doing it now, when she was alone in the woods with Liam, felt different.

To his credit, Liam turned away as she slipped off her shorts and tank top. Quid was putting her clothes on the large rock, appreciating him for allowing her time, when she realized he still hadn't taken off his shirt.

"Liam…. Are you okay?" Quid reached out to him, gingerly touching his bicep.

He didn't say anything to her at first. He just stood, silently staring at the water. As if shaking himself from whatever bad memories had held his mind captive, Liam quickly ripped his shirt over his head. A deep sigh shook his chest as he threw the shirt down next to hers.

Quid tried not to gasp as she realized the extent of his scars. The left side of Liam's back, then down his waist and reaching towards his elbow was a collage of scars. Thin, white lines, and deep red scars wrapped across him like waves.

"Our house burned down when Nia and Nua were babies." He shrugged his shoulders but said nothing else. As if that explained everything. She knew it wasn't a story he wanted to tell.

Quid didn't know how to respond. It didn't seem like he talked to anyone about it.

She realized that that was why Nua was surprised Liam was going to go swimming. She was willing to bet that he kept his scars hidden from everyone.

She watched as he shrugged off the severity of the scars on his back like it was no big deal. He didn't say anything else, walking silently towards the water. Quid didn't press him. She knew what it was like to have secrets. She also knew what it was like to have a past you didn't—or in her case, couldn't—talk about.

"You know there is no way in hell that I'm jumping from the top of that thing, right?" Quid gestured towards the waterfall, trying to ease through the awkward moment.

Liam's smile returned as he walked back towards the center of the stream. He playfully kicked water at her as she followed him.

"Don't worry. It's not as bad as it seems…" He stuck his hand out for hers again. This time, she didn't hesitate.

Chapter Thirteen

After watching him jump from the waterfall three times and not die a horrific death, Quid allowed Liam to convince her to jump. Maybe, just a little, because he promised to hold her hand and not let go.

With a grin that she knew she would remember forever, Liam waited for her to take his hand. His eyes were full of excitement and mischief as he counted off.

Quid leaped through the air; sure, she was crushing the bones in Liam's hand. The wind rushed around her as she plummeted. Her adrenaline surged and her heart pounded in her throat as she breached the cool water.

As the cool water pushed her under, a different kind of fear come over her. *What am I thinking?* She knew better than to lose control like this. Disastrous things happened when she let go of her control. Hadn't she learned that?

As she came up for air, she expected to see the water of the small pool thrashing like the waters of the wave pool. Instead, the water was calm except for the waves caused by their splashing and the flow of the water over rocks. The summer breeze came across the air to greet her.

A few heartbeats later, Liam emerged. True to his word, he had not let go.

For almost an hour, but what felt like an eternity, the two of them swam in the waters of the creek. The sun was warm, and the water caressed her skin like a sweater. Quid had never spent so long laughing. Her cheeks filled with a strange tingling feeling— like the tickle in your cheeks from blowing up too many balloons. Now she was the balloon, filled to perfection with laughter. She was finally floating.

The more time she spent with him the more she felt like she had known Liam for years and not hours. She realized that he was much less serious without everyone around. He deflated as if he had finally shed the weight and responsibilities he carried.

They talked about everything. He told Quid stories about Nia and Nua. They were always getting into trouble as kids. How they had been raised by their grandparents. She told him about her strained relationship with her mom, though she left out some of the larger reasons.

When they weren't talking, he challenged her to all sorts of hilarious games and contests. Like the kids she had watched at the pool for so many summers, they wanted nothing more than the opportunity to enjoy their scorching, summer afternoon.

The two of them played a game to see which one of them could dive the deepest. To her surprise, Quid realized the pool was even deeper than she expected. She won that contest, and it was the first time Quid had seen Liam frown since their leap from the waterfall. It didn't last long though, as he immediately challenged her to see who could hold their breath the longest.

Liam counted the two of them down as quickly as he could. She watched as he ducked his head violently under the water.

Quid lost that game in a matter of seconds, despite her ability to hold her breath for much longer than the average person. The problem was she could see underwater perfectly. Quid ducked under the surface, and within only seconds she took in a lung-full of creek water because she came face-to-face with Liam.

He was turning red from holding his breath. His cheeks were poking out, enormous and puffy, filled with air. His dark hair floated around him like some sort of crazed sea creature shooting tendrils from the top of his head.

Quid shot from the depths of the pool, water spewing from her lungs and out her nose. As she laughed harder more water spewed out her nose, until she was a cycle of coughing, laughing, and spewing.

Liam's wet hair crested the water. One eyebrow was cocked as he watched her, waiting to see if she was okay. The bridge of his nose was still below the water, half his face lurking below the surface, like a frog peeking on a predator. *The most handsome frog-man I've ever seen*, Quid thought to herself.

Liam wagged his furry eyebrows at her now. Most of his face was under the water, but the corners of his cheeks peeked just above the surface. He was grinning in triumph.

Quid went for his shoulders, trying her best to push his cocky smile back under the water. Despite her best efforts to dunk his head into the murky water, he didn't budge. He wrapped his arms around her waist in the water and held her.

Quid draped her arms around his neck, pulling him in close to gain a better grip.

"If I go down, you go down with me." She whispered to him, eyes locked on his, daring him to try.

Her eyes met his with the challenge, but his eyes met hers with something else. Her throat went dry as he moved closer.

Liam leaned in and pressed his soft lips against hers. He had been making her smile and making her heart pound all day. Now, time stood still.

She leaned into him, pulling him closer, filled with an intense longing. His kiss gave her confidence she hadn't felt before. All worries that she might lose control, all desire to maintain control, melted away.

His tongue danced with hers as they floated in the water.

Quid was thinking that she could stay there forever, that she could spend eternity in the cool waters, playing games and kissing Liam, there was shouting from atop the waterfall.

The two of them broke apart and embarrassment washed over Quid as she finally stepped back into reality. She fought to catch her breath, as she looked up to see Nua and Nia peering over the waterfall.

"Guys… You have…to come see this!" Nua shouted down to them. He was leaned over, hands on his knees. His breath was short and ragged as he spoke—like he had run all the way there.

Something in the tone of his voice had them both out of the water and climbing up the steep rocks along the side of the waterfall within seconds. They hurried to grab their things from the rock, as Nia and Nua moved towards the opposite side of the water.

"There is a trail that's faster up through here!" Nia urged them all. She was already disappearing into the thick woods, a flash of pink against the green and brown of the trees.

Quid pulled her shorts and tank top on over her wet bikini. Her clothes were warm from waiting in the sun, but a chill went up her spine as she hurried. Worry and urgency hung in the air as she trudged across the stream. Without thinking, without saying anything, Liam reached his hand out to hers. She was instantly comforted.

The four of them swept through the forest with Nia at the lead. Whatever the emergency was, they moved towards it with incredible speed. It was no wonder Nua had been so out of breath.

They quickly covered miles of ground, despite the rough terrain of the thick woods.

We have gone way beyond Kid Camp. The ground continued its rise and Quid realized that they were following the stream north, towards its source.

Quid was used to hiking and she could go for hours, but she admired the way the three of them moved. They were one with the forest, moving confidently, dodging branches and brambles, making no noise, and leaving no trace behind. In their own way, they were almost as in-touch with the forest as she was. Almost.

Quid could go for miles without getting winded, but the farther north they went, the heavier Quid felt. At first, she thought it was the incline, but as the trees around her grew thinner and thinner, she could feel her chest tighten and her feet grow heavy.

She reached out silently with her influence, searching the forest in front of her. She felt out for the animals and the trees that she had been pushing away all morning, expecting to feel a flurry of life around her. There was only emptiness coming from the trees. The animals around her screamed their pain. Like a punch to the gut, it hit her, knocking the wind out of her as she struggled to catch her breath.

"We are almost there!" Nua shouted from ahead of her and Liam. He stopped to look back at the group. His eyes were full of pain and panic. A look passed between them all. Quid knew she needed to prepare herself.

She could feel the change in the land and the trees around her. A cough rose in her throat and the pain intensified with each step. She had to see it for herself.

Quid pushed aside the thin branches of a low tree that blocked her path. She could see the sun shining down. The leaves littered the ground before them.

That doesn't make any sense. Fall isn't for weeks.

The branch in front of her fell as she pushed it out of her path. Thin and broken, it hit the ground with a thud, stirring dust around them. Quid's breath caught in her throat at the horror in front of her. Pain settled over her, causing her to clutch her chest. Pressure from her influence began to build inside her. Next to her, the four of them stood in stunned silence.

Like the scene after a wildfire, the forest was bare. Trees crumbled over one another. Their once-proud trunks were flat on the ground, decaying in the sun. The undergrowth had withered to nothing and lay bare and brown. A blanket of death was spread across the ground. Where there should be damp, healthy ground, there was a hard, thick crust. The slightest breeze spewed dust across the flat basin. The blue sky could be seen for miles. What should have been a lush forest was bare, lifeless.

Quid gasped at the scene before her. Her hand rose to her mouth to keep the bile from spewing.

Hundreds of animals had gathered all around the depleted stream. Deer, foxes, birds—it seemed every type of animal that called the forest home lay near the water. Most of them were dead, some called out to her in pain.

She listened to their cacophony of tortured songs as they stretched out as far as she could see.

Her whole body shook, and her eyes welled with tears as she tried to take in everything. Their weakened bodies pressed on her mind, begging her for help or to end their suffering.

Behind her, Liam, Nia, and Nua stepped silently from the woods. Next to her, Nia's sharp gasp filled the silence as she came to stand by Quid.

Flint and Sap stood on the opposite bank, staring out as well. Another weir, this one older, its sticks worn by the current, stood in the water. It had done its job. Hundreds of fish were trapped. Most had gone belly up, but some flipped their tails and fins weakly. The poison was slowly, torturously, killing them all.

Behind them, pinned to a tree, a sheet of paper flapped loosely in the breeze. Thick red ink bled down the paper, dripping from a strange symbol and onto the ground. Quid examined the symbol curiously. A circle, divided in half by a crescent moon, was speared by arrows in every direction. The symbol sat like a memory on the edge of her mind. Underneath the symbol was a single word written in dark, black ink, "Profectus."

"What does that mean?" Nua asked the group. He walked over to the paper as if to tear it down, but as he grabbed for it his hand dropped, as if thinking better of it.

"It's Latin." Liam's voice was full of venom as he spat out the word.

From across the stream, she heard Sap whisper, as if to himself, "—it means progress."

Quid's mind was full of questions as she tried to understand the connection between the paper and the horrors in front of her. *Why was Liam so angry at seeing the paper? What was the Profectus?*

Quid's breath came out ragged. Her shoes were full of lead and her legs protested painfully as she walked forward. The weight of the poison pressed down on her, dulling her senses. Her mind flooded with questions and she tried to wrap her mind around what to do.

Her lungs began to protest painfully. Quid's breath came out in a wheeze and she clutched at her chest, forcing herself to take deep breaths. She had only gone a few feet, but it was harder and harder for her to stay upright.

"Quid. Don't…" she heard Liam say. She could hear the worry in his voice and knew what she must look like. She must seem crazy. Part of her knew that she shouldn't get closer. She shouldn't do it. She had never used her gift like this before, but she couldn't just walk away.

She ignored that voice of reason, and she ignored Liam's words of warning. For the first time in a long time, she stopped pressing against and stopped pushing away the animals and plants. She welcomed their influence on her mind.

Quid took a shattered breath and opened herself to it. The sounds of the animals grew to a deafening roar around her. They were in pain. They were dying and only she could help them.

Quid couldn't think about the fact that her friends stood behind her, watching her with curiosity. She couldn't think about the fact that they would learn her secret. All she could hear and all she could feel was a thousand voices, a thousand souls, calling out to her.

Enough. It was all she could think as she sunk her hands into the warm water. Like the wave pool and again this morning, she sent it out like a command. No more. No more death. No more destruction. She couldn't let it go on. She couldn't let it spread any further.

Enough. Quid sent the command into the stream, picturing it in her mind once again full of life. She imagined the trees lush and full. She pictured their branches alive with leaves. She pictured the birds flying over the trees. She longed to see the foxes running, their tails swishing back and forth in the underbrush. She prayed for the animals to be full of health again. Then, she was filled with overwhelming fury at their pain.

Quid felt a wave come out from her and across the land. It came from the center of her and spread out through her fingers and toes. She felt her arms stretch wide with the power. Her head filled with pressure. It kept building until she thought it might crack. It pulsated with the need to be released.

Go. When she couldn't take it anymore, she urged the power out of her. Like getting the wind knocked from your chest, it stole her breath and went out into the field of death before her. The wave left her body as the world swirled around her, pitching her into darkness.

The first thing she felt was the throbbing pain in her head. Someone was hammering on both of her temples. Her eyes were heavy as she pulled her surroundings into focus.

Quid peeked her eyes open as a breeze greeted her face. She was warm, wrapped tightly in something soft against her arms and legs. The hard ground underneath her and the ache in her back told her she had been laying on the ground for some time.

Quid listened to the crickets sing around her and the wind's soft breeze passing through the trees. The night's songs filled her ears as her eyes fought to adjust to the twilight around her. Spots covered Quid's vision as she struggled to keep the world right-side up. A wave of dizziness threatened to spill the contents of her stomach across the ground.

As the humming in her ears stopped, loud voices drifted in from somewhere nearby.

"I don't understand what you mean, it's better?" a thick, husky voice that Quid didn't recognize asked.

"I don't know, Grandfather. It was like she did it. She touched the land and within minutes there was growth again. She changed it all. She made it better…" Quid recognized Liam's voice. "You have to see it for yourself. It was incredible."

Liam's voice was filled with wonder as he spoke. At first, Quid felt a sense of relief. *At least he didn't think she was a total freak.*

The relief at Liam's words was short-lived as a wave of something else washed over her. Images of the death at the stream flooded her mind as her breath caught in her throat. Dread sunk into her gut as she realized that if his words were true, they would want an explanation. She would not be able to give them one.

Quid's thoughts raced as she tried to come up with an explanation they would believe. Liam and the others might not understand everything that happened, but that didn't mean they hadn't seen a lot more than she wanted.

"I'm sure it was a coincidence. The animals were probably spooked by your presence and ran away…" Vernie's voice was filled with denial. Quid sat and listened to her mother lie. "Quid probably just got scared and fainted."

Fainted. Quid almost laughed out loud at the obvious lie. Only fragile maidens in fairy tales actually fainted. Her mother was a terrible liar. From the pounding in Quid's head, she knew she hadn't just "fainted." She had overdone it. She had pushed herself too hard without really meaning to. She was lucky it hadn't killed her.

"You could have told us she was special. That she was—-"

"She's not!" Vernie yelled over the female voice that had spoken.

"If you know something about this…if you know something that can stop it you must tell us." The male voice was angry, full of rage.

"We could make her tell us." Quid recognized Flint's honey-filled voice. The threat hung in the air as he spoke.

Quid had heard enough. She angrily threw back the soft, heavy quilts wrapped around her. A twig snapped underneath her heavy palm, shattering the tense silence of the night.

Within seconds, a ring of people emerged from the growing darkness and surrounded Quid. Vernie emerged first. Quid noticed again how loose her clothes hung from her thin frame. The laces of her shoes were once again untied, dragging the ground behind her, as if she just hadn't bothered to fix them. Liam's grandfather towered over Vernie as he emerged. He wore a dark green flannel shirt now, but the fox fur had disappeared from his shoulders. His hair stood up at every angle—as if he'd spent his day running his fingers through it again and again.

Liam shuffled in. He had his green t-shirt back on and he still smelled like the water of the creek as he approached. He silently dropped her yellow bag to the ground. Quid realized he must have grabbed it when he went back to the stream. *How had she gotten back to camp? Had Liam or someone else carried her back from the stream?*

Liam walked back silently to stand behind the adults as Grandmother Dana approached. She was wearing a thin white dress that ruffled with every step she took. A small kerosene lantern lit her path, giving her a strange ethereal look.

In the darkness, lit only by the flickering light of the lantern, the adults formed a half-circle around Quid. Their eyes were full of questions.

Quid watched Liam rock to the side as he tucked his hands deep in his pockets. From her position on the ground, Quid watched him shove a piece of paper into his pocket. Before he crumpled it, she saw the edge of the symbol she had seen earlier. He must have brought it back with him from the stream too. Quid noticed that his eyes never met hers.

"Honey, are you okay?" Vernie's voice was filled with worry as she helped Quid continue to pull off the multitude of blankets.

"I'm fine, mom." Quid couldn't keep the venom from her voice. Not after hearing her mom do everything, she could to deny how much of a freak her daughter was.

Silence fell around them again. A strange, tense, awkwardness hung in the air. Each of the adults stared down at Quid. Vernie's eyes were full of concern as she gently stroked Quid's damp hair away from her face.

"What happened?" Liam's grandfather was the first to break the tense silence. His voice boomed down at her. His eyes were dark under his thick eyebrows. A tremor of fear went through her as he stepped closer.

Iktomi..." Grandmother Dana whispered his name. Her voice was full of warning. In the glow of the lantern, Dana smiled sweetly at Quid. Her silver hair fell in loose locks, a stark contrast to Iktomi's wild look.

His piercing eyes were cold and intense as he studied her face.

Quid watched as Vernie also took a step closer, part of her body now blocking Iktomi from approaching.

The wind whipped around them, tossing the branches of the trees about, and blasting through the group. Quid knew it responded to her sudden discomfort, the feeling of being interrogated.

"I..." Quid searched for a lie that wouldn't betray her secret.

"I just saw the animals and got scared. I must have fainted."

Repeating her mother's previous words, Quid shrugged her shoulders, as if that explained it all.

"That's bullshit." Flint came forward from the darkness in a rush. He marched towards Quid, pushing past Liam to stand next to Iktomi at the center of the circle. Again, Vernie stepped in front of her protectively. She said nothing, but Quid noticed that Vernie suddenly stood a little taller. Her feet were set further apart. Quid's head swiveled between the two of them. Her heart swelled with pride and gratitude at her mother's sudden, protective instincts.

Still shuffling awkwardly behind the adults, Quid looked desperately towards Liam, expecting him to speak up, but he made no move to defend her.

Quid stood up now, fighting to maintain her balance. Iktomi's eyes watched her as she rose. The suspicion in his eyes glared into her. "I'm sorry for scaring you." Quid said it to the group, but this time she looked at Liam.

His eyes were unreadable as he finally looked back at her. Tears burned in her eyes, threatening to spill. *Why had he not defended her? Had their time in the creek not meant the same to him? Maybe he kissed lots of girls. Maybe he thought she was a freak now too.*

She could tell that he had questions, but she couldn't answer them, even if he asked. It didn't matter. It must have not meant the same to him if he wouldn't stand up to Flint and Iktomi.

"Could we get food? I'm starving." She asked the air around her before stepping out of the circle of interrogation. She felt another twinge of sadness as she realized that she never did get to try whatever Liam had packed for lunch.

Her feet were lead once more and her head swam as she walked, but she did her best to pretend that they didn't. There was no reason to make anyone more suspicious than they already were.

She stumbled slowly into the dark woods, knowing the eyes of every person in the circle were watching her walk away. She could hear the faint sounds of music and laughter float through the trees. The sounds of the camp were growing as she struggled with tired feet through the underbrush.

She nearly tumbled into the undergrowth, until a hand gripped her elbow. Vernie placed one hand around Quid's waist, guiding her and keeping her upright. The two of them walked in silence back towards the larger group, both carrying secrets. She knew they were both wondering how much of Quid's secrets had been discovered that night.

Quid sat outside their orange tent, in one of the metal folding chairs. The cool metal greeted her, keeping her grounded as she listened to Vernie pack their things up. The world continued to swim around her.

The cool night air brushed her face as Quid sat watching people around the camp carry on with their fun. Young children roasted marshmallows again, teenagers huddled together, listening to music. The couple wearing the matching red flannels had changed into matching camo shirts but had apparently made up.

They were holding hands while they too watched the world around them pass by.

They have no idea what happened today. Quid pondered this for a few moments.

As the laughter and conversations drifted across the night Quid's head pounded in response. She still couldn't believe what happened. *Was Liam right, had she really healed the stream and the animals?* She knew tonight was their last night at camp and she still had so many questions, but no one to help her find answers.

So much had happened that day and she was drained by it all. Quid closed her eyes and tried to reach out with her influence into the earth around her. Pain filled her head and her stomach tightened. Her body was exhausted. Kid Camp and the stream were much farther away than she had ever sent her influence out. But she had to know. She had to know if things were better like Liam said.

A few yards away, she felt a small trickle of water flowing through the dirt. Up, around trees and rocks, she connected that trickle to the larger stream. Like she was one with the slow, moving current, she followed the stream north. All around her was life.

Hundreds of fish, frogs, and minnows now flourished. They eagerly splashed their way downstream. With her mind, she followed the current as far as she could. The water felt different as she traveled. It was thicker, still recovering from whatever had poisoned it. But she could feel that it was healing.

When Quid opened her eyes, she was coming back into herself. The wind caressed her face and the sound of laughter and music fill her head once more.

As Quid walked to the center towards the fire, she noticed that the large kerosene lanterns that had lit the campsite the night before didn't fill the corners of the camp with light like before. There was only the blaze in front of her, dwarfing the one from the night before. Its light cast shadows across every face.

Slowly, the noise died down. Music was cut off mid-song. Conversations were halted. Like the night before, someone walked across the circle, towards the fire.

Quid sat down on the hard log as the heat warmed her face and the orange and yellow tendrils danced for her. The air shifted and something was different this time. Quid felt it and apparently so did everyone else. The mood in the camp changed as Liam's grandfather circled the enormous blaze. Quid shifted anxiously against the hard log underneath her.

His voice was clear as he spoke. He did not yell, though she was sure everyone could hear him. Only the crackle of the fire dared to interrupt. As he began, it was as the story overtook him, emerged from him. He became the story as he paced around the camp.

"Last night Grandmother told you the story of the history of our people." Quid watched as several people nodded along as Iktomi spoke, entranced by his words. "The Believers have been persecuted for centuries. We came from many lands. We were Druids running from the persecution of the church. Many of our children get their names from these ancestors…" with this he nodded approvingly towards the outer part of the circle. Quid turned to see Nua and Nia watching adamantly. Neither looked in her direction.

"Most of us come from and respect the traditions that were passed down from the great Nations that truly founded this country." Quid jumped as someone behind her whooped loudly.

"But now our nations and the lands that they once called home are suffering. Pollution, contamination, have begun to take over our land. It kills the animals, the trees, everything it touches. Our people who work as migrant farmers have reported to the Council that the contamination is becoming more and more wide spread. It affects many coasts, but none more so than here."

It was Quid's turn to listen intently. She had no idea that the contamination was so bad. She never even considered that there could be other places affected. *How many other places were dying? How many more animals would die? How many ecosystems would be destroyed?*

"We must find the sources of this contamination and stop them. We must find who is behind this!" Iktomi's voice boomed across the silent camp now.

"As you go back to your communities, implore them to report back anything you learn to The Council. Those who help us end this plague will be greatly rewarded..."

Iktomi circled the fire again, but this time his eyes never left Quid. She felt them bore into her, questioning her, trying to get her to spill her secrets. "Those who aid our enemies will be greatly punished. We must do whatever it takes to rid our land of this plague."

Chapter Fourteen

After Iktomi's speech, the oppressive mood in the camp sent everyone to bed. Within a few minutes, everyone's dinner was cleaned up and chairs and tables were hurriedly put away. Iktomi's words still hung in the air as tents all around were zipped tight.

Quid's heart raced and goosebumps crawled across her skin at the thought of Iktomi. Worry filled her. *Why was he interested in her and her abilities?* She needed a chance to get some answers.

Quid dragged herself back to their campsite shortly after Iktomi's speech and Vernie had nearly everything loaded into the truck. The back of their truck was nearly filled to the brim as Quid approached. Boxes usually kept neat and tidy were thrown about, items threatening to spew out the top. A tremor of fear raced through her as she realized how frantic Vernie had become, but still, she implored her mother to let them stay until morning.

She finally convinced Vernie to stay, explaining that she wasn't well enough to ride yet. Vernie was insistent at first. Her face full of worry, eyes darting all around the campsite as if expecting the boogeyman to spring from the trees. Vernie was even more spooked than Quid, but she finally gave in.

Disappointment filled Quid again as she trudged towards the orange monstrosity. If she was honest, she was hoping to see Liam and talk to him again. Her head buzzed with questions about how she had gotten back to camp. *Who was the Council Iktomi had talked about?*

She needed answers.

How had so much happened in only a few days? Meeting Nia and Nua. Meeting Liam. Her kiss with Liam. Healing the stream. The weird interrogation between her and Liam's grandparents. *And what the hell was that speech? How was a ragged group of campers going to fight the contamination if it was so widespread?*

Quid wondered all these questions again and again as she lay on the air mattress under the stars. This time Vernie insisted on sleeping on the floor, hoping Quid would feel better if she got a good night's sleep. Quid lay in the bed in silence, staring at the cocoon of fabrics snoring loudly.

It felt like hours, but Quid couldn't stand it any longer. She wasn't going to leave until she got some answers. Within moments, Quid had thrown back her covers, slipped on her shoes, and tip-toed out the tent. She was going to find Liam and demand some answers.

The moon filled the campsite with its soft white glow as the stars stared down at Quid. The sound of noisy crickets and the incessant call of frogs filled her ears as her feet crunched through the grass. Quid walked towards the center of the camp, headed for where Nia had come bursting out of the old RV this morning.

Quid couldn't be sure if Liam would be in there, but it was certainly a start. But, like this morning, she felt something burn into the back of her head. The sense that she was once again being watched overwhelmed her. The hair on the back of her neck stood up. For a moment, she regretted her decision as fear swept across her.

As she paused in her determined stride, Quid looked desperately around the campsite for whomever or whatever may be watching her.

The smell of smoke still filled the air as she hesitantly walked across the campsite. The fire had burnt out long ago, but the ring of rocks sat charred and waiting for its return. Red embers waited in the center, glowing against the darkness. Crouched next to the fire pit was a figure, dressed in a worn, white robe. A small black lantern peeked from behind the log.

Dana stood; the colorful beads that adorned her white robe swished with a kind of music. Quid watched as the old woman hobbled over to sit on the large log once more. She turned towards Quid with an arm outstretched, inviting her to sit.

A lot had happened, and Quid filled with apprehension. Perhaps leaving the tent had been a bad idea. Dana wasn't exactly who she was hoping to find, but as she looked at the old woman, with her silver hair dancing in the moonlight, she felt inclined to join.

Quid sat and was comforted at the presence of the old woman. Dana was such a warm contrast to Iktomi's intense nature. Quid felt heavy as she tried to decide which of the hundreds of questions she had to ask first.

"I know that I am not who you were looking for tonight." A peaceful expression sat on the older woman's wrinkled cheeks as she spoke. Her gray eyes shined at Quid with mischief as she smiled slyly across the log. "But thank you for joining me."

Dana let out a long sigh as she continued. "So much has happened today. So many things have been put into motion." Dana's warm hand squeezed Quid's. Her fingers felt thin and fragile.

"Our lives are often full of turmoil, full of chaos. Sometimes it feels like we will never gain control."
Nervousness filled Quid's stomach as she looked down at their interlocked hands again. A breeze swept around them, tossing Dana's silver strands about, and pushing against Quid's back.

"I feel I must apologize for my husband's behavior tonight. Even the wisest among us forget that there are things about life that sometimes we cannot control." Dana's eyes were sad as she spoke. Her eyebrows furrowed together, and she squeezed Quid's hand gently. "Sometimes all we can do is find that person who completes us. The person who helps us pull ourselves together and be the best version of ourselves that we can be."

For the first time, Quid wondered why Iktomi and Dana were together. They were so opposite to one another. He was hot-tempered and fiery while she was calm and steady like water.

"I hope you can forgive him for his ways. Sometimes we find ourselves…lost."

Dana stood, and Quid went to help her. The woman placed something cool in Quid's hand. A thin, dark leather strap held a gold circle in its center. The cool metal reflected in the white moonlight as Quid turned it over in her hand.

"It is customary for the hosts to give out gifts to their guests. I did not want you to leave without giving you yours." Quid examined the thin metal of the bracelet as Dana's deft fingers tied the leather around her wrist.
"The sun is the protector of us all. It is the giver of life, but it can also be the taker of life. Without her, we wouldn't have anything that grows in the ground. But she is nothing without her partner, the moon, who reminds us all that darkness must reign as well."

The two of them say in silence for several minutes. Quid thanked Dana for the bracelet as the older woman walked off into the night. It wasn't until Quid was under the soft blankets again that she realized she hadn't gotten to ask a single one of her questions.

As she drifted off to sleep, Quid thought about everything the old woman said. She stared up at the white orb against the dark sky, silently hoping that she would get to say goodbye to Liam in the morning.

Quid was still reeling from everything that happened when she awoke the next day. She watched out the window as Bald Eagle slowly faded from view. They had been on the road for several miles, still following a few cars from the caravan.

All around them, the silence filled the spaces, like another person sitting between them. Compared to the raucous noise that had filled her ears the night before, it was hell.

Quid knew that they both had a lot on their minds. She didn't understand why Iktomi was so interested in her or why he appeared to hate her so much, but she knew that whatever was going on was bothering Vernie too.

Quid's mind was full, thinking back to the look that Liam had given her. He hadn't come to find her at all last night or this morning. She had waited as long as she could.

As another car broke off behind them, she found herself wondering which one Liam and his grandfather were in. Despite everything that had happened last night, the past two days were still great. Nia and Nua had come to say goodbye this morning, leaving Quid feeling like she finally had friends. *If only Liam had also shown up.*

For the next several miles, Quid thought about these people who called themselves The Believers. Then, every few minutes, the image of a handsome, crooked, smile dancing behind the firelight would also return. It was hard not to let the image linger.

Her mind drifted to the stream. She could feel the fatigue wrap around her all morning, but she felt better than she had last night. She had reached out again this morning and felt even more life and growth throughout the forest. Pride swelled inside her. She had healed so much of the forest.

"Did you have a good time?" Vernie asked, breaking the silence. The question was kind of absurd and Vernie's awkwardness as she said it hung in the air around them.

"It was the most fun I've had at a funeral." Quid admitted, shrugging her shoulders.

A long pause passed between the two of them. Each of them glanced at the other and burst into laughter. Despite the way they had fled the campsite, Quid felt a surge of happiness go through her. She couldn't remember the last time she and Vernie had laughed together like this.

As quickly as it came, the laughter died with the clinking of water droplets on the windshield.

"I didn't know it was supposed to rain today." Whispered Vernie, leaning over the steering wheel and pulling the lever to turn on the windshield wipers. More and more droplets splattered across the windshield as Vernie increased the speed of the thin, black wipers. The rain became a sheet in front of them.

The hair on the back of her neck stood on end as a shiver passed over her spine. She always, *always* knew when it was going to rain.

"This isn't you, is it?" asked Vernie frantically, her head whipping back and forth from Quid to the windshield.

"It's not! I swear!"

Thunder rumbled across the sky. The wind whipped around them, shaking the frame of the truck. Vernie's knuckles turned white as she gripped the steering wheel.

The windshield wipers were frenzied, trying to clear the deluge now covering the glass.

"Mom…" Quid whispered. Vernie grabbed out towards the passenger seat, without taking her eyes off the road.

With her eyes closed, Quid reached out to the storm, hoping to urge it in another direction. Storms rarely listened to her, but she healed the stream. Surely, she could lighten a little summer torrent. Normally she couldn't control this kind of natural event, it took too much energy, but she thought back to yesterday. Maybe she could redirect it to the acres of empty farmland near here. Quid followed the whips of wind as they strayed from the clouds to the ground.

In her mind she approached the clouds, expecting to be greeted by the playful gusts. Instead of feeling a natural power, she felt only darkness. As with the water of the creek, the storm was unnatural. Tainted.

Panic set in and Quid's heart pounded in her chest. She had never felt anything like it before. It was as if something else controlled the storm, something that was cutting it off from the rest of the natural world. The storm was headed right for the line of cars, targeting them.

Her breath came in quick bursts, increasing as a gust pushed angrily against their car. She wanted to help, but she didn't know what to do and she was losing control.

As if sensing her panic, Vernie squeezed her hand tightly.

Quid took a deep breath, trying to calm herself. She looked down at their entwined hands. She studied her mother's fragile bones and the old-age spots that spread across her skin. Her parents never showed how old they were.

They were always so active and energetic. Sometimes she forgot. *Maybe she shouldn't be so harsh to Vernie, moms were supposed to be protective, weren't they?*

She covered Vernie's hand with hers. Worry gripped her chest, followed by a sharp pain. The seatbelt tightened, squeezing the air from her body. The squealing of tires and crunch of glass filled her ears. Then, the world went dark.

None of it made any sense. Sirens from the firetrucks and ambulances pulsated around her, piercing the air. The red lights flashed in her peripheral as Quid opened her eyes. She looked down at something scratchy against her palms. Someone had placed a thick wool blanket across her.

It was like 80 degrees today. She thought to herself sourly. As she sat up, she realized that one of the straps on her tank top was torn. It flapped uselessly at her side, exposing the thin strap of her bra. The clothes against her skin felt wet and clung to her stomach and thighs as she shifted positions. She looked down at the soft, blue sheets of the gurney and the mud dripping from her.

Why was she so wet and dirty?

Quid pushed the heavy wool, trying to sit up.

"Hey… stay right there…" said a gentle but firm voice from behind her. A young paramedic squeezed out from between the large silver doors and hopped onto the ground next to her. His gloved hands gently pushed on her shoulders and Quid couldn't help but cringe at the feel of the latex against her skin.

Quid let him push her back down on the gurney, too sore to resist. She clutched her injured wrist to her chest. A sharp pain shot up her arm like lightning.

Quid felt the panic growing inside of her as she looked out at the carnage before her. The blonde paramedic's navy-colored uniform filled her vision as he shined an annoying light in her eyes, getting in her way again. A part of her finally realized he was speaking to her through the haze.

"Follow the light with your eyes." He instructed her again.

Instead, she pulled away, trying to see around him, back towards their car.

Quid searched her foggy mind. She frantically tried to remember what had happened. All she got was flashes. The image of laughing with Vernie. The clink of rain on the windshield. Then, Vernie's panicked face and the feel of the wind pushing the car.

Quid pulled at the ache in the back of her neck. She wiped the mud from her hands across the heat of her skin as she remembered.

The reality of the situation came rushing back to her and the fog in her brain began to lift.

Lights continued to flash and all she saw were steel cabinets full of medical supplies. She whipped her head around towards the back of the ambulance in stunned terror. Her heart pounded in her ears now, a drumming she couldn't turn off. All around her sirens blared and people moaned or screamed in pain and panic.

Black smoke billowed from the wreckage of cars and trucks. From about twenty feet away she could make out the edge of the small, red, compact she knew they had been following behind. Its front bumper was now mangled with the black Jeep in front of it. Chunks of glass of all sizes and shapes littered the ground, like dark confetti for a party no one had ever wanted to attend. The country road was a tangled array of rust and metal, glinting and smoking in the sunlight.

A bandage was placed gently on her head. The paramedic brushed the bloody strands of her hair back from her face. Pain pierced the left side of her head. She must have cut it somehow.

"You most likely have a concussion and maybe a small wrist fracture." He said to her softly, shining the annoying white light in her eyes again. He moved towards her and she gently handed him her wrist.

Cool liquid poured against the warmth of her skin as he washed the scrapes off with a small, white squirt bottle. She was transfixed by his adept hands as he wrapped a thick, white gauze around her wrist.

Quid looked down at the cloth as she took stock of her injuries. Her wrist was probably broken. She wiggled her toes— thankful she wasn't paralyzed. A breeze swept across one foot as she realized that she only had on one of her black Converse. A sharp pain went up the foot as she wiggled it around. She looked down, surprised that it too had already been wrapped in a tight gauze.

She looked at the bandages on her foot and her wrist. Her mind was still clearing off the fog of pain and noises, so she focused on it. The white glared back at her in the morning sun. The air was thick with the smell of burning rubber, smoke, and gasoline. But this cloth was so clean, even though the rest of her was covered in dirt and grime.

Dirt. Quid stopped for a second—the fog in her head cleared by the adrenaline coursing through her veins. She closed her eyes and took a deep breath. She searched out for the connection that was always there. The wind always made her feelings known first. When she was too happy wisps and little swirls danced in the air. When she was too angry it pushed everyone around like a school bully on the playground. If she wasn't careful, the sky and the rain would come, sometimes plants and animals if she didn't concentrate hard enough or she didn't get control fast enough. She reached out with her influence, searching the landscape around her, but felt nothing.

Terror gripped her. She had never been this defenseless before. She had never been without the connection. Whatever it was that helped keep her in check, whatever tether was tied naturally on the chaos she felt inside had completely stoppered her abilities.

She opened her eyes to see the paramedic looking at her questioningly. Despite all the pain, she thought to herself that if he shined the light in her eyes again, she was going to hit him with her good wrist.

"It is going to be okay." He said to her again. She knew that he meant it to reassure her, but the way his eyes kept darting back to the cars around them and how he flinched each time someone screamed in the distance did nothing to support his words.

His words were long and drawn out like there was something wrong with her brain and not her leg. "You're—going—to—be—okay…" he looked over her wounds again, "I'll—be—right—back…"

Quid suppressed an eye roll and thought to herself that if her life had suddenly turned into some sort of horror movie, he would surely be the next to die for uttering the cursed phrase. He took one more unsure glance at her.

She decided to keep her bitter thoughts to herself and nodded that she was fine. *Why am I reassuring him?* She wondered to herself. The aches in her body were impossible to ignore and her ankle throbbed under the weight of the bandage.

She closed her eyes as he turned to step away. The first two steps crunched on the broken glass as she wondered again which ambulance Vernie was in. Against the sirens and the screams, she heard his radio go off, "DOA. Red truck."

The paramedic took even longer to process. He was more than an arms-length away, with no chance of catching Quid before she burst off the gurney. Her feet raced through the macabre scene, heading towards Vernie's truck.

Quid didn't register the glass as it crunched under her feet. She ignored the ripping of her dress and the gash that opened on her thigh as she came sliding around the front of a black compact.

Her feet carried her closer until she saw the wreckage of the truck. It had flipped onto its roof, blasting the glass from the windows and the windshield. The metal passenger door was crumpled and bent. It had been ripped from the frame like the page of a book. Quid trembled in shock and fear as she realized the firefighters must have pulled her from it.

A sob rose inside of Quid as she took a hesitant step towards the truck that had always been like another member of their family. She was processing the loss as her eyes fell to the white sheet spread across the pavement.

Time stood still as she looked at it, confused at first. Her ears filled with the sound of the pounding of her heart and her breath came in short bursts.

Her mind raced with a thousand possibilities and a thousand different emotions. *It isn't her because Vernie is in another ambulance. It isn't her because whoever was in that sheet was too tall. Vernie isn't that tall, is she?* The thoughts went on and on. All she knew as she stood frozen in fear was that couldn't possibly be her.

She stood, staring down at the sheet. Her mind fought to process what was happening. Several feet away, on the other side of the upside-down truck, another EMT stood next to a tall firefighter in his luminescent gear.

All around her was noise and chaos. A woman screamed—a high-pitched guttural scream that echoed Quid's cries. The sirens from the firetruck screeched their warning to other drivers of the danger ahead. The smell of gasoline and burned rubber burned her nose and eyes.

Quid waited and watched in all the chaos as the two men whispered to one another. They talked calmly, as if their conversation were over coffee and not a body they had just covered in a crisp, white sheet, pulled from the wreckage of a life that was now gone.

Her eyes moved back and forth between the two men and the ground.

Quid was a statue of pain for what felt like hours, maybe years. She spent an eternity waiting for permission or instructions on what to do next.

The EMT had a clipboard in his hand, "Female. Driver of the vehicle." He said it aloud to himself as he wrote.

His words struck her from her stupor, and she looked again at the sheet on the ground. The clean, crisp white of the sheet stood out against the black pavement and the glittering glass. *Mom.*

Quid's throat constricted. Her heart pounded painfully across her chest and somewhere in her mind, she thought it might explode. *Maybe that would be better.* The thought came across before she could stop it.

Maybe her heart would stop beating, right now, in the middle of this road. Maybe she wouldn't have to live in a world where her mom wasn't alive. Quid waited for it to come. Her breathing staggered. She wanted to drop to the ground. She sank into the pain like a stone dropped into a pond.

A strangled cry came from somewhere deep in her body. It struggled from her chest and once it wrenched itself free her anguished cries poured out from her soul.

Instinct took over. She was running again. Beneath her, the ground disappeared, and her vision blurred. Her feet carried her into the wooded area along the side of the road. She ran for the trees. Like her body believed it could somehow outrun the pain.

She stumbled through the sharp branches of honeysuckle bushes, falling on to the warm earth again and again. Behind her, she heard the voice of the medic and firefighters yelling at her to stop.

Time crept by slowly. Her breath came in sharp gasps and her lungs screamed for oxygen as she continued. She ran and ran through the trees, every step felt like trudging uphill through deep mud. Somewhere in the back of her mind, she heard it. It was like when someone whispers your voice from another room, barely enough to hear it. Someone told her, *stop.* If she hadn't left Fen at the house, she would have sworn it was him.

Something inside her took her, guided her, through the patch of woods, to an enormous oak tree.

Like a desperate child, she clung to its hard trunk, slamming her body against it, scraping her arms, and digging her nails deep in its bark. The image of the white sheet flew across her mind again and her stomach retched.

She heaved the contents of her stomach onto the forest floor a and let out the only noise that she had left. It was a strangled, tearful, sob that broke through the terrible silence of the forest.

The woods had no comfort for her this time. She had never been here, but nothing reached out for her. No plants or animals pressed on her mind with their familiar itch. There was nothing. She was disconnected from the natural world.

The blonde medic pulled up alongside her moments later. He heaved for breath as he bent over. His hands gripped his knees as his eyes searched hers. His long, blue stethoscope now hung haphazardly about his neck. The clipboard and medical supplies were long forgotten, tossed aside during his chase. Leaves and twigs clung to his neat, blue shirt.

Around them, there was no wind. Nothing stirred at the tumult of emotions coming from inside her. No rain came pouring. Someone guided her back slowly through the forest. The emptiness sat in her stomach. She stared at the dirt and leaves on the ground as she walked. Every step she took she hoped that the ground underneath her would somehow open and swallow her whole. She wasn't sure how long it took, but they finally reached the ambulance.

Before she knew what had happened, she was being loaded into the back of the ambulance and strapped to the gurney for transport.

A small wisp of air tousled her hair as she rested her head back on the gurney. As the doors slammed shut the wind touched her cheeks and she couldn't help but feel like it was consoling her, apologizing for the disaster it had reaped.

As the ambulance slid into motion Quid waited again for something disastrous to happen. Surely, the feeling eating away at her merited some sort of reaction. She willed earthquakes, rain, or anything to take her away from the pain.

Nature was still for her. There was no anger, sadness, or even grief. She was empty.

Chapter Fifteen

The fluorescent hospital lights shined harshly in her eyes as the world came together. The cold of the room settled over her as she opened her eyes. The chill throughout the small room was like another presence. It hung in the air mingling with the sour smell of antiseptic. It invaded the space around her, creeping under the thin, eggshell-colored hospital blanket and through the hospital gown, layering her with the thick smell of sickness and death.

Next to her, Merle rested in a brown recliner. The wooden armchair was pressed tight against the bed. One thin arm propped up his sleeping head, another lay outstretched, gripping Quid's hand tightly in his sleep. As she stirred on the bed, Merle sat up in the chair and Quid thought to herself that she would never forget the look in his gray eyes. His head hung low, even as he tried to smile at her. His eyes stared at her with an intensity she had never seen before.

There were wrinkles she had never noticed. His eyebrows furrowed like he had been waiting to ask her all the questions about what had happened. They stared at each other. Their shared grief hung in the air between them. The answers to his questions wouldn't change the outcome of the day.

Merle smiled weakly and squeezed her hand tighter.

"Well, I don't know where the hell Fen is." The old man shrugged his broad shoulders. He rose slowly from the armchair. An awkward pause hung in the air between them.

Merle was the first to break the silence as tears welled behind his eyes. He choked the words out as he grabbed Quid in a hug that squeezed the breath from her. "I'm really glad you're okay."

"I'm really glad you're here." Was all Quid could think to say as warm tears spilled down her cheeks. She buried her face into Merle's shirt, breathing in the sawdust and earthen smell that always lingered around him.

The two of them clung to each other like that for what seemed like hours. Quid sobbed into her father's shoulder until she had nothing left.

Merle finally shuffled awkwardly. His face was red and puffy as he looked down at Quid. He rubbed her cheek with the pad of his thumb, pressing his forehead into hers before turning towards the door. "I'll get the doctor. Maybe we can go home."

Merle left, moving slower than Quid had ever seen him move. His face had aged ten years since she last saw him.

I am here. Replied a voice in her head as soon as Merle left the room. *Outside the window.*

Quid turned to her left to see that Merle must have opened the blinds, though it was now dark outside. The hospital's large parking lot was below. The towering lights illuminated the reflective surfaces of the cars below.

The bough of a thick oak grew outside the window. Its branches stretched across the windows of several rooms. From the tree, she could see two large eyes reflecting off the light of her room. They were a beacon in the darkness, letting her know Fen was close by.

I will break this window down if you need me to. They took you once to do... Fen paused, *pictures of your bones?* She could hear the confusion in his voice. *I was forced to make myself a small rodent and hide. I did not enjoy it, but I am not allowed to harm humans without cause.*

She could hear the irritation in his voice. She knew it must strain him to remain outside. He had been out there this whole time, waiting. He had wanted to give her and Merle space.

Quid. I—am so sorry. I should have been there. Quid heard the emotions behind his voice and thought back to all the times she had caught Vernie sneaking Fen bacon. There were so many mornings she would find them sitting together. He had lost someone too.

It's not your fault. Quid watched the large bird hang its head low on the branch.

I will take you away from this place if you wish. Fen's voice promised her as she rolled to her side. She didn't know why Fen had chosen to be her unshakeable companion but felt comforted by his words. She knew that he meant it. Part of her wondered how big of a bird he would have to become to break the hospital's double-plated window.

A small smile escaped her. *I wish you could come in here too.*

A few minutes later Merle returned, followed by a doctor in a pristine white lab. The doctor took her blood pressure, checked the beeping monitors above her, and shined another annoying light in her eyes. Finally, he told her that if she 'promised to take it easy' she could go home in the morning.

Quid wasn't sure if she should feel relieved or not. She stared at the ceiling tiles for a long time, as the doctor's words played in her head. It didn't matter if she got to go home because she wouldn't go home with Vernie.

Merle seemed to be processing the doctor's words as well. Hours crept by and neither one of them turned on the television. No one spoke for the remainder of the night. There were no words of comfort. The time for questions and stories would come soon enough. For now, there was only the endless silence of grief.

Merle lay in the hospital lounger by her bed as he slowly fell asleep. Quid watched for several hours as he tossed and turned. At one point his long arm reached out in the empty air. She knew he was reaching for a hand that would never grip his again.

More tears spilled from Quid as she turned away from her father. She waited for the numbness to wear off. She waited for reality to come crashing down. From the foot of her bed, there was a scuffle under the sheets.

I am coming.

Quid lifted the covers to find a small, brown field mouse. Surprise filled her. Part of her thought Fen was joking about following her into the x-ray. Quid lay her palm flat against the sheet, as tiny paws scurried onto her outstretched hand. The warm body of the mouse comforted her as tears came once again.

I will not leave you again. Fen's mind whispered to her as she pulled the tiny body to her chest.

The night crept by as nurses and doctors arrived periodically. It never failed that each time Quid came close to falling asleep someone would come to check her monitors. Each time, Fen would scurry off to hide and each time the nurse pulled on the painful IV in her arm.

Quid's exhaustion grew and her patience withered. Her anger reached a new peak. The nurse woke Quid again and again. Each time she would smile down at Quid, but her eyes were full of pity.

It was around midnight when Quid started to fall asleep again, just as the nurse came in for the third time. Every time the nurse returned to check the bags that hung on the pole next to the bed, she would try to assure Quid that everything was fine.

After checking Quid's vitals, the nurse started to leave the room and Quid had to resist the urge to hurl a pillow at the back of the woman's head. As the nurse opened the door to leave, she reminded Quid again how much she needed to rest. She assured Quid in her sweetest voice that someone would be back soon to 'check her condition.'

How stupid is that? The bitter thought filled Quid's mind. *My condition is terrible.*

The night passed by and Quid squeezed her eyes shut, trying to tune out the beeping of the monitors and murmurs of hospital personnel.

Fen crawled silently back into her palm. She stroked the silky, brown fur of Fen's mouse body. He silently offered her the only comfort he could. When she finally fell asleep, all she dreamt of was laying in the forest on the cold, hard ground. In her dream, a white sheet drifted down from the sky and wrapped around her, pinning her to the dirt. All around her, the rain poured.

It had been three weeks since the accident. Quid had once again been in bed all day. Her sleep was fretful and sparse. Most days she just watched as the sun fill the room and then watched as the light slowly left the room. Even when the room was stifling hot, she could not bring herself to care enough to move.

Neither of them left the house. The shop and the greenhouses were closed. The only change from day to day was when neighbors brought food to the door. News of the crash spread through Kutz like wildfire. Quid would listen as Merle politely thanked each person. Their voices filled the house for a while. Then, the crushing silence would fall over the house again.

Once a day, Merle would come to her room to check that she was breathing, but ever since the funeral, the two of them hardly spoke. There was a sense of loss between them that couldn't be described. She didn't know how to help him, and he didn't know how to help her.

Quid curled into herself on the bed. All she could think about was how unfair it was and how unprepared they had been. All the movies and the stories people tell about tragedies are always about weeks or even years later. They're all about getting over or getting through it.

No stories prepared Quid for the excruciatingly long, silent ride home because the hospital was in the middle of nowhere. No one had ever talked about what happens in the hours afterward. No one prepares you for what to do when you wake up and you don't have a mom.

Quid thought again to the morning she had left the hospital. It had been two days since the accident when a young female volunteer in pink scrubs finally wheeled Quid out the double doors. The doctor had told them that morning she could go home. She would never forget the rage that burned through her as the doctor clapped Merle on the back to tell him, "how lucky they were that Quid hadn't sustained more serious injuries."

The sun was warm on her skin as she waited for Merle to get their truck. Fen arrived first, having taken the time to leave and come back in his preferred form, an enormous brown wolf. Quid heard the volunteer gasp as Fen rounded the corner. He said nothing except, *I will go in right now and tear apart that doctor if you wish.*

Quid shook her head in response, as Fen rested his enormous head on her lap.

Merle had pulled to the curb in his faded blue truck. The yellow sunflower logo a bright contrast to her dark mood. Out of habit, Quid moved into the back seat as Fen clambered onto the truck bed. The seatbelt clicked in place and it wasn't until then she realized her mistake. Merle hesitated in the doorframe as his eye brimmed with tears. The realization settled over them that Quid could sit in the front now because Vernie would no longer be there.

Neither of them had said anything as the hospital disappeared from the rearview mirror. Quid spent the entirety of the drive trying to control herself so she wouldn't flood the road and lose both parents. Still, the rain came.

The entire drive home she held it together. Hours passed and no one spoke. Quid said nothing, just tried to control her feelings long enough to make it home. Neither of them spoke what was on their minds—that they weren't prepared to leave Vernie in the cold hospital morgue.

Merle pulled the truck in front of the house and Quid's breath caught in her throat. She looked at their home through the grim light of the day and couldn't hold back the pain. The sobs came out in waves, clutching at her gut. Around them the rain poured in sheets, flooding the yard. Merle held her tight against his shoulder and from the back of the truck Fen let out a long, high-pitched howl of grief.

While they were gone, Merle had fixed the porch.

It isn't fair, Quid thought for the hundredth time that morning. She was out of tears, but her whole body ached. Every day the pain continued and every day it got worse. It was constant and permanent like someone had carved a piece of ribcage out.

Quid hadn't done more than relieve herself and get snacks in a very long time, as evidenced by the small mountain of trash that surrounded the bed. Like clockwork though, she had to go outside and soak in the sun or sit in the greenhouses to avoid the fever. She dragged herself outside and back, only allowing herself the bare minimum, and only because Fen threatened to drag her out by his teeth if she didn't.

The day waxed on and Quid was still in bed. She floated in and out of sleep, haunted by dreams of thunderstorms that were out of her control and rain that never ended.

The room was dark when she woke up to the sound of Merle yelling. She turned over in her bed, sure she was losing her mind because Merle never, ever yelled. Even when the mailman refused to bring the mail anymore because he had found the bobcat that Quid was caring for eating his lunch. Years before that the county tried to force Merle to pay for an "exotic animal" license for Fen. Merle refused because he never claimed to own the wolf. When the man from the county came Merle didn't yell, even when the man got beet red and screamed at Merle that the wolf would be confiscated without a permit. Merle simply told him to give it his best shot at catching the enormous wolfhound.

Fen still laughed about it all. He had enjoyed chasing the man away. Still, in all of that, Merle had never yelled. Quid suspected that Merle also enjoyed seeing the man being chased away.

Quid threw back the heavy quilt, sitting up for the first time in hours. Her feet met the cold wooden floors. Fen rose as well. His ears perked forwards, listening intently. She silently left the room, and he was at her heels.

What is he yelling about? She heard him ask in her mind. His voice in her head feigned disinterest but she looked back to see his lowered head. His, long, brown tail was pointed down towards the floor and his hackles were up. She knew that he sensed something.

The two of them crept through the kitchen, carefully avoiding the ancient wooden, kitchen chairs that whined in protest whenever you touched them. Finally, they entered the 'gift shop' towards the front of the house—which was really their renovated living room, filled with carefully placed merchandise.

Quid stopped and looked around the lime-green walls. Shelves painted an even darker shade of green lined the room. When she was little Quid often told Vernie that it was like being on the inside of a tree and looking out at the branches.

Each shelf overflowed with decorations. Clocks, baubles, animal statues of all shapes and sizes, and signs that read things like "Home Sweet Home" or "Home Is Where the Garden Is…" filled every surface. Art from local artists covered every wall. The floor was littered with Merle's various woodcraft creations.

Tall rocking chairs, benches for small children to sit on, and even a few of those creepy hide-and-seek dolls leaned against the walls. The room was filled with things Vernie knew people would buy.

Quid stopped and looked around the room as she realized that she hadn't been in here since they got back, avoiding the place in the house that most reminded her of exactly what she had lost. Part of her wondered who would fill the tree's branches with treasures now?

They walked slowly, avoiding the places where the old, wooden floors creaked the most. Fen's large, brown paws touched the floor but made no sound.

As they got closer to the front of the house, the voices got louder.

Wait. She urged Fen, who had been headed towards the front door. The large wolf stopped and cocked its enormous head towards her. His eyes questioned her.

She didn't have an answer for him. All she knew is that she wanted to know what was going on, but something told her that Merle might not want her to.

Quid stopped near one of the front windows, trying to hear what Merle had to say and trying not to be seen. She peeked from behind one of the thick, red curtains to the two men on the front porch.

Merle was standing on the front porch. The yellow glow of the porch light cast a shadow over his face. She could see that he was as disheveled as her. His gray hair stood out at all ends. He was still in the thin, worn, red flannel nightshirt that he had on this morning. He stood at his full height though and his fists were clenched at his sides. She watched his body tremble with fury.

Quid heard nothing but the sound of the crickets in the distance and her own soft breathing as she waited for Merle to continue.

Merle pointed a finger towards the other figure. "You have no idea what we are going through. And now you want me to just let you take her?"

Quid struggled to see the other person now, as she pressed closer to the cool glass. The dark shadow ducked under a porch beam and Quid immediately recognized him.

Taller than Merle, with broad shoulders that filled the air around him, Quid could barely see the bright yellow tree imprinted on the shoulder of his t-shirt. The same tree Liam had printed on his shirt weeks before. His beard was grizzled—like it hadn't been combed or cleaned. He stepped towards Merle again and his dark eyes were full of desperation. The whites around them stood out against the yellow porchlight, giving him a crazed appearance. Iktomi was on her front porch.

Merle put down his finger and stepped back towards the porch swing. Iktomi walked towards him. For a moment, Quid thought he may have seen her, as she jerked back away from the window. Her heart raced as she waited. Finally, she inched back the thick curtain again.

"You have no idea what we are up against." He slowly spat the words. His eyes raised to the window as he paced in front of Merle. A chill went up Quid's spine as she listened. She had a distinct feeling Iktomi knew she was listening. "We all must make sacrifices to beat this."

Quid waited for Merle to speak again as she remembered Iktomi's words that night at camp. *Was he talking about the contamination?*

Merle's voice was low and full of defeat as he spoke, "I know it's bad. It keeps getting worse around here as well." Merle cleared his throat as his shoulders sagged even lower. He placed his head into his hands. "But this isn't our war. We never wanted to be a part of this. We left that part of Vernie's life behind...."

A soft sob escaped Merle as he looked up at Iktomi, "We wanted to find a way to help Quid. They never...she never would have even been there if..."

A small gasp escaped Quid. She traded a glance at Fen, whose ears were flat against his head. He let out a short, high-pitched whine but said nothing to her through their shared connection.

Hot tears welled in her eyes. She didn't need to hear him finish. She knew what he was about to say.

That's why they had really gone to the camp. They had gone to meet the Believers to help Quid.

Her body went numb and her heart pounded against her chest.

Her stomach tied itself in knots, as Quid doubled over, trying to catch her breath. *They never would have been there. Vernie never would have gone.* They wouldn't have even been there if it weren't for her and her inability to control her powers. It was Quid's fault she was dead.

Quid stumbled back, crashing into a small table.

Silence fell outside. She knew that Merle knew now that she had been listening, but she was already gone. Tears flowed down her face and her gut wrenched. The crushing reality of her father's words settled over her.

"Quid! Quid wait!" Merle yelled from the porch, throwing the screen door open wide, but she was already tearing through the house to her room, slamming doors behind her.

Quid slammed the hard wooden door of her bedroom behind her, jamming the lock in place. Fen was in the hall with Merle but remained silent.

"Quid…" Merle, whispered through the wood, knocking softly. "I didn't mean it. I'm sorry…"

She couldn't bring herself to respond. His words ricocheted inside her head and confirmed everything she had been thinking for the last three weeks. Even though she hadn't known, they had gone to the meet-up for her. All the people in the wreck, Vernie fighting with Ayasha, it was all over what to do about her. Vernie wouldn't even have gone if it weren't for her daughter, the freak. She wouldn't have died if Quid had been able to stop the storm.

The weight of it was too much and she couldn't hold herself up any longer. Her knees buckled. She crumbled to the ground, leaning her head against the icy wood of the door. Outside the house, the wind ripped, and the rain poured against the roof. She struggled to breathe.

Let me die right here. Let me take her place. Quid sent her bargains to the universe. From the other side of the door, she heard Fen whine in protest.

She continued to sob as she waited for the universe to answer. She begged someone, anyone, to hear her prayers. The rain demanded her attention, crashing against the windows, as the weight of her mother's death threatened to crush her from the inside.

Hours later, Quid's mind faintly registered the sound of Merle's retreating footsteps. She knew he would fall asleep in the same place he had every night since they came home without Vernie. His snores emanated through the house from the center of the gift shop. He waited in a cushioned rocking chair for a wife to wake him and remind him to come to bed. But she would never come.

Merle didn't stir as Quid placed the note on the small table. No other words would be shared between the two of them.

You don't have to do this. Fen implored her again, but she knew he was wrong. Quid crept into the kitchen and opened the cabinet above the stove. She quietly took all the 'rainy day' money from the pickle jar.

As Merle slept, she closed the kitchen door and took her worn, yellow suitcase, packed with all the clothes she could fit in it, out to Merle's blue truck. She tossed the suitcase into the back seat as she looked over at Fen.

His black eyes looked at her expectantly as she sent the thought to him, *you should stay here with Dad.*

Quid stared down the large wolf. Fen let out an angry snort in response. He hopped into the truck and sat in the passenger seat. *I don't need you to get hurt too,* Quid explained to him again.

I should have been with you before and I will be with you from now on, was Fen's only reply. She knew he felt guilty for letting her and Vernie go without him, but it wasn't his fault. She had done this to them all.

Quid closed the heavy door of the truck and turned over the engine. She couldn't stay here and ruin any more lives. She may not have created the storm that caused the crash, but she didn't stop it either. The guilt of knowing Vernie wouldn't have even been on that road if it weren't for Quid was too much for her to bear.

Behind her, the house faded from view. The familiar connection to the greenhouses faded and she wondered how soon it would be until the poison took that from Merle too.

Chapter Sixteen

Quid's lungs began to fill with a horrible, acrid smoke. Her eyes were open, but she could see nothing. There was only darkness. Her breath came in short, fast bursts. Panic began to take over her.

Her hands searched around, but there was nothing but the cold, flat walls. The smell of the smoke got stronger and filled her lungs as she pulled the thin fabric of her shirt to her nose. She looked at the dark expanse above her. Embers began to flicker and fall. They were tiny sparks at first but grew larger as they fed. Something was burning above her. The flames began to reach for her.

Something white-hot and molten dripped down the walls, filling the small space with bursts of light. The liquid settled on the floor around her, pooling at her feet. The thick smoke choked her and burned her lungs. The heat in the room rose. It burned her toes first, as the pool of molten debris grew. It scorched her ankles, then crawled up her calves. Her flesh burned away to nothing. The pain was unbearable as she fell to her hands and knees.

Quid woke with a start, heart pounding. A flush came across her cheeks as sweat dripped down her face. Her whole body was drenched. Startled by the realness of the dream, she sat on the soft cot. Desperate to shake off the fear still creeping across her spine, Quid rubbed the sleep from her eyes and breathed in the frigid air of the greenhouse.

All around her were potted plants left by the previous owner. Even though the flowers and shrubs flourished with her presence, she knew their presence alone wouldn't be enough for her to "recharge" like she needed to. Long gone were the days when a short walk under the stars was enough to keep her going.

Even though being surrounded by so many tall structures and cars left her feeling cut off and worn down, she loved being in downtown Philadelphia. She loved passing people on the street and wondering if they were hiding as many secrets as she was. Was the tall man on the street carrying a briefcase coming from an important business merger? Was the young boy running along the sidewalk late for his bus? Maybe he was skipping school for the first time, hoping to not get caught. The culture and life of the city were infectious, and she was happy to be sick with it.

Quid thought about all of this as she quietly got dressed. Her dark gray sweater sat atop her pile of clothes in the corner of the room. She anxiously pulled it over her head, eager to get out the door. The icy chill of the fabric wrapped around her legs as she threw on the pair of faded jeans. She felt out around her, trying to judge how long it would be until the sun would warm her face, hopefully, it would rejuvenate some of her energy.

The tiny bathroom at the back of the greenhouse flickered to life, barely pushing out the shadows. It was nothing more than a sink and toilet, but she was thankful. After all, she didn't pay rent here. She was lucky the water worked at all.

To improve the place, she had placed a few succulents on a small, upturned wastebasket. The lightbulb shined brightly against the dark, sending spots across her vision as she waited for her eyes to adjusted. She splashed the icy water on her face, still trying to shake off the nightmare. She would need a shower later. She silently thanked the heavens she had met Ms. Rose downstairs, who was sweet enough to let her shower whenever she needed it.

She grabbed up her bamboo toothbrush from the corner of the sink. A familiar twinge of pain greeted her as she remembered how excited Vernie had been when the toothbrushes came into the shop. Quid pulled on the new-to-her pair of white Converses she had purchased at a local thrift shop. The pickle jar money had helped her survive at first. When it ran out, she made money by using her influence to grow and sell fruits and vegetables to the people in the building. Lately, Ms. Rose had been bringing her to the Clark Park market and she had been making a killing selling her out-of-season produce.

Quid tied her shoes as she prepared to leave. For much of her life, she had preferred to go without shoes. Her feet being in the grass or covered in dirt had always felt natural to her, but that wasn't an option in the city.

Be in control. She reminded herself as memories of walking around the woods left her feeling homesick.

Quid looked at Fen, who was finally asleep on the rug next to the door. He hadn't slept much since they arrived in Philly. It had been almost two months since they pulled into the city, the old truck sucking fumes the last few miles. They both felt like fugitives, but he seemed permanently on edge. Every day, he urged her to return home.

Fen was curled in a tight ball, half-buried under the pile of clothes. She listened to his soft snorts. She couldn't deny it. She was grateful for his company. It hadn't been easy for either of them to lose Vernie and then lose their home. She owed it to him to let him rest.

Her internal clock told her it was still early in the morning, probably before five. The nightmare lingered at the back of her mind and she swore she could still feel the heat of the flames. There was no way she could go back to sleep. This would be the perfect time to visit the river.

Quid grabbed her bike from beneath the stairs of the abandoned high rise. The morning air was unseasonably warm. In the back of her mind, she considered that this late in October it should be freezing outside for most people. Although she had learned from a young age her body temperature didn't regulate the same way most people did, she could feel something was off. In the wintertime, she usually would only need a light jacket or nothing at all, whereas normal people would freeze without an extra thick coat.

Worry filled Quid's mind at the strange weather. She had even bought a coat last week, hoping to blend in once everyone else started to wear theirs. This morning though, the wind was calm and there was almost no nip to the air at all.

She unlocked her bike from the stand next to the building and took off. The cool metal greeted her arms and legs as she sat down. This early in the morning the city was quiet. Everything and everyone around her still slumbered. Normally this block of the street was filled with noisy street vendors, tourists, and shop merchants. But right now, the only sound disrupting the silence was her breath. For the first time since she had arrived, she was alone in the metropolis.

The streetlights illuminated the sidewalk in little patches of light as she pedaled along. The wind greeted her, flowing through her hair, and wrapping its long fingers around her waist as she went. It invited her to let go, to loosen her control.

For a moment, she smiled and relaxed, enjoying the peace of being able to relax for once.

Electricity had always been a problem for her. She could never allow herself to feel out of control. In the heart of the city, she was constantly surrounded by so many devices and couldn't imagine what might happen if she scrambled a traffic light or crosswalk.

Immersing herself in all the technology, instead of hiding from it, had given her a sense of control she never had before.

Shortly after arriving, Quid stashed the old truck. She felt guilty for taking Merle's only remaining vehicle, but with the logo on the side she couldn't exactly drive it around. Ms. Rose was gracious enough to give Quid her apartment's assigned parking space—since Ms. Rose didn't own a car. Quid had decided never to drive it though, she never knew who could be looking for her and technically it was stolen. Since Quid couldn't use computers, she definitely couldn't drive any of the small, zippy cars that were perfect for the city life—even if she had been able to afford one, which she couldn't. She had been getting around using her bike or busses. It seemed the larger the engine the less susceptible it was to her influence.

One of the biggest challenges of living in a small town was that specific types of bulbs behaved erratically when she was near. This was especially true for streetlights. Since they depended on the sun to tell them when to turn on and off, her natural energy often overpowered them. If she wasn't careful and in control, she could blow a whole block.

At home in Kutz, where things moved a bit slower, people often noticed the odd things that happened around her. But in the city, everyone was so busy that no one seemed to care.

Quid was just another person on the street. At home, she always had to be calm and collected. In Kutz, Quid couldn't allow herself to lose it. The consequences of her emotions getting the better of her could be disastrous. She could never let herself forget or lose control. When she was sad it sprinkled, but when she was depressed it poured. When she was five, she had woken up to find out her favorite kitten had run away, and she flooded the ground by the barn.

Quid couldn't allow her emotions to control her, because she could control everything with them, but living in the city was a chance to practice her control. Every day was an opportunity to train what she could do. After a few minutes of riding, Quid arrived at the top of the hill that led down to the river walk.

She looked around her, nervous for anyone to see. She loved this hill. She loved the feeling of the wind pulling around her as she raced towards the river as fast as she could. The morning was still dark as she rode. The only lights around were the small solar lamps along the path.

Quid peered towards the bottom of the hill to see if anyone was down there, but the lights ended before the sharp curve that would take her to the dock by the river. In the daytime, the dock was used for paddle boats and canoes but right now it would be empty. That made it a great place for her to put her feet in the river and let the flow of the water wash away her weariness.

Confident that no one would be out this early in the morning, Quid pushed her pedals forward, towards the hill's crest.

The wind greeted her like an old friend. Her excitement caused it to stir into a bluster. *Be calm*, she silently urged it.

Quid pedaled the first few feet of the hill, but ultimately let them go and lifted her feet out of the way. She zoomed down the hill, listening as the wind whipped past her ears. Popping noises filled the air behind her as each lamp went out like lights on a race-track. Her energy was too much for them.

The hand brakes on her bike let out a high-pitched squeal as she pulled at them. The wind continued to urge the bike on—a small child too excited to know when enough was enough. She had about twenty yards left until she could try to curve right towards the dock or dead-end into the river.

The shrill screams of her breaks continued to disrupt the silence of the morning as she hurtled down the hill. She smelled the faint burning of the rubber as she tried to pull to a stop. She was nearing the end of the hill and the edge of the river. Her heart pounded in her chest as she tried to gain control. All of a sudden, she watched a dark shadow run towards the center. It stopped right where she was headed.

"Watch out!" she screamed through the darkness.

The shadow did not move. She prepared for impact, squeezing tighter and dragging her shoes along the ground. Panic set in but she sent her panicked thoughts through the morning air, into the wind. *Stop! Now!*

A whoosh of wind from the opposite direction slammed into her, seconds before she made impact.

Two arms grabbed her handlebars. She came to an abrupt stop, but she went forward, over the bike. She toppled to the soft cushion of the person before her. They met the ground in a tangle of limbs.

Pain shot up her back and the world spun around her. Quid let out a low moan as she the impact hit her all over. Quid felt gingerly at her head, checking for damage. She seemed to be stiff, but generally uninjured. She rubbed her neck as she sat up, trying to rid herself of the stiffness down her spine. She rolled her ankle around as she sat up. Miraculously, she hadn't sprained it again. It had just returned to normal from the car wreck.

A cough came from next to her, and she realized she still had her legs tangled with the person she had crashed into.

"I'm so, so sorry!"

Quid went to move her legs, as the person lifted themselves onto all fours. She watched through the darkness. From the faint light of the streetlamps a few yards away, she could see the frame and broad shoulders of a man.

His dark jeans were now covered in dirt from their tumble. His green, flannel shirt hung off him as she stared at the back of his head. The sleeve had ripped and all of it was covered in thick dust from the concrete.

"Are you—are you okay?" she asked frantically. The wind continued to whip their hair and clothes playfully, always unaware of the chaos it caused.

"Just bruised. Are you?" replied the man, slowly turning around to face her.

Before she even saw his face, Quid recognized that voice. His dark brown hair was even longer now. It had been months since she had seen him. Months since the summer day in the stream. Immediately, Quid felt a sting of pain. It had been months since Vernie died.

"Liam?" she asked across the darkness.

"Quid?" his voice was filled with surprise as they both stood up, dusting themselves off but eyes never leaving each other. "What are you doing here?"

"Oh, you know…" Quid tried to sound nonchalant. "Just mowing down pedestrians with my bike."

"Ha! Am I not your first victim then?" Through the growing morning light, Quid could see his eyes were full of laughter.

"No way. I'm trying to make a name for myself. The Hillside Flattener." Quid laughed aloud. The sound of her voice broke through the morning silence as she surprised herself. She couldn't remember the last time she had laughed or even made a joke.

"What are you doing here?" Liam walked towards her bike,

helping her to pull it from the bushes it had rolled into.

Quid searched frantically for an answer but opted for a version of the truth. "I live in the city and I couldn't sleep. I come down here sometimes to think."

Liam's brows furrowed tightly as he considered her answer.

"It seems dangerous to be riding around in the city by yourself, in the dark."

"I can take care of myself." Quid spat at him, a little more aggressively than she intended. He had once had the opportunity to defend her when she needed it. Instead, he had stayed silent. *Why should he protect her now?*

"What are *you* doing here?" she replied, looking around them. She knew why she was here, but why would Liam be skulking around the river this early?

"I'm in town working for my grandfather." Liam shrugged his shoulders as if that explained everything.

His lax reaction piqued Quid's interest.

"How is Iktomi?" Quid tried hard to keep the venom from her voice, remembering the way Liam's grandfather had questioned her after they returned from Kid Camp. She thought back to the crazed look in Iktomi's eyes. She couldn't prove it, but she was sure he knew she was listening to his conversation with Merle. He had been desperate for her to go with him. Maybe even desperate enough to take her by force.

Liam let out a long sigh. "He is grieving."

Quid watched as Liam's shoulders sagged as if he too were bearing some heavy burden. When he spoke it was soft, a gentle whisper in the night. He choked on the words like they were hard to speak aloud. "We lost Grandmother Dana a few weeks ago. She got hurt in the crash and just never really recovered."

Quid couldn't breathe. Images of the crash flew through her mind. Her mother laughing. Rain droplets falling on the windshield. The feel of the storm. It's unnatural response to her. Then, the sound of sirens filled her ears. The smell of gasoline stung her nose, making it hard to breathe. She grabbed her chest as her heart pounded wildly. An image of a white sheet against dark pavement filled her vision as the medic's voice filled her head ahead, "Driver. DOA."

The sensation overwhelmed her. The wind whipped her hair. Droplets of rain began to fall from the night sky.

Then, like someone had pulled the panic plug, she came back to herself.

The muscles of Liam's arms were wrapped around her, holding her tight. Their strength held her in place, calming and comforting her. Quid leaned her forehead against his chest, absorbing his warmth. Slowly, she focused her breathing, as she forced herself to take long, deep breaths.

"Where did you go?" Liam whispered into her hair. His voice was thick with concern and she realized she was holding him too. Her fingers wound tight around the cloth of his shirt. The wind died down and the rain stopped. Quid's heart finally slowed its desperate attempt to escape her chest.

"My....my mom...." Quid's eyes burned with tears as she tried to choke out the words. Liam squeezed her tighter. One of his hands rubbed her back.

"I didn't know that she was one of the ones..." his voice trailed off again.

The two of them stood there, arms around each other, for what felt like hours. It was the first time Quid had tried to say it aloud. Her mother was dead.

Finally, Quid leaned back to look up at Liam. The air around them showed no signs she had temporarily lost control. *Why does he calm me so much?*

Liam looked down at her. His eyes were full of questions and to her surprise, tears.

"Thank you." Quid whispered to the air between him. It was hard to meet his intense stare. She waited for him to speak, but he just looked at her, examining her face. There were no other words to say.

Quid found herself studying the buttons of his shirt, uncertainty had settled over her. Liam still had one hand resting at the small of her back, but the other he brought up between them. Quid felt his thumb against her cheekbone first. The calluses on his hand rubbed gently across her face before he lifted her chin.

Her stomach fluttered as she looked up at Liam. She had just managed to calm her breathing, but now she felt it stop completely. His face was inches from hers. Their warm breath mingled in the cool morning air.

Quid thought back to the day at the creek. They had been alone before. They had even kissed. Somehow, this was different.

More intimate. The beating of her heart was almost painful in her chest as she waited for him to cross the few inches between them.

Instead, Liam dropped his hand from her face. Quid watched as something seemed to pass behind his eyes. Almost like a thought or decision he had made without her knowledge.

Quid broke from him, trying to regain control of herself again. She leaned down once more to grab her discarded bike from the sidewalk.

"Let's—go sit by the river." Quid urged her bike towards the awaiting dock as Liam silently followed.

The sun was rising as they approached the river. Pink and yellow lines filled the sky and pushed away the dark around them. Quid deposited her bike at the end of the dock before walking towards the water. The wooden planks protested underneath their feet. Once again, Liam looked at her nervously as he slipped on the thick moss growing across several of the boards. Like they had in the creek, Quid grabbed his hand and guided him along.

At first, they sat on the end in silence, watching the morning sun reflect on the water, but when Quid took off her shoes and placed her toes in the water Liam looked genuinely shocked.

"The water is freezing!" he watched in awe as she sank her toes and most of her calf into the water without flinching. "You're crazy!"

His eyes were filled with disbelief and Quid couldn't help but smile. If he noticed that her hair regained some of its color, or that her skin regained its healthy appearance, he didn't say anything.

"Have you ever been to the ocean? We should go some time." Liam asked next to her. His eyes were full of hope.

"Oh no. It would be too over-powering…" she replied before she could stop herself. It was the truth.

Rivers, creeks, woods left her feeling replenished. They gave her body and her abilities strength when she was feeling drained. She had always dreamt of going to the ocean, but she was also afraid of what might happen. *What if it was too much for her to handle? What if it got out of control?*

"What? You're an awesome swimmer. You'll be fine." Liam replied, nudging her gently with his elbow. "I won't let you get swept away."

"Sometimes I think it would be okay to get swept away…"

Quid whispered across the early morning.

She looked at Liam for a long time, enjoying the way his whole face lit up. He leaned closer to her when she talked, like his whole body was listening, absorbing whatever it was she had to say.

She talked to Liam in a way she had never talked with anyone. She explained to him why the ocean was so important to her and why she was so afraid to go there. At least as much as she could without revealing her secrets.

When she was done, she closed her eyes, picturing the two of them splashing in the waves like a normal couple. Liam listened to her in a way no one else ever had. She rested her head against his shoulder, soaking up the magic of the morning.

They sat in silence, listening to the sounds of the river. Slowly, the first light of the day pushed away the chill of the night. She knew Liam was watching her, waiting with hundreds of more questions. For the first time in months, she felt truly relaxed as she kicked her feet in the icy water.

Chapter Seventeen

The city was waking up all around them. The sound of voices and engines slowly filled the air, forcing Quid to realize that her time alone with Liam was coming to an end. Like coming out of a great dream, she shook off her stupor.

Liam was the first to rise to his feet, reaching his hand out to Quid. As they reached the end of the dock Quid feared he would have to leave. He did say he was in town working for his grandfather. Disappointment washed over her as she realized he would have to go work at some point.

A sinking feeling came over her as she picked her bike up. She prepared herself for goodbye again. She grabbed the rubber of the handlebars as Liam exclaimed, "Well, obviously, we have to get breakfast."

A smile spread across her face. Liam took the bike's handlebars and began steering back up the hill. Her smile fell as she shifted uneasily. She would have to go back and get some money first.

As if sensing her hesitation, Liam glanced back at her, a sly smile spread across his lips. "I know the best diner. It's so cool. It's like stepping back in time and it's not too far. We can ride there!" His eyes were full of the happy mischief that she loved as he urged, "Please? My treat."

How can I say no to that? She thought to herself as she waited for Liam to rent a bike from one of the city's rental stations.

A half an hour later, the two of them arrived at a gaudy, 50s style diner near the river. Its blue neon sign flashed in her eyes as they rounded the corner. Drenched in metallic chrome, the front of the restaurant stood out against the rest of the buildings nearby. Every surface reflected the soft, orange morning light back at them.

Quid and Liam parked their bikes along the side of the old building. As they walked towards the front a pair of flashing blue signs in the window boasted "The Only 24-Hour Jive in Town!" and "World's Best Waffles!"

Bells dinged as the heavy red door closed behind them. The smell of fryer oil and bacon filled the air. A small sign stood at the front told customers to "Please Seat Themselves." Liam led her towards the back of the restaurant.

Quid slid into a high-backed booth covered in hotrod-red and black. Liam slid into the space across from her and Quid realized the glossy table was actually painted to look like an old a cassette. Along every inch of the walls were old vinyl records and black and white photographs of celebrities like Marilyn Monroe and Elvis.

This place is so tacky that it's come full circle back to cool again Quid thought to herself as she watched Liam grin wildly. "I am not putting those skates on this early in the morning, Harold." A shrill voice declared from the back of the restaurant. An older, red-haired waitress emerged from the kitchen.

The stern-looking older waitress approached the table, carrying a small brown tray under one arm. Her flaming red hair was streaked with gray and contrasted starkly against her bright pink poodle skirt as she took their order. Sure enough, she was wearing a comfortable-looking pair of white Reeboks. Although, Quid would have paid good money to see the older woman on skates.

After a few seconds of indecision, Quid decided to order a chocolate chip waffle at the waitress' behest. Apparently, they were "The best in the whole, damn, city…"

Their food came out quickly but the two of them sat in their large booth in the back of the diner for the better part of the morning. Liam was right, as soon as they walked in, she felt like she surely must be walking back in time. All around her was a sea of chrome and leather. The high-back booths sheltered them from the few other customers beginning to trickle in. As the morning waned on, they had privacy to talk, but they could also people-watch out the large front windows.

Quid was on her third cup of stale coffee, watching a group of birds peck at the trash outside, when Liam said something unexpected.

"I want you to know I'm sorry."

Quid thought for a second she should be polite, smile, and say, 'For what?' but they both knew what he had to be sorry for. That night in the woods still sat in her gut.

"Okay," was all she could think to say. Her first instinct was to shrug off his words, reply that it was fine but a voice in her head reminded her that it wasn't fine. Nothing about that night was fine.

"I should have defended you when everyone was freaking out about what happened with the creek and all the animals. I should have told Flint to keep his mouth shut."

Quid could see the anger in his eyes as he said Flint's name.

He stared at her from across the table. She felt herself forgive him a little. After all, surely, she had done worse. She was keeping quite the secret from him and everyone else.

"It's okay I guess." Quid shrugged her shoulders and gave him a weak smile.

"So, what did happen that day? How did you fix the stream? How did you heal the animals?"

Quid wanted to tell him she didn't know what he was talking about, but she knew he had seen more than probably anyone else of what she could do. She let the question hang silently in the air.

"I can't talk about it." She didn't want to lie to him anymore. She just wanted to sit and be normal a little while longer.

Liam grabbed Quid's palm gently. He played with her bracelet for a few moments. Quid noticed for the first time that he had one too. The dark, leather straps of his matched hers perfectly. They jingled softly against the hard table. A gold crescent moon shape rested on his wide, caramel-colored wrist.

Liam stared at their bracelets. A look of confusion spread across his face as he watched the two symbols fall together. She watched as he opened his mouth several times as if to say something but decided against it.

After a few minutes, he finally circled back to what he asked her at the river.

"So why are you *really* in the city?"

Quid choked as she sipped her coffee. For a moment, she considered lying, telling Liam she was visiting a friend or something. As she met his eyes over the cup though, she felt the overwhelming urge to tell him the truth.

"I ran away." She stated, shrugging her shoulders like it was no big deal. The weight of her words held her down though. It was the first time she had acknowledged it, even to herself.

He didn't say anything, waited patiently for her to continue. His eyes never left her face as he sipped his coffee. Quid told him the whole story. She struggled through telling him about the funeral. She told him how she and Merle barely said a word to one another for weeks. His eyes were hooded as she talked. He listened to her intently, offering her a napkin from the small, silver, holder when she began to cry.

Liam waited as she continued. She tried desperately to keep herself together as she spoke, choking back tears of anger, hurt, and guilt. *How many times am I going to cry in front of this guy today?* She scolded herself.

As she rambled, Liam said nothing. The only emotion he showed was a flash of surprise when she mentioned his grandfather's role in it all. Through it all, he waited until she was done.

Once again, Quid shrugged her shoulders as if that said everything. "So now I'm here in the city."
Liam spoke slowly as he reached for her hand across the small, linoleum table. "You have to know that it's not your fault. It was just an accident." This time it was Quid's turn to listen. She watched Liam's smile slowly drop as he spoke.

"Your dad…" Liam sighed, shaking his head as he spoke. "He shouldn't have said that. That's just not okay and I'm not defending him. But…" Liam spoke slowly, watching my reaction. Quid's anger rose as she thought back to it.

His face grew tense. His eyes were serious but sympathetic as his hand touched her elbow, the pad of his thumb began running smooth circles. She didn't pull away as he continued. "People don't know what to say in a crisis so sometimes they say crazy stuff they don't mean." Liam shrugged his shoulders like he was telling a joke, but there was no laughter behind his eyes.

"Grandmother Dana told me once that the day after the fire, a man pulled up to our house. They didn't know him, but he must have been a neighbor. I was still in the hospital, both my parents were dead, and my Grandparents were in charge of figuring out what, if anything, could be salvaged from the fire, along with suddenly caring for three kids…." Liam's eyes got dark again. He shifted back in his seat, shoulders shrinking against the soft leather of the booth. He twirled a spoon from his coffee cup in between his fingers.

"Anyway. They're pulling all this charred stuff out from the house. Things they think can be salvaged or things to take pictures of before they get thrown in the trash. Suddenly, this man pulls up in a big, white pick-up truck. He pulls to the end of the driveway and says to Grandma Dana, as she is holding the scorched remnants of her dead daughter's wedding gown in her arms, 'Gosh. All those fire trucks pulling up was the most excitement this neighborhood has seen in years…'"

A sharp breath escaped Quid's lips and a flush of anger warmed her face. *How could people be so stupid?*

"Then, he just drove off, like he had told some hilarious joke." Liam shook his head. "I can't understand why he even stopped in the first place."

Liam took another deep breath as he finally rested the spoon next to his cup of coffee. "He was the focus of my anger for a long time. When I was recovering from my burns in the hospital, I thought about him a lot. I thought about taking a bat to the windshield of his stupid truck. Of breaking his front door down. I briefly considered setting his house on fire, so he knew how it felt…"

Quid could see the guilt in his eyes as she spoke. His head hung low and it was her turn to squeeze his hand. She rubbed her thumb across his palm as he continued, "It took me a long time to realize sometimes people just don't know what to say. They say something they think is the right thing or they do something that is the wrong thing because they don't really understand what the other person is going through. That man didn't know that my parents had been trapped in their room. He didn't know that I had to leave my mother and father in the house in order to save Nia and Nua."

His words shocked her. She couldn't imagine having to leave either of her parents to perish. Liam paused, shifting in his seat. He took a deep breath before continuing, "I had to learn to forget about this man and his stupid words and eventually forgive him."

Quid nodded. She knew they would have to forgive each other eventually. There was a hole in her life where her dad used to be. She missed how easy their relationship had always been. She missed having a dad to talk to and lean on. But guilt still sat in her gut, eating away at her. It reminded her again of what it would be like when she faced him.

As if they both sensed it, sensed their perfect morning together coming to an end, Liam excused himself and went to pay the bill. Quid was gathering her things as she heard a familiar voice boom across the small diner.

"Well, if it isn't Miracle Girl." Quid's head jerked up, surprised to see Flint gallivanting across the diner towards her. Flint walked past Liam, smacking him roughly on the back—a gesture that from anyone else would have appeared friendly.

Liam's eyes flashed with anger and she watched as his whole body went rigid. He hurriedly passed the cash in his hand to the red-haired waitress. She eyed the two of them sourly but said nothing as Flint crossed the dining room. A look of curiosity crossed behind her eyes and Quid wondered if her slow movements were a direct result of wanting to know what was about to go down between the two young men.

"Who knew you'd be here." Flint sneered down at her as he took Liam's seat across the booth. Something about his tone told her he knew she would be.

"What do you want?" Quid snapped at him, in no mood to play games, though she wondered why he might suddenly be interested in her.

Flint wiggled his thick, black eyebrows at her as he leaned forward. His voice was low as he whispered across the table, "Looking for you of course. Lots of people are looking for you." His eyes flashed at her. His crooked smile, revealing his missing tooth once more. The way he looked at her sent a shiver up her spine. Everything about him screamed at her to stay away.

Liam rushed back to the table, ignoring Flint's presence completely. He turned his back to his 'cousin' and stuck his hand out for Quid to take.

It was Quid's turn to ignore the hand before her. She looked between the two of them, suddenly wondering if it was a coincidence bumping into Liam this morning. *How did Flint know we were here if they weren't together?*

She wanted to trust Liam, but a warning in her gut told her that he was lying.

"Grandfather sent me. We have work to do." Flint spoke to the back of Liam's head. Liam let out a sigh as his shoulders sagged. He lowered his hand and turned to meet Flint's intense glare.

"I'm sure he did. I'm going to ride with Quid back to her place and then I'll meet up with you." Again, Quid questioned what was happening. Fiery anger grew in her chest as she watched Liam choose his words carefully.

What is going on?

She wasn't stupid and didn't appreciate them treating her like she was. The two of them were being weird and cryptic. Heat rose in her face now. *Enough of this crap.*

Whatever was going on with them, she wasn't interested in secrets or being lied to, especially if Flint and Iktomi were involved.

Quid slid across the booth, pushing Liam out of her way. She watched as a flash of hurt crossed his face but forced herself to ignore it. "I don't know what's going on with you guys. But I'm not interested in it."

She turned and stared Liam down angrily as she rose. Liam made a move towards her, but her hand came out to stop him. She felt the warmth of his chest on her hand. Flashes of that first morning in the woods, when she thought he had been following her, danced across her mind.

Liam looked down at her hand on his chest, as if he were having the same thought. She could feel his heart pounding beneath her palm. His eyes were full of worry as she looked between the two of them.

Quid ripped her hand down as he reached to grab her palm. "He said he was looking for me. He said that lots of people were, so I don't know why you're really here, but you need to leave me the hell alone."

"Wait—" Liam tried again to grab her hand, but she pulled it back. Quid all but ran across the tiled floor, closing the heavy glass door behind her with a clang of bells. She hadn't even gotten to where their bikes were tied up before Liam and Flint were behind her.

The wind whirled around them in response to her anger as she fought to control her emotions. *Why had she trusted him so easily?*

Liam stood behind her. His arms reached out to her, begging her. For a moment she let him grab her wrist. That familiar calming sensation came over her. Her heart rate slowed and the anger began to seep from her shoulders.

His eyes were full of panic and desperation, as he gently held her wrist. "You have to let me explain..."

Part of her wanted to. Part of her was desperate for him to hold her and explain what was going on, but Flint's glare peered out from behind Liam. Reality came crashing down again as she looked at Liam's hands clutching hers. This time she didn't fight the rising fury.

"Actually, I don't." she spat at him. "I don't know why you didn't tell me that you were looking for me or why you were waiting for me this morning..." The look of guilt as face fell and his mouth hung open, empty of explanations, told Quid she was right.

"Leave me the hell alone. I'm. Not. Interested." Quid wrenched the long, metal chain off the bike.

"We need your help, miracle girl." Flint was leaning against a light pole now, arms folded across his chest. Quid turned her bike slowly as she processed his words.

Her gut sank at his words as her heart began to pound. They were looking for her. Iktomi had wanted her to go with them that night on the porch. She didn't know why, but she knew she shouldn't. Her whole body shook, repulsing from the idea. They saw what she could do. They wanted to use her abilities for something. And now they had found her.

Liam spoke calmly as he placed both hands on her handlebars. He was blocking her from leaving. He was between her and home. Liam's voice was low, pleading. "We need to know what you can do…"

"What I *can* do is throw a mean right hook, so why don't you back off?" Venom filled her voice as she fought to keep it from shaking. It wasn't entirely true. She had never really punched anyone before, but she knew the basics and she was pretty sure she could at least stun someone long enough to run away.

Quid's eyes met Liam's and a small spark jolted through the metal handlebars, zapping Liam in the process.

"Damn." Liam cursed, jumping away from the bike. The air around her stirred as Liam jumped back, startled. It startled her as well. She had never done anything like that before.

This was different from the blast of wind that stopped her this morning. She hadn't done that on purpose. This one was.

Flint left his perch and approached her. He stalked closer to her, reminding her of a feral cat waiting to pounce. His eyes were full of anger. His words that night in the woods rang in her ears. "We will make her talk…" he'd suggested.

"You need to come with us." Flint's threat hung between them.

Liam stepped between them, his hand against Flint's chest. "Not like this." His voice was a low threat. The two of them stood together, facing off.

Quid's heartbeat quickened as she wondered how far they were willing to go to get her to join them. As Flint took another step forward, trying to push Liam out of the way, Quid raised her hand defensively.

The blast came out of her hand without a thought. Cold as ice and solid as gale-force winds, it sent them both flying. Paper and leaves flew through the air as the wind ripped across the sidewalk.

Shock rippled through her at what she had done as the two boys hit the ground with a thud. Quid lifted her hand, examining the soft pads of her skin. The wind continued to wrap around her fingers, caressing her with gentle encouragements. It was hers to control now.

Flint let out a slew of curse words, but it was Liam who looked back at her. His face was a mask of fear.

Flint made a move to stand first, but this time the blast that came from her was intentional. It left her hand, swirling in the air around her. She watched as the air stirred. The gusts pulled her braid loose. Her hair flew in all directions. Power emanated from her. The dark clouds covered the sky and thunder shook the air behind her. She pinned the boys to the ground.

"Leave. Me. Alone." She spoke each word with force, looking first in Liam's eyes and then Flint's.

Blood was forming from the scrapes on their hands and elbows as they struggled. Liam shouted at her, but she couldn't hear him over roar of the wind.

Finally, she hopped on the hard seat and pedaled her bike as fast as it would go. The wind urged her forward, helping her escape. As she raced towards home, she was uncertain which hit the ground first, the rain or the tears.

Chapter Eighteen

Quid rode back to the greenhouse, but before she got within five blocks, she could hear Fen's anxious voice in her mind. He was circling overhead again, changed back into the enormous crow.

Where have you been? Why didn't you wake me? Where have you been?

Quid relayed what had happened that morning as she once again chained her bike to the rack. Her mind was racing but she had finally calmed down enough to stop the deluge around her.

Of course, Fen knew what happened on the camping trip, including her weird encounters with Flint, although both chose to glaze over the parts with her and Liam kissing in the water.

What do they want from me? Quid asked as she began the climb up the stairs to the greenhouse.

It does not matter. They will not get it. Fen's heartfelt response filled her head and she was immediately comforted. He had always been there for her, especially the last few months, and she was secretly glad he had not decided to stay with Merle.

You still should have woken me. You must not go anywhere alone now. His voice was an angry command in her head. Quid nodded in agreement.

Quid finally reached the door that led to the roof and opened it with her key, stepping out into the crisp morning sun. In front of her, Fen sat impatiently, returned to his favorite wolfy form.

The two of them sat on the edge of her bed. The sun shined overhead, but she had used her influence to create a canopy of vines across one of the panes of glass during the day. Like a shady tree on a hot day, the thick brown cords and their glistening leaves offered a reprieve from the constant onslaught of light. In the corner a small fan buzzed, cooling the air around them.

Fatigue wrapped around her as she sat, rubbing the soft fur of Fen's long ears. *I am glad you are okay and even happier that you can defend yourself now.* His voice in her head was once again filled with concern. *We need to work on that.*

Quid ruffled the wolf's ears, which she knew he despised. Quid lay her head back on the pillow, ready to nap the afternoon away. *Why? Are you tired of me?*

Always. Was his tart reply.

Quid slept for the rest of the afternoon and into the evening. When she woke, she was famished, and someone was insistently ringing her doorbell. Quid stirred from her nap, trying to wipe the sleep from her eyes. At first, she thought the ringing was in her ears, but quickly realized it was coming from the small speaker at the corner of the greenhouse roof.

The bell worked both ways and was installed so workers in the greenhouse could be let in and out.

I am going to eat whoever is behind that door. She heard Fen growl across her mind. He had not slept at all, instead keeping a watchful eye out for anyone suspicious.

It's probably Ms. Rose again. Quid replied, forcing herself to be awake and friendly to the neighbor who was always so kind to her.

Quid walked through the first door with a suspicious Fen behind her. They stepped out into the chilly evening air as it swept over the roof. She cranked open the second door to the main building, pushing the heavy door open against the intense wind.

Sure enough, Ms. Rose waited anxiously for Quid. Her slippers swished against the concrete floor.

Ms. Rose's gray, wiry hair was filled with streaks of light brown. She always wrapped it in a messy bun that stuck out in all directions. Tonight, her face looked tired and sickly. There were dark circles around her eyes. Her skin was pale, except her nose which was so red it was almost luminescent.

Her pink cotton nightgown and robes were pulled tight around her as Quid stepped through the door. The old woman was hobbled over, smiling weakly as a horrible, hacking cough shook her whole body. Quid waited patiently as Ms. Rose finished the coughing fit.

You're gonna catch a disease... she heard Fen tease from behind her.

Ms. Rose continued to hack, pulling tissue after tissue from the deep pockets of her robe. Quid helped her lean against the railing. "Do you need me to go get you some medicine?" She guessed, as the woman took a long, rattled breath.

"...could you?"

Despite sleeping most of the afternoon Quid was still exhausted. She thought back to her argument with Liam and Flint. Anger and fear rolled over her, as Fen let out a whine behind her.

Still, she knew she needed to help Ms. Rose while she could. She owed the sweet older woman a lot. As Quid helped Ms. Rose back down the stairs, she promised herself that she would never let her anger or fear keep her from helping someone who needed it.

Ms. Rose gave Quid a twenty to walk the few blocks to the shop that tripled as a corner store, pharmacy, and vegan barbeque pit.

Quid repeatedly assured the old woman it was no problem. She owed a lot to her. Ms. Rose was always so kind, and she let Quid stay in the greenhouse free of charge. All she asked was a little help here and there—which was great because Quid had long ago run out of pickle jar money.

With knowing eyes, Ms. Rose looked her over when Quid promised to bring back a receipt with the change. Quid knew what the other woman saw when she stared at her in the dark hallway. Quid had lost weight since leaving home. She didn't have a lot of money and even when she felt hungry, often couldn't bring herself to eat.

"Get yourself some dinner too. It's not like I'm gonna be eating much." Ms. Rose hobbled into her apartment, pink robe billowing behind her. The smell of patchouli and pot filled the air as Quid closed the door behind her.

For the first time since leaving the diner, Quid smiled.

Quid and Fen left the dilapidated apartment building and headed towards the pharmacy.

That creature should be committed. Fen commented again. He dropped the Milkbone Ms. Rose always forced him to take onto the sidewalk. Quid laughed as she watched him glare at the abandoned treat.

Fen was the size of a normal dog now, or at least the size of an abnormally large Great Dane. Usually, he was very skilled at not drawing attention as they walked from street to street.

They continued down the sidewalk in silence. The warm air wrapped around Quid like a coat as she tried to force herself to relax. She tried not think of everything that happened.

The wind pushed across them though, as if sensing her trepidation. With each step she glanced behind her, wondering if Flint or Liam would spring out. Her chest ached at the thought because she knew part of her still wanted to see Liam, but another part of her was scared.

The sounds of the city were loud as they walked. Cars honked at one another and people laughed loudly as they passed a few shops. The smell of coffee and bread filled her nose as they passed a local coffee shop. Rap music drifted in from somewhere behind them.

Next to her, Fen revealed his nervousness as well. His head hung low as his eyes looked over every shadow. He growled at every nook, cranny, or hidey-hole, waiting for someone to spring out.

It didn't take long before people eyed them suspiciously, noting the wolf's aggressive behavior. His hackles stood on end as if daring her pursuers to jump from a doorway.

Okay. Quid sent the thought to him. *You're going to have to stop with the Cujo act before you get us into trouble. You're drawing way too much attention.*

Fen's scoff was apparent as he looked at her and then across at the small crowd of people sitting on the nearby patio of a cafe. Faces full of alarm, people stared in their direction as they approached

And what is the worst they could do? His voice was full of arrogance.

Quid watched as a young couple across the street walked a well-groomed poodle on a short leash. The dog's grooming bill was probably more expensive than all of the haircuts she had ever had combined.

Well, for one, technically there are leash laws in the city. Quid pictured having to put a collar and leash on Fen. She thought of him at a dog park, being sniffed by little fluffy chihuahuas and bichons with bows in their hair. The idea brought an eruption of laughter as she doubled over. Maybe she would buy a matching pink collar and leash.

Absolutely. Not. Was Fen's reply as she pushed the image across their link.

And I'll get you a tiny bowtie to match all your friends. Quid laughed so hard she had to fight to catch her breath and struggled to right herself.

Fen gave her a disapproving stare, rolling his enormous brown eyes, but shook off his predatory stance. His hackles lowered and he held his head high. When he began to wag his tail, the picture of the perfect puppy, Quid nearly peed her pants with laughter.

A few minutes later, Quid delivered the prescription to the pharmacist. Following the smell of hickory and barbeque, she walked over to place the food order while she waited for the medicine to be filled.

Quid sat down with her meal, once again enjoying the sounds of city life. Mr. Sims always let Quid try his new creations. Everything in his shop was faux meat, made with plants instead of animals. It was always fun to watch the older man try to convince Fen to take a bite.

She was waiting at a small folding table in the corner as her prescription was called.

Ms. Rose's antibiotics, Quid's leftovers, and the soup she had found on sale for Ms. Rose weighed Quid down as she walked.

Fen walked casually next to her, but his eyes were always alert. Quid couldn't argue with his sense of unease as she tried to remain calm. Her anxiety was building, a feeling of dread crawling across her. The streetlights popped behind her, overpowered by her influence. Next to her, Fen gave her a knowing look as she rubbed his ears for comfort.

They finally reached the apartment and Quid began the long ascent up the stairs as Fen growled deep in his throat. The sound filled the silence of the hallway, sending chills down her spine.

Something smells wrong. Fen's voice warned her as he squeezed alongside her in the tiny hallway. His nose continued to sniff the air and along the walls.

It's probably the Johnson's attempting to make curry again. She assured the wolf.

Quid dropped off the soup and medicine inside Ms. Rose's door, as she was sure the older woman would be asleep by now.

Her legs were aching as she reached the top of the stairs. The weight of the day hit her as she pushed open the heavy metal door. All she wanted to do was crawl into bed and not leave until tomorrow afternoon.

Fen came up behind her, sniffing wildly. Quid looked at him as she stepped onto the roof. His hair was on end. His hackles stood up. His growl was different now, filled with warning.

Quid was startled as she looked across the darkness at their home. The emergency light above their door cast a low red light, illuminating the short walkway. It took Quid a moment to process everything before her.

Several windows in the greenhouse had been broken and the wooden door stood awkwardly off its hinges. Every light in the greenhouse was on, though she was certain she had flipped the switch.

As the door closed behind Quid with a thud, she turned to see a strange shape, painted in red, across the back of it. It was the same as the shape from the creek, a crescent moon, encircled and pierced by arrows in all directions. She took a step closer to examine it just as she felt Fen's warning crash into her.

Wait— he urged but was too late. A pair of hands stretched out from the darkness, grabbing Quid, and covering her mouth roughly with some sort of cloth. She struggled to breathe, to conjure her defensive blasts like this morning, but the world went black.

Fen pounced on Quid's attackers, seizing the one who grabbed her. He would tear the limbs from whoever had dared to touch her. His teeth tore into soft flesh, just a sharp pain pierced his side. He looked back to see another man in a dark mask plunging something into his fur. Fen struggled to stay upright as the masked man ripped free of his jaws. He stumbled as he watched the pair open the door to the stairwell.

The light spilled from the building onto the dark roof and Fen crawled across. *He couldn't let them take her.*

Fen woke with a start from where he landed on the ground. The world struggled to right itself. The lights around him twinkled like stars. His paws were too heavy, and he struggled to stand. He had no idea what time it was, but the darkness told him it must be either very late at night, or maybe even early morning.

Flashes of the attack flew across his mind, bringing him back to his senses. Anger rippled through his fur. A furious growl emerged from deep in his gut.

Fen sniffed the air, ready to distinguish the thousands of different city smells in search of Quid. But the air was flat, stagnant. There was nothing.

Suddenly, there was a shift. A ripple of air turned into a loud rumble, blasting down the street. Like an earthquake, it set off car alarms, rocked streetlights, and startled dogs barked. Each noise continued to grow. The few people who walked the sidewalk instinctively ducked to the ground. Small trees planted along the sidewalk shook with anger, though there was no breeze in their leaves. The sky rumbled and lightning struck, filling the night with streaks of red light.

Fen waited, scanning the sky. The storm stood still, growing, reaching out across the sky. Dark, heavy clouds blacked out the tops of the skyscrapers overhead. Cold swept around him. The warmth was swept away. An unnatural frost formed on every surface.

Electricity and panic filled the air. The world itself had become kindling, waiting to be ignited. The energy came from everywhere—the clouds, the earth, the trees, even the water in the ground. The fury reached down from the heavens and swept across the land.

Quid was gone. Nature was without her daughter and the world was in chaos.

Chapter Nineteen

The trunk popped open with a deafening creak. Light flooded her vision. A pair of rough hands grabbed her bound arms and wrenched her from the car. Whatever they had drugged her with was beginning to wear off, though an unsettling buzz filled her head as she opened her eyes.

She did her best to ignore the splintering pain in her shoulders as they were yanked up behind her, she asked groggily, "What is this place?"

Quid glanced around as the world continued to correct itself. In front of her, a familiar face sneered down at her. Flint's eyes were full of fury as he pulled her along the dirt road. Quid tried to wrench herself free, digging her heels in the hard dirt and pulling in the opposite direction.

On the other side, another hand grabbed at her arm. This one was gentler, hesitant, as it pulled her along. As she expected, Quid turned her head to see Sap walking alongside her. He refused to meet her gaze as he followed his brother's lead.

Quid and her captors approached what appeared to be a large, abandoned factory. The giant, dark, steam stacks were spread throughout the wide area. Although nothing came from them, they stood over her ominously, stained with black soot. She searched frantically for a sign of something familiar, but as she whipped her head around all she saw was empty land.

In front of her, she could see one main building. But behind the building were dozens of looming towers, different than the smokestacks. It took her a moment before she realized they were some sort of storage stack.

The car was parked on a narrow, dirt road that led to the factory. She looked behind her, but where the road started, she couldn't see. It stretched on and on. Even if she escaped, she could run for miles and not reach help. The flat, barren field around the factory stretched on for eternity.

The dark sky overhead pulsed with anticipation. The air was tense and full of electricity, like a storm waiting in the distance.

A storm. It hit her, and she stopped cold, digging in her heels once more. Her slightest mood shifts had caused the wind to knock limbs and leaves from the strongest trees. Her sadness had caused floods. Here, she was terrified, but there was nothing.

No wind whipped at her hair. No rain fell from the sky. If she had not been panicked before, she was now. Even as the drugs continued to wear off, she knew something bigger was at work. *How can anything or anyone have the power to separate her from nature?*

"Oh, you noticed, did you?" sneered Flint from in front of her. "Your tricks won't work here."

He was right. Her panic and adrenaline were causing the drugs to wear off faster and faster, but she could tell it was something more. Like the time she accidentally got trapped in Ms. May's basement as a child, she could feel her body's desperate need to return to the earth. Her steps were growing weaker. Her body was beginning to numb much faster than it should.

There was something more to all these dark towers. As the three of them approached the closest tower, her sense of foreboding multiplied. "Where are we? What do you want?"

"You don't need to worry about it." Chuckled Flint darkly. His hands were firm on her arms as he pulled her along. Every time she resisted his touch he pulled and shoved her again.

The three of them walked for what felt like miles. Her mouth grew dry, her feet heavy. Her body was protesting the broken connection.

As they urged her on, she realized her two captors were waiting, or perhaps looking, for something.

"He said it would be marked and we would be able to get in." Sap spoke for the first time with his brother. His voice was filled with confusion as he looked up at the looming towers.

So, they are looking for something. Some sort of sign. Who are they waiting for?

As they continued to shove and pull her across the barren land, she wanted desperately to summon wind or rain or something to aid her, but when she tried to draw on the earth, it drained her even more.

Deep in her gut, an emptiness was developing, and she quickly stopped seeking the connection. Like sitting up too fast, the dizziness sloshed around her brain.

Sap and Flint continued to drag her around the outside of the factory, staring up at tower after tower. The longer they lingered the more she grew weaker and weaker. She was certain it was much more than fatigue.

Sap walked away to study a smokestack and Flint finally released his grip on her arm. She dropped roughly onto the hard dirt.

Her knees touched the hard ground and she felt it. She realized what was wrong. There was something wrong with the *Earth* here. There was no life in it at all. She reached inside her and sent her influence down into the ground and all around her, but there was nothing. There was no water in the ground. No life from plants. Nothing. Like the day at the lake, all life had been wiped out here.

Desperate to try anything, she sent her influence into the air and all around her, pushing it further than she ever had before. The rays of the sun were beating down on her. She could feel the heat, but not the internal light and comfort they usually gave her.

No animals were reaching for her. Nothing for her to call to. An emptiness sat in her stomach where their presence should be. It was like she was completely cut off. Without nature, without her influence, she had nothing. Her mind was growing groggy as her body tried to figure out what to do. She was growing weak and she was alone.

Despite her fatigue, she continued to search around for some string of nature to hold. She searched with her mind, trying to find anything to draw strength from. Something dark lashed out, reaching for her through the connection. It was like the hand from her nightmares. It reached out to touch her, desperate to grab hold. Her heart pounded and sweat fell down her face as she internally wrestled to get free. Like the pool and at the campsite, she tried to send out a command for whatever it was to stop.

Quid pictured the blast she had sent into Flint and Liam yesterday, knocking them off their feet. This time she pictured the darkness being pushed back. A small burst of energy left her and went into the ground, into the darkness, barely strong enough to set her influence free.

She opened her eyes. Flint still stood close to her, waiting for Sap to finish his search for whatever it was they were looking for.

Quid struggled to catch her breath. Sweat was pouring from her, despite the cool of the day. *What was that?* She had never felt something so dark, so sinister, and it left a mark on her. Whatever power grappled for her it was more than just a bad feeling. She remembered back to the warning Iktomi gave at camp. This was the thing causing the contamination across the country. It wasn't just pollution from a factory or a company. It was so much more. It was a silent, deadly omen waiting to come true.

The men were so intent on their task they barely noticed how much she slowed as they began their examination of the stacks again.

"What is this place?" breathlessly, she asked again.

"Am I interested in your questions? Shut your mouth." Snarled Flint, striking her violently across the face and forcing her to hit the hard ground with a crash. Dust swirled around them as Quid gasped for breath.

The hard earth came up to meet her. Her head pounded as the world swirled around her. Sap's gentle hands rested on her shoulder, lifting her to her knees.

Quid spat a mixture of blood and dust onto the ground in front of Flint. She looked up at Flint as shock poured through her. She knew he was an angry guy, but as she looked into his eyes there were no emotions, only darkness. Something dark had latched onto him.

"You didn't have to do that." Sap's words were full of anger as he held his hand out to keep Flint from striking her again. "Iktomi said we were supposed to bring her and leave her."

Quid was stunned by his words. Sure, she figured Iktomi hadn't liked her. But kidnapping her? That was an extreme move just for refusing to join their community.

"So Iktomi sent you? Why?" Quid asked again, meeting Flint's fierce gaze as she spoke. He could hit her all he wanted, but she was going to get answers and the angrier he got the more he talked.

"He's one of the parties interested in what you can do." Flint looked her over as he spoke. His gaze lingered a little too long on her chest where her sweater had torn. His eyes were full of malice. Her skin crawled as she shifted, craning her neck away. Slowly, he leaned down until he was level with Quid.

"He thinks you can fix all this." Flint opened his arms wide, gesturing around them. "We all saw what you did with the creek, with the animals. Hell, Sap and I went back, and we couldn't believe how fast you undid our work. It took us weeks to poison the stream."

Quid's heart raced as she listened.

Flint continued, pacing wildly before coming back to her. He grabbed her face roughly, but she pulled away. This time he clenched the back of her neck, exposing more of her chest as he wrenched her hair.

She met his stare with her own. She refused to show him the fear he was obviously enjoying. "But some other people, they want you to stop fixing things. Stop interfering."

Once again Flint pushed her to the side where Quid fell with a thud. With her hands tied behind her, she fell with a hard thwack. Her head smacked against one of the sharp pieces of rubble.

"That's enough." She heard Sap spit angrily at his brother. She looked up as spots filled her vision. He had stepped in between them again.

"Don't be weak," Flint whispered before hastily beginning his search again.

Quid struggled to sit up again, trying to pull herself up to her knees without being able to use her hands. Sap gently pushed against her shoulders to right her. With a look she thought might be regret, he wiped the blood streaming down her face with his shirt sleeve.

Her head pounded; a splintering pain impossible to ignore. A warm stream continued to drip down her face. She struggled to hold her head up. The pounding was intense and clouded her vision. Crimson drops dripped to the cold soil at her feet.

Everything went dark. But soon again the pressure of rough hands pulled at her and she was on her feet.

Her head reeled as the piercing pain filled her shoulders, combining with the fatigue from the dark presence of this place. Her feet were heavy as she tried again to gather a blast of wind to attack her captors.

Suddenly, the darkness struck at her again. It came from deep within the land. A tendril grabbed at her and choked back her command. Instead of a blast, what came out was a small breeze that barely ruffled Flint's greasy hair.

"Ha." He scoffed at her. "That's all you got?"

She met the man's eye as he watched her. "This is going to be fun." Flint's hot breath lingered on her face as he leaned closer to her. Quid was ready this time, moving as fast as she could. Before he could pull back, Quid slammed her forehead into the delicate bridge of his nose.

Flint dropped her arm as he screamed in pain, clutching at the fountain of blood now pouring from his face. Quid urged her legs to run faster as she made a break for the car. *Maybe they were dumb enough to leave the keys in there.*

Quid's mind filled with options to tear free of the ropes binding her wrist as she ran. She didn't make it more than a few feet though before someone grabbed her around the waist.

Quid kicked and screamed, slamming her body against the one holding her. Sap hoisted her above his shoulder, as he carried her back. This time he was silent as he plopped her onto the hard ground.

Flint came up to Quid's side, one hand pinching his nose. His shirt was covered in blood now and he wrenched her arm even more violently than before. A new sense of dominance behind his eyes.

As they began to trudge on, fear threatened to overtake her. *What am I going to do?* She couldn't defend herself and she had no idea what else she might need to defend herself from.

A chill went down her spine as Quid realized, Fen and the rest of them had no idea where she was. Without Fen and without her gifts she was helpless. How would anyone find her?

"Look! Here it is!" exclaimed Flint. He pointed to a symbol across a lower part of one of the towers. Quid realized with fear, it was the same one that had been drawn across her door and on the sign by the stream.

Under the symbol, rubble had fallen. A wheel stuck out from the front. Flint turned the wheel, opening the heavy door into total darkness inside the silo. Quid didn't know what was behind that door, but she could sense the darkness was stronger the closer she got to it.

Frantically, she fought against the two men as they pushed her. She began kicking and screaming, trying to press against their hands as they shoved her inside. She knew—as surely as if someone had whispered it in her ear—if she went through that door, she wouldn't be coming back out alive. Quid hurled her body against the heavy door again and again.

Darkness surrounded her as the door closed with a final, deafening creak.

Chapter Twenty

Liam pressed the small doorbell like the old woman downstairs instructed him. So much had happened, and he was desperate to talk to Quid.

Silently, Liam cursed again. He didn't know how his cousin had found him today at the diner, but he had to explain to Quid what was going on. Liam pressed the small doorbell again in vain and almost gave up. Out of curiosity, he turned the knob, only to realize the lock was broken.

Liam pulled his coat tighter as he stepped out from the door. The air was full of thunder and lightning as an outcry of both city and natural noises filled his ears. Liam looked around, trying to find his bearings against the onslaught. As the door slammed shut behind him, he turned to see a pair of enormous yellow eyes staring back at him from across the distance.

It only took a heartbeat, but the enormous wolf crossed the distance between them, slamming Liam to the ground.

Where is she? The angry voice filled his mind, clouding his thoughts, and overwhelming him. Pain, like the pressure of diving too deep in the water too fast filled Liam's head. He clutched at his temples just as his back slammed to the ground. Everything swam.

The wolf had him pinned to the ground and Liam waited for the bite to come. Its enormous jowls dripped with what appeared to be blood and its claws dug through his shirt. His heart was in his throat as he spoke in what he hoped was a soothing voice, "goo-good boy. Easy...."

Tell me where you have taken Quid, or I swear I will take off your head. As if to show its sincerity the wolf bared its sharp fangs inches from Liam's face.

"Wha-what? Quid? I haven't..." The wolf's words rang in Liam's mind as he quickly realized.

"Where is Quid?"

Liam struggled to free himself, trying to push the wolf's heavy paws from his chest. The wolf narrowed its dark eyes down at Liam. He craned his neck as far as he could away from its mouth as it leaned closer. His heart hammered in his chest as the hound's hot breath touched against his scalp. It sniffed him again.

Silently, the wolf stepped back, temporarily releasing Liam.

You smell of the ones who came here. But you also smell different.

A different kind of panic and confusion hit him as he struggled out from under the wolf's claws. "Hang on there, bud." Liam shuffled backward, sitting up and placing distance between them. "So, you can communicate with me?"

Obviously. The voice in Liam's head was full of fury and impatience. *Why do you smell of the ones who took Quid?* The wolf inched closer to him again.

An image of what happened the night before flashed through Liam's mind. The onslaught of the memory brought tears to his eyes as he fought the sensation. He saw the memory through the wolf's eyes. A masked man grabbed Quid, placing some sort of tissue over her mouth as another stabbed the wolf with a needle.

Why do you smell like these men? The wolf was insistent as the image faded. The yellow eyes watched Liam.

"I don't know!" Liam put his hands up in surrender.

You are the one she was with yesterday, yes?

"Yes..."

She came home yesterday and smelled like you. But she also smelled like one of the men who grabbed her.

It all came together as Liam jumped to his feet. The wolf bared its teeth in response and let out an angry growl.

"Flint! Oh, my Goddess! What have you done?"

You know them! The wolf blocked the door as Liam raced towards it.

"Yes, and we need to go see my grandfather right now."

You will take me.

Liam began to protest, but the angry, fierce look in the wolf's eyes made him think twice.

Iktomi and the others lived near the edge of the city. As always, The Believers liked to stay in places like campgrounds or RV parks. Places they could leave in a hurry and without a fuss. This had been Liam's way of life almost his entire life, ever since the fire. He had always loved traveling, but as they approached the group of tents and campers it was like he was seeing it all for the first time.

The entire drive there all he could think about were all the times he had listened to Iktomi rant, preach, talk, about doing whatever it took to fix the contamination in the land. He had always pushed the other Believers to go as far as was necessary to get things done. He secretly urged the younger ones to destroy construction equipment or burn buildings and structures to stop production. He said they must do whatever it takes.

Grandmother Dana had always urged restraint. She gathered different Believer communities together for peaceful protests. She attended community councils, spoke to leaders and factory owners, trying to teach them how to be productive while reducing their impact on the environment. Of course, a lot of times they didn't listen.

Liam's heart was heavy as he threw the truck in park. He had always believed in balance. Like Iktomi, he believed fiercely in protecting what was sacred, but like Dana, he wanted peaceful solutions.

With the passing of Dana, her seat as Matriarch on the Council was vacant. It was supposed to go to the next female, Nia. Soon his sister would have to decide about her role in the community, especially as it seemed Iktomi was interested in controlling it at all costs.

The wolf leapt from the truck before Liam had even turned off the engine. He hurried to follow the creature as people emerged from their campers and tents. Slowly, its long, brown fur standing on end, the creature strode across the camp.

Liam watched from the corner of his eye as several mothers grabbed their children and pushed them back. He met the eyes of several men and shook his head as he watched them reach for their shotguns. Usually, the guns were only to warn off predators like bears or mountain lions, but Liam wasn't going to allow anyone to harm the wolf while Quid could still be in danger.

The wind continued to whip around them, as thunder and lightning raged above them. No rain fell, but there was electricity in the air as they walked towards the center of the camp.

Time slowed as Iktomi emerged from the doorway of the large RV. The metal door banged open as he stepped down. "What is going on, Liam?" The old man spoke slowly, choosing every word carefully. His eyes never left the wolf.

"Where are Flint and Sap?" Liam's voice was filled with venom as he said their names. His temper flared as he looked around the campground for them.

"They went out." Nia hopped from the RV but stopped short

when she saw the wolf. Nua stepped down behind his sister, slowly placing himself in front of his twin. Their eyes were full of fear as both stood frozen, looking back and forth between the three of them.

"Where?" Liam stepped towards his Grandfather. His fists were clenched. He had no time for games.

"They went out to do a job for me." Iktomi's smile was smug as the words left his lips.

His smile faltered as a clap of thunder shook the air around them. The wind stopped its panicked whirl but the air around them filled with heat, choking them, and making it hard to breathe. Liam's lungs struggled for air and he grabbed at his chest. Around him, the others began to panic as they too strained to breathe.

Pain radiated through Liam's temples as he grabbed wildly at his head. Trying desperately to alleviate the sudden pressure. A voice full of fury brought everyone in the camp to their knees.

I am Fenris and I am the protector of the Daughter of the Goddess. You will tell me where you have taken her, or I will decimate this camp. There was a promise in his voice as the words rattled inside Liam's brain. Sharp pain filled his head. It grew and grew.

He grabbed his ears instinctively and watched as others in the camp did the same. Fen was speaking to all the Believers and they too were feeling the power of his words.

Liam looked up from the ground to see the wolf towering over Iktomi. He couldn't believe it, but the wolf was even larger. *Had it doubled in size in seconds?*

It bared its fangs closer to Iktomi's head, and Liam watched as they dripped sizzling red drops onto the earth below. His eyes grew wide.

The wolf's teeth were stained with the blood of Quid's captors. Liam smiled in approval, a new appreciation for the wolf-god before him.

"I… I didn't know. I had no idea. Goddess, forgive me." Iktomi struggled to get out the words as the wolf growled in his ear. "They were just supposed to take her and test what she could do. Scare her a little to see if she could fix the land like she did the creek."

Liam's heart dropped. Until that moment he hadn't fully wanted to believe his grandfather's role in it. He wanted to believe that whatever Sap and Flint did they did without approval. But as Iktomi cowered Liam's stomach sank and bile rose in his throat.

The old man was willing to do whatever it took for what he believed to be the greater good. Even if it meant hurting an innocent girl.

Liam saw red as his heart pounded and his hands clenched. At that moment, it was all Liam could do to not wrap his hands around his grandfather's throat. Perhaps that would be for the greater good.

Chapter Twenty-One

It took no more persuasion. Iktomi told Fen and Liam where to go to find Quid. Sap and Flint were at the center of the closest major contamination, a factory a few hours away. The factory was near the coast and the poison had been wreaking havoc on the land nearby for years. The plant had suffered a major malfunction and spilled toxic chemicals into the ground. The aftermath was now destroying the local ecosystems.

Liam grabbed his Grandfather's collar when Iktomi told them where they had taken Quid. The place was toxic. "I don't know how you could do this. But rest assured I'll be back to bring forth formal charges with the Council." He wouldn't stop until Iktomi lost his position and was exiled from their community forever. Liam walked away as his Iktomi stumbled back.

You will hold him here Fen told the camp, *I promise you, if he escapes, I will hold every single one of you accountable.* A tremor of fear went down Liam's spine as the words echoed through his mind. He knew the wolf would keep his promise.

Nua climbed into the truck without a word and Liam didn't protest. He was sure that Fen could handle the twins by himself, but that didn't mean he would turn down anyone willing to help.

It was nearly nightfall as they pulled up to the old factory. Much to Liam's shock, Fen leapt from the back of his truck about a mile before, transforming into a huge bird. Liam and Nua stretched their necks out across the dashboard, straining to see through the dusty windshield. Both of them were in awe as they watched him fly away.

I will fly ahead was all he said in their minds—as if that explained the fact that he transformed effortlessly into a completely different creature.

There were no lights in the main building of the factory, so Liam drove around the outside, forcing his truck over the rough ground and tossing them around in the cab.

Liam swerved, as Fen landed in front of the truck with a thump, stirring up dust as he turned back to the brown wolf in a flash of white light.

Liam stomped hard on the brakes as he and Nua slammed into the dash. He threw the truck into park and followed Fen, whose nose was to the ground, sniffing wildly.

This way.

The only sound that broke through was the crunch of gravel under their feet and Fen's nose in the dirt.

They followed Fen all around the factory, in between the enormous silos. Behind him, Nua stumbled over a piece of rubble on the ground.

"Are you okay?" Liam asked, helping his brother from the ground.

Nua lifted his hand to examine it, but it was covered in blood. "Nua are you—"

Nua cut him off, holding out his palm in disbelief. "It's not mine."

A nervous growl escaped Fen as he came over to sniff Nua's hand. *It is hers.*

The sun was beginning to set, leaving streaks of pink and orange across the fading sky. It had been more than fifteen minutes since they found the blood and there were still no other signs of Quid.

As they rounded another stack, Nua brought a finger to his lips to quiet them. Liam listened as voices came from up ahead. He recognized the arrogant tone of the loudest voice.

Flint.

Fen was not in a waiting mood though. Liam watched as the wolf lowered its head and stalked towards the two boys. A low growl emanated from deep inside the creature and filled the air around them.

Sap and Flint both scurried from the base of the tower, but the wolf descended on them. Its enormous head lifted Flint, sending him flying across the darkness. He hit the ground with a crack and Liam waited, but the lifeless form did not get back up.

Sap didn't make it far before the wolf cut him off, using its body to block his escape. The young boy didn't have the heart to stand up to his fate. Instead, he dropped to his knees.

"Where is she?" Liam grabbed Sap by the collar as Nua grabbed the boy's arms behind his back.

"I—In there!" The boy pointed a shaky arm at the silo.

Liam nodded to Nua, knowing his brother could handle Sap if necessary. He followed Fen to the edge of the stack, where he finally found the door.

Wait. Fen urged, but Liam had already grabbed the wheel. A searing pain shot across his hand.

Fire.

Liam stepped back as Fen charged the door. It didn't take much, the door blasted into the room as smoke billowed out. Fen and Liam charged in.

Flames filled the room as pieces of something burning on a platform above them fell to the ground. The glow of the fire was growing, and Liam struggled to breathe. Smoke filled his lungs. If Quid was in here, he had no idea how she could have survived. *Please,* he sent his prayers out, *please don't let her be...* but he could not bring himself to finish the thought.

Liam scanned the darkness. His eyes struggled to adjust as he ducked piece after piece of falling debris. After what felt like an eternity, he spotted Quid from across the vast room.

"There!" he shouted to Fen, pointing to Quid's lifeless body.

As they ran across, Liam walked through a cloud. The air was hot and Liam and Fen dodged piece after piece of falling debris.

The largest pieces seemed to surround her. The white-hot flames reached around her. Their tendrils shot out in a dome, missing her again and again.

Quid's desperate eyes looked through the smoke towards Liam as Fen fought to push debris out of their way. To his absolute astonishment, she was still breathing.

She created a shield of air. Fen's voice was filled with amazement. He spoke with reverence and respect as they made their way through the blaze.

Liam's heart pounded as sweat poured down his face. Images of weeks in the burn unit as a child flashed through his mind as terror swept over him. Quid slowly stretched her hand for him, desperately seeking help.

He watched as the gold circle on her wrist shined in the lights of the flames. He knew the first time he saw it that she had received it from Grandmother Dana the same night he received his. The circle represented the sun and all of nature. The weight of his crescent moon scorched against his wrist, heated by the air around them. He looked across the flames for her outstretched hand.

His was the sign of the moon, the protector. The sun's other half. He pulled Quid from the cocoon of air and felt her fall into his arms. Her protection began to fail as he ran with her towards the door.

He needed to get her out. He had to get her out so he could explain everything. He needed her to understand. Even if it meant she still hated him, she deserved to understand the bigger things at play.

Everything would be okay, as long as she made it. She was everything they had been waiting for. She was the only one who could save them.

Debris continued to fall around them. Liam watched as enormous, flaming logs began to fall from the platform above them. The flames on the ground had grown, blocking the path.

Liam wrapped Quid's legs closer, trying to protect as much of her as he could. Flames burned at his denim jeans, and more than once he had to kick off embers. The flames reached from him as fiery fingers scathed his back.

Fen ran by his side, smoke emanating from his brown fur. Liam watched as the wolf shoved log after log from their path.

Horror struck Liam as he watched a shadow teeter towards them from above. As they reached the door, a full-sized tree trunk began to fall. With Quid wrapped tightly in his arms, Liam flung them through.

He looked back for Fen, but the doorway was completely blocked. Flames began to spill from the door, reaching out as if desperate to pull them in again.

Moments passed, and Liam silently debated what to do. *Should he run back in?* He knew Quid needed help right now.

Slowly, the enormous wolf limped out from the darkness. Yellow eyes reflected against the brightness of the flames. Its thick, brown fur billowed with smoke.

Liam watched as the wolf stared first at Quid. Its long maw hung open, struggling for clean air. As it took a breath, the wolf started. Its nose jerked in the breeze.

Its head turned towards the darkness. A tremor of fear slid down Liam's spine as he turned. Through the light of the flames, a lone figure stood in the distance. Liam struggled to see the man's face.

A warning growl emanated from Fen, shaking the air around them with its boom. Liam breathed a sigh of relief that the terrifying beast was on his side. It must have been enough.

Without a word, the figure faded away into the darkness.

Before Liam or Nua could say anything, Fen collapsed to the ground.

"Li-am…" Quid choked out his name in two long breaths. Liam stared at her in his arms. Her bright green eyes stood out and he tried to wipe the soot from her face. Her pale skin was soft beneath his palm as he trailed his fingers down her cheek.

His mind raced to catch up, but before he could worry about what to do next Quid took a rattled breath. Her lungs were struggling to fill with air. Chaos reigned on them.

Chapter Twenty-Two

Liam drove down the abandoned road, urging the engine to continue against the wind. The gusts threatened, again and again, to push the truck off into the deep trenches on the sides. He sped down the abandoned highway. Rain battered his windshield. Hail quickly followed. The noise was deafening as it pelted the sides in a furious torrent. The temperature fluctuated from searing heat to freezing temperatures on the digital thermometer of his car.

He fought the truck's air conditioner. Then, he cranked the heater to keep the fog and frost from clinging to the thick glass of the windshield. All around them nature screamed her fury and confusion. As if demonstrating her anger, the season, what temperature, what time of day shifted again and again. Nothing made sense anymore.

Her daughter was in danger and nothing else mattered.

New fear that this treacherous tempest would sweep everything clean before he could get to the shore flooded his mind. He pushed the truck to its limit and hoped—prayed the Goddess was listening. He prayed that he was right. *Please, let this work.*

He thought back to Quid talking to him on the dock. Had it only been such a short time ago he found her speeding down the hill?

"Calm waters hold a deep power. The ocean is the mother of all waters and what connects them. She is nothing but unrivaled power above all beings…" she had said it in a whisper to herself. She spoke with reverence and he knew she was repeating the words her mother had taught her. He wasn't even sure he had heard her correctly. *What if he was wrong about this whole thing? Should he be taking her to the nearest hospital?*

Liam took a sharp turn, narrowly avoiding a massive, overturned tree that had lost its battle to the blustering wind. He caught a glimpse as he sped by. The deep roots of the tree looked as if they had simply released their grip on the earth and the mass of wood had tipped violently across the city street, shattering the pavement. It left nothing behind nothing but a gaping hole where it once stood.

He approached the road stretching along the beach and slammed to a halt, skidding to a stop in the middle of the road as he looked ahead, dumbfounded by what he saw.

Before moving to the east coast, Liam spent a lot of time up in the mountains. The Believers were normally wanderers, but after his parents died, he had gone to live with his grandfather to fight the logging companies.

On the mountain where they had lived, he had been caught with his grandfather numerous times in the dense, early morning fog. He had seen it roll off the peak and envelop the land. He was no stranger to a morning mist, but he had never seen anything like what lay before him.

There was fog and then there was this. A blanket of white surrounded the shore. The boardwalk was gone, lost to the clouds around him. There was no inviting warmth of the sand before the eventual chill of the surf. The fog surrounded everything. An impenetrable wall. The air was thick and heavy. A chill sat on his shoulders as he opened the door.

Liam clambered out of the car, carefully keeping one hand on the hood as he ran across to the other side. He welcomed the cool air against the burns dotting his back.

He peered in the back seat and was starkly reminded why he was here. Opening the back door, Liam gently placed one hand underneath Quid's head.

Her once lustrous brown locks appeared dim and depleted, as if all the color had drained from them. Her skin was cold to the touch. Liam choked back his anger at the bruises across her arms and legs. A large gash across her head had stopped bleeding. He wondered if it was a good thing or bad. Every inch of her appeared to be covered in dirt and grime.

With a heave, he lifted her gently. As he pulled her closer to him, he took a step towards the shore, and all at once the hurricane of wind, rain, and hail stopped. A whoosh of pressure lifted from the air, calming the winds and the rains. He continued towards the shore.

A tremble of fear crept up Liam's spine. He instinctively pulled Quid closer to his chest. The air was still, a sense of calm swept down the beach. *Did this mean he was supposed to do this or that he wasn't? Was this an answer or a warning?*

Nature was holding her breath and so was he. Still, the fog remained. With it came the sound of the ocean he couldn't yet see. The ocean left a deafening roar, blocking all other sounds.

Liam carried Quid across the boardwalk and down into the soft sand. She had been right. The fog was heavy, and he couldn't see the water, but he could feel the power of the ocean through the roar of the waves.

The ocean was angry today, furious, like the rest of the natural world. The power coming from it could surely be felt from miles away. Although he couldn't see the expanse of it before him, he knew he was getting closer as the roar increased with each hesitant step.

Liam trudged in the sand, alone with hope and with dread. Across the damp grain of sand and the sharp shells, he realized even if this did work, they might both meet their demise in the angry waters. If something, anything, were to go wrong nothing and no one in this small ocean town would realize their absence. Even if the two of them got lucky, even if someone might notice a lone set of footprints in the sand, it would be far too late.

Would someone follow his footprints to the edge of the water, only to realize no steps in the sand lead back out? The tide would come in and wash the prints away. *Would it wash him and Quid away too?*

Liam looked down at Quid's helpless form in his arms as he stumbled across the sand. She was so strong, and she had been through so much she didn't deserve. He hadn't meant to betray her trust, but he knew he had. Every moment since the day at the creek when they realized she was the one The Believers had been looking for. Ever since Iktomi first began talking about what she could do, what she could mean, every opportunity he hadn't taken to tell her the truth he had betrayed her, again and again. He hadn't known what Iktomi would do, but maybe if he had shared with her the whole truth this never would have happened.

Finally, Liam's feet touched the edge of the shore. His shoes filled with freezing water. Hesitation filled him. He looked down at Quid again. The breeze from the water brushed her long, brown hair from her face.

The waves crashed against a nearby rock jutting out into the ocean. The tall waves sprayed his face. He knew that if he walked into the waters, even if by some miracle the ocean brought back her power, brought her back —they may be swept away before either of them even realized what happened.

A gasp escaped his lips as the icy winter waters wrapped

around his legs and the sting of the salt filled his burns. He knew he couldn't turn back, so he pushed forward. A lap of water touched Quid's hand as it dangled lifelessly.

He listened as she took a shattered breath. The first wave washed over them.

Chapter Twenty-Three

The first thing Quid felt was intense, unimaginable pain. The fire had been terrible. The sting of the smoke was just like in her dreams. When she could no longer stand it, she had waited for death to take her. This was different.

The pain started in her chest and radiated outwards. Deep in her chest was an all-encompassing feeling, a combination of both panic and power. Like a jolt of lightning, the power of the waves washed over her and absorbed into her body. Each time the water ebbed she pulled in more of its natural force.

She had always been afraid to visit anything larger than a river. She was terrified of losing control, of losing herself. Now, she felt the strength of the water and she knew why. This water had touched and remembered every year, decade, and millennium earth had ever had. Its memory contained every life that had ever lived.

The ocean drew its power from the moon, from space, and from the universe itself. The power reached for her, bringing her back from the darkness.

Quid's influence expanded in a way it never had before. It shook her like an earthquake. For one brief second, she felt the millions of fish in the sea, the birds in the air, and the plants and animals of all kinds, for miles around. It cast out of her in waves. She knew that if she let go, if she stopped fighting, she could succumb to it all and become one with it. She could stop floating and become everything and nothing.

For three heartbeats Quid closed her eyes against the current and considered the release she would feel if she never had to fight for control again. She would never have to control her emotions, control the wind, control the rain. She wouldn't have to worry about flooding if she was too sad. She wouldn't have to worry about draining another wave pool. She wouldn't feel the weight of so many animals push on her. She wouldn't worry about Liam's grandfather wanting to sacrifice her. Maybe she could let go. Maybe she would join Vernie if paradise really existed. Maybe she could sacrifice herself and heal everything. She was so tired, so exhausted, from trying to control so much.

Quid held her breath and quit fighting. The waves pushed her around and she allowed herself to stop kicking.

Something in the water reached out and squeezed her hand.

Quid opened her eyes at the touch of Liam's hand in hers. Like the day at the creek, a sense of calm washed over her. His touch brought her calm. It slowed her pounding heart and gave her the control she needed. The deep waves tossed them around, but Liam didn't let go.

In the dark of the waters, Quid watched as Liam fought for them both. Through the tumultuous water, he tried to meet her eyes. Liam's grip was forceful as he held both hands to her face. He peered across the water.

He was begging, pleading for her to try, to not give up.

He held tight to her hand as he struggled to get his head above the crest of the water, but the under-tow threw them around again.

Quid watched as he flailed about. His legs kicked wildly, and his arms pushed against the water. Like their leap from the water-fall, he never let go of her hand. He hadn't given up on her yet. He had saved her, brought her all the way here.

Part of her wondered if it was all meant to be. Maybe meeting the Believers, all her desperate attempts at control, the weight of the responsibility, maybe it was all to bring her to this moment.

With an icy grip, Quid wrapped her arms around Liam's neck. She held him tight against her body in the freezing water. Her influence filled around her again, reaching out. The power was being pulled from the universe itself. It was stronger than she had ever felt, though exhaustion lay around her like a wet blanket.

Liam didn't fight her, though she was sure he was nearly out of breath. His hard frame pressed against her as the waves tried to pull them apart.

In a voice that didn't sound like her own, she sent the command. *"Enough."* The waves wrapped around them in response.

Please Leave a Review!

Leaving a review helps in more ways than you can imagine! Self-Published authors rely on reviews for exposure. This tells Amazon to advertise our work and, of course, helps the Natural Born community grow!

Amazon: **https://tinyurl.com/y467obgx**

Search for us on Facebook, Instagram, and Goodreads
@MorganPerrymanAuthor

Read Along in the Next Step of Quid's Journey!
Natural Born—Wildfire

About the Author

Morgan Perryman is from Dayton, Ohio. She is a mother of three beautiful kids (Chloe, Carter, and Catalina) and two beautiful husky pups. She is a middle school English teacher and has a Master's degree in Education and a Bachelor's of English degree. She is an ABSOLUTE bibliophile! She will read anything, but particularly enjoys classic literature like *Pride and Prejudice* and young adult literature authors like Tamora Pierce.

Dear Readers

Wow! Hello, amazing, incredible, wonderful readers!
Thank you so much for taking the time to read *Natural Born.*
This book has been a long, long, long time coming. I have dreamt of Quid and what she could do since I was in middle school.
Whenever the wind whips my hair or wraps around my fingers, I always wondered what I would do if I had power over it. I hope after reading this book you do too!

Please feel free to follow us on all our platforms by searching @MorganPerrymanAuthor or visit our website
www.morganperrymanauthor.com

Natural Born Lore

Natural Born uses the names and lore from a variety of different cultures and beliefs. This includes some elements from Norse mythology as well as elements borrowed from various Indigenous nations throughout North America. It was my hope to introduce these names to my readers so that they might be more inclined to seek out their origins, backgrounds, etc.

Writers often use allusions within their work to characters and stories of other cultures. Throughout my life as a reader and as a writer, I rarely—if ever—encountered the lore of Indigenous nations. After months of research, I decided to use some of these names within my characters for "The Believers." It was my hope to bring more representation of these figures and cultures to the young-adult genre, as well as to portray the importance of making crucial environmental changes. I have included a list below where you can support Indigenous authors and hopefully learn more about Indigenous stories, culture, and more.

Thank you for reading!

https://www.goodreads.com/shelf/show/indigenous-authors
Goodreads List of Indigenous Authors

This Land is Their Land—The Wamanoag Indians, Plymouth Colony, and the Troubled History of Thanksgiving
by David J Silverman

As Long as Grass Grows: The Indigenous Fight for Environmental Justice, from Colonization to Standing Rock
by Dina Gilio-Whitaker

Please help support the Indigenous peoples across the United States, who were drastically affected by the pandemic by following the link below!

https://www.firstnations.org/covid-19-emergency-response-fund/

Acknowledgements

Thank you so much for taking the time to read *Natural Born*. This book has been a long, long, long time coming. I have dreamt of Quid and what she could do since I was in middle school. Whenever the wind whips my hair or wraps around my fingers, I always wondered what I would do if I had power over it. I hope after reading this book you do too!

So many people have made this book possible. My wonderful husband, who supported me taking a year off from teaching, which became two years off and now has turned into so much more! I love you more than I can describe, and this book is truly dedicated to you.

Thank you to my wonderful family. My cousin Trema has been such a fantastic supporter. She talked me through so many scenes and really made me feel confident enough to call myself a writer.

Thank you to my sisters for their support. Your excitement made me more excited and I didn't even know that was possible.

Thank you especially to my mom and dad, who have always fostered my love for reading. Thank you for buying me the Lynn Ewing books when I was young. Thank you for taking me to the bookstore and the library. You had no idea how much you were shaping me.

To my wonderful team. Thank you to Joyce for helping edit the book. I had no idea how much I would need your thorough eyes for checking and editing. To Abby. You insisted you didn't need a blurb or even acknowledgement, but I owe this gorgeous cover to you. Thank you for sitting through zoom meetings with me and reading my way-too extensive meeting notes. You have truly become a friend.

Trigger Warning
(Spoiler Content)

This book contains scenes that may be distressing for some readers, including injured and hurt animals, parental (maternal) death, violence with fire and near-drowning.